R

Life in the Brohouse – Book 2

By Carmen Black

Published by Scarlet Lantern Publishing

Copyright © 2021 by
Carmen Black & Scarlet Lantern Publishing

All rights reserved.

This is a work of fiction. Names, characters, businesses, places, events and incidents are either the products of the author's imagination or used in a fictitious manner. Any resemblance to actual persons, living or dead, or actual events is purely coincidental.

This book contains sexually explicit scenes and adult language.

1

RACHEL

I wade through the crowd of people, holding my purse close to me while stepping onto the escalator which would take me to baggage claim. The flight was long and annoying. There was something wrong with the plane, so we were delayed by an hour. Then when we arrived at Colorado, there wasn't space for the plane to land. So, of course, the pilot was forced to flying the plane round and round until we could finally land.

I was so close to grabbing the vomit bag.

I still feel dizzy, my stomach twisting with every step I take towards the conveyor belt. I take out my notebook, fanning myself with it after stopping in front of the carousel. Even though it's the middle of winter, my face feels like I have been sun tanning on a beach for the past several hours.

I just hope the boys aren't pissed it's taking so long.

I purse my lips, taking out my phone and hoping Lucas hadn't sent me a million messages that they were here and waiting for me. Thankfully, he had sounded understanding when I called him in New York, explaining the situation.

"We haven't even left yet," he had said. "Don't worry. We won't leave without you."

I smile down at the phone now, happy to see only one message reading: *Did you land safely?*

I type a quick message back: *Yep. Waiting for my suitcase.*

I shove my phone back into my purse, sighing when a bell rings and the conveyor belt begins moving.

Today is January 1st and the boys and I are going skiing in the mountains. Never mind the fact I have never been skiing, which my mother pointed out to me so eloquently when she dropped me off at JFK.

I remember rolling my eyes while grabbing my suitcase and slamming the door shut. "I'll be fine, mom," I had said at the time, though I genuinely wonder if that's true. I'm not really a sports girl and I've been known to trip up the stairs and stub my toe on the bed.

Knowing my luck, I will probably break my legs on the first day and spend the rest of my semester walking around campus with crutches.

I shake those thoughts from me and pause, spotting my bag heading towards me. I reach for it, lugging it out and stumbling back from the force. Smiling, I look for the exit and head in the direction, feeling excitement and nervousness brim within me.

Two weeks. It has been two weeks since I last saw the bros, and that is two weeks too long. I recall mom eyeing me when we were at the mall, there to spend a bit of cash and, of course, she caught me looking at the lingerie. I probably should have been a bit more secretive, but then again, I didn't know my mother was going to be following after me as if she were a puppy demanding attention.

"Are you dating anyone?" she had asked.

I, of course, remained completely chill by dropping the matching bra and panty set I had been holding and yelled, "Huh?"

Yep. Really chill.

And of course that means now I have nothing cute to wear at Lucas's cottage. I guess my usual raggedy bra and mismatched set would have to do. At least until I get paid from the running store and I can go shopping for something a bit more… risqué.

I pause at the exit, feeling my jeans rub against my gut, which had definitely expanded since the holidays. Maybe I should go running with Seth as soon as we arrive.

I don't know if I can get naked right now with my belly still so bloated from all the ham and biscuits I ate.

But it was totally worth every last bite, I tell myself while striding through the doors.

The Colorado air hit me immediately, the breeze whipping my hair, making it impossible for me to see. I gasp, grabbing my hood and tossing it over my head to give me some sort of protection. I frown at my ungloved hands. *Bad move.* Looking around, I pray Lucas is somewhere nearby, yet I don't see his car anywhere.

It isn't until a black SUV opens that I notice Seth running out wearing only a black sweater and long shorts. He smiles at me and all my anxiety evaporates as my feet take me to him.

"Lucas got a new car," says Seth, grabbing my suitcase and dragging it towards the large vehicle.

"I can see that," I say, my smile widening when I enter, seeing Hunter sitting in the front seat.

"Rachel, long time no see," says Hunter while turning around.

I slam the door shut and giggle, happy to see my Thor-like man. Although, he looks a bit thinner than he was when I left him. Dark circles shadow his eyes, and his smile doesn't quite meet his gaze.

Maybe something happened with his mom?

I don't want to ask him here, in front of the bros, so I make a mental note of it to store for later and turn to Seth as he slams his door close.

"Ready to disembark," says Seth with a salute.

"How was your flight, Rachel?" asks Lucas while pulling out from his spot next to the curb.

"Ugh, it was terrible," I say as I buckle my belt. "I really thought I was going to throw up all over the plane."

Hunter chuckles, still facing towards me. His belt is all twisted around his broad shoulders. "The fresh air will definitely help."

"Family wasn't upset about you leaving early?" asks Seth.

I wince and give him a shrug. "What can they do? I'm eighteen."

Hunter chuckles, his tone a bit awkward to my ears. "You got that right." He turns back around before I can look at him. Something is off, I can feel it, but I don't know how to broach the subject.

And sadly, I can't stop thinking about it.

I try to focus on the mountains in the distance, appearing ever closer as Lucas continues driving. Lucas puts on the radio, blasting rock music which I bob my head to, enjoying the 90s alternatives and cringing at each metal song assaulting my ears, which the bros continue screaming to. I laugh, feeling at peace, feeling like I had finally returned home.

Snow begins falling as Lucas approaches his parents' cottage, which is more like a mansion. *Lucas calls this place a cottage?* I think as he parks the SUV, my eyes growing wider while I take in the brick path leading to the huge home with large extravagant windows.

It's at least two stories, if not three, with a balcony overlooking where we just drove from. The lights are on, illuminating the massive place. I open the door, my eyes still glued to the windows, trying to take in as much as I can. Trees surround the area with more mountains, higher up, peeking behind the cottage.

Is that a chandelier? I wonder while stepping out of the SUV.

"Jesus, Lucas," says Seth while opening the back door and grabbing the suitcases. "This isn't a cottage. It's a freaking mansion."

Exactly what I thought.

Lucas chuckles while rubbing the back of his head. "I guess it's a bit over the top."

"I'd say," says Hunter while grabbing his backpack and throwing it over his shoulder. I see him still, yet I don't see his face. I suppose he's wincing. *Did he ever see a physical therapist about that shoulder?* I wonder while taking my suitcase and dragging it towards him.

I touch his arm lightly and try not to frown when I see his forced smile again. "I'm fine," he says quickly, already knowing what I'm about to ask. "I just moved too quickly. Still need to be careful and all."

I nod, taking his word, yet I still can't help but worry. Last semester he was taking painkillers from his coach. Even though he messed up his shoulder and broke his hand, he was still playing regardless of the pain and the detriment to his body. Not to mention his mother was suffering from cancer and his father was absent.

I really want to speak with him and see how he's doing.

Maybe when the others are skiing we can have some personal time.

Lucas walks ahead, leading the way down the brick path towards the home. Snow is stacked on either side of the path and icicles hanging from the roof, threatening to fall. We walk onto the porch, waiting for Lucas to unlock the door before striding in through the massive foyer.

Yep, there's a chandelier.

I look around, expecting a butler or a maid to pop out from nowhere, carrying a tray of martinis or a platter of escargot. I'm actually a bit miffed when I see none of that.

"Is it just us?" I ask, dropping my suitcase down and striding towards one of the large windows. I plant my hands on the glass, finding a steaming infinity pool in the back overlooking a beautiful view of snow-covered peaks. I pinch myself, wondering if I'm still asleep on the plane, but I don't seem to be waking up.

I hear Lucas chuckle behind me and turn around, finding him shaking his head while staring at me, a mischievous glint in his eyes. "Yep, just us," he says while crossing his arms. "I had Mom send the attendees home. I wanted some... personal time."

My cheeks heat and I feel my stomach twisting for an entirely different reason. "Oh," I say simply while tucking a stray blonde curl behind my ear.

"I can give you a tour of the place if you want," says Lucas while looking between Seth and Hunter, who both shrug in response.

"I'd rather get in the pool," says Seth while striding towards me, placing his forehead against the glass and looking at the pristine blue waters.

"Is it really warm?" I ask, not sure if I can trust my eyes.

Lucas nods while dumping his bag on the kitchen counter. "Yep. The whole thing is heated during the winter." I still when I feel his hand brushing my hair away from my neck, his knuckles caressing my nape.

My anxiety heightens immediately and I walk around him, striding towards Hunter and grabbing his arm, leading him through the foyer. "Let's have that tour, shall we?" I call, forcing a smile while looking around the large place.

I hear Hunter chuckle next to me and Lucas's grumbling behind. I can't help it. We haven't been together in two weeks, and even then my relationship with the bros is... different. Having one boyfriend is strange for me, never mind three. And all of them are sexy, God-like creatures with perfectly toned abs and strong arms while I have been busy feasting away on chocolates, scones, and bread.

I'm not quite ready for them to see me naked just yet. Maybe after some heavy dieting and lots of running, I can think about having some naughty time with them, but now? Now is definitely out of the question.

"You alright there, Rachel?" asks Hunter.

When I peek over at him, I see he is genuinely smiling. "I'm fine," I say, grimacing at my high pitched tone.

Hunter chuckles and pulls me to him. He brushes his lips against my temple and I nearly jump out of my skin, my face heating so much I must have put it in the oven.

"You look very pretty," he says while turning and leading me upstairs.

"Do you guys want to choose your rooms?" I hear Lucas ask from behind.

"I call the biggest!" Shouts Seth while running up the stairs, whizzing by us with incredible speed.

Lucas rolls his head and I stifle a giggle, watching him slowly approach us up the steps. "I hope he realizes that bigger does not necessarily mean better," he grounds out while going past and I stifle another onset of laughter.

My gaze meets Hunter, and I see he's also trying to contain his laughter. "Although, it does help," he whispers into my ear.

"This is mine!" I hear Seth shout followed by another groan from Lucas and Hunter, and I burst into a fit of laughter as we quickly run up the rest of the steps.

I look through the rooms, finding each and every one of them absolutely beautiful. I peek inside one, finding Seth and Lucas in a glaring match.

"This is my room, numb nuts," says Lucas while throwing his arms open.

"Not this time," says Seth while going on his tiptoes. "I shouted dibs."

"Yeah, but this is usually my room."

Seth scoffs, tossing back his head and smiling bitterly up at Lucas. "Sharing is caring, asshole."

I shake my head, closing the door and continuing down the hall to the one in the far corner. Opening it, I smile at the white canopy bed and the beautiful vanity sitting underneath a large window, showing another beautiful view of the mountains surrounding us. Beige pillows litter the bed with a matching comforter. Pink slippers rest at the foot of the bed with a matching pink robe hanging in the closet.

I peek inside the small space, finding black snow pants, a large ski coat and some goggles. Becoming extra curious, I open the drawers and I see each and everyone is filled with a variety of sweaters. *This must be his sister's room? Does Lucas have a sister?* I frown, realizing I don't know much about the rower.

"I see this will be your room?"

I turn, finding Hunter in the doorway, leaning against the frame with arms crossed.

I nod while closing the closet door. "Where are Lucas and Seth?"

Hunter shrugs. "Still arguing."

I chuckle and shake my head. "Why am I not surprised?"

Hunter strides towards me, taking my hands in his and placing them on his shoulders. He closes his eyes, breathing me in and leaning closer to my body. I wrap my arms around his neck, fiddling with the blond locks at his nape.

"I like that," he breathes.

I go onto my tiptoes, feeling especially brave as I brush my lips against his. "Do you now?" I whisper, watching his eyes open and a soft smile lift his lips.

"God, I missed you," he says before capturing my lips and pushing me up against the wall.

I moan as he deepens the kiss, his body pressing against mine, touching every inch of my skin. He wastes no time sliding his hand up my front, his fingers fondling with the cup of my bra as his tongue becomes entwined with mine. I gasp, feeling his hard cock press against my core, igniting a fire in between my legs that I had so missed. His fingers pulled down my bra, his thumb and index pinching my nipple and I whimpered, bucking my hips against his.

My fingers dig into his hair, keeping him from straying far. I gasp as his lips pull away from mine, kissing down the length of my neck and back up. His other hand reaches towards my front, cupping my womanhood and pressing his fingers in the perfect spot. I moan, arching my back and thrusting myself against those fingers as he continues ravaging my neck.

"Hunter," I whisper, feeling myself growing wet with desire.

I don't even care at this point how much weight I've gained from the holidays. I want his cock in me. Now.

I slide my hands away from his hair, caressing his shoulders before dipping to his front. His lips capture mine once more, his teeth tugging at my bottom lip while my tongue slides against his. He moans, shivers racking his body while my fingers toy with the top of his jeans, undoing the button before sliding the zipper down. His fingers still as I palm his manhood. I smile against his lips, feeling him rub himself against me. I kiss him deeply, my teeth nibbling on his tongue before sliding against him once more. He moans, thrusting himself against me, leaking pre-cum through his underwear.

"Hunter!" Lucas calls from the hallway.

Hunter doesn't stop. His thrusts grow more fervent as his fingers press deeper against my jeans, hitting my clit. I grab his cock while I move my hips against him, shivering with each flick against my little bundle of nerves.

"Hunter! I'm going for a beer run. Might need your help."

"No," Hunter moans, not stopping with his movements.

"Hunter!"

Hunter grabs cups my ass and drags me up from the floor. My legs wrap around his hips and we grind against each other. "Don't stop," I moan while he undoes my jeans and pushes his hand inside.

I moan, tilting my head back, my arms clinging to his shoulders. Just a little bit more. My feet point, feeling myself going closer to that wonderful edge filled with bliss.

"Hunter, where the fuck are you?"

Hunter growls, dropping me to the ground unceremoniously. He scowls at the wall, inhaling deeply before shoving himself back inside his underwear and buttoning his pants. I reach for him, my skin tingling with need.

"Don't go," I whisper, grabbing his hand and pulling myself towards him.

"I'll be back soon," he says, pushing my hair away from my face and kissing me.

I moan, holding onto him and sliding my body against his very hard dick. He groans, pushing me away. "Tonight," he says, before quickly striding out of the room and down the hall.

I frown while I quickly button my pants and stalk out of my room, hearing Lucas and Hunter slam the door shut. *What the hell was that?* I think while continuing down the steps. *One minute we were sexing each other up and the next he's blue balling me.*

I head downstairs and scowl at the refrigerator, opening it to find absolutely nothing inside. *Well, maybe it's a good thing they went out, but hopefully they know we need more than just beer.* I close the door, looking around and wondering where Seth ran off to.

My question is immediately answered when I see a naked man out of the corner of my eye jump into the pool.

I stride towards the French doors, opening one and walking out onto the brick veranda. Seth's head pops up, and he flicks his hair, splashing water that drips right in front of me. I chuckle while watching Seth rub his eyes while I rub my shoulders. I should have brought more clothes.

"Come in!" Shouts Seth as he waves at me. "The water's great."

I shake my head, striding past his clothes in a crumpled pile near the edge. "I don't have a swimsuit."

Seth rolls his eyes. "I don't either." He waggles his eyebrows. "Come on. I'll make it worth your while."

I laugh, tilting my head back and looking over my shoulder. It's too bad Lucas and Hunter will be gone for a bit. It's been too long since all of us have been together. Honestly, maybe I should be waiting for everyone. I feel a little guilty that Hunter and I had already had a moment just minutes ago.

But I'm all stirred up.

I can still feel Hunter's fingers rubbing against me, still feel his lips sucking on mine, and I couldn't help myself from wanting more.

I unzip my coat, my gaze not deterring from Seth's interested blue eyes. I fling my coat behind me, smiling coyly as I kick my boots off, not bothering to unlace them.

"Ooh, baby," Seth laughs.

I giggle while sliding up my sweater, shivering when I feel the chilled air bite at my skin. I can't work slowly anymore. Being sexy has totally left my mind as I quickly unbutton my pants and slide them down, needing to jump into the hot water immediately. My underwear soon follows my pants and I unblock my bra, throwing it behind me before stepping into the water and following into wondrous heat.

I gasp as I resurface, flicking my hair away from my eyes and rubbing the chlorine away. The water feels absolutely amazing on my body, although a part of me wonders how I will ever be able to get out. Maybe I just sleep here, spend the whole trip in the water. Maybe just live here until summer comes and I can finally leave the water.

Seth wraps his arms around me and his chin digs into my shoulder. I feel something stiff brush against my ass and I smile, leaning into his touch. "Did you and Lucas finally settle on the rooms?"

Seth hums his answer, kissing my nape while his arms tighten. "We missed you, you know," he breathes against my ear, before kissing my jaw, my shoulder. He rains kisses upon me and I sigh, feeling content in his arms.

"I missed you, too," I say, feeling very conscious of his hand slowly making its way down my front.

I gasp, feeling his fingers slide against my already engorged clit. Seth hits the wall of the pool, his lips mouthing my neck as I slid my ass against his cock. I whimper, feeling a finger enter me while he continues strumming my pleasure button.

"Seth," I breathe, my head lulling from one side to the next.

He isn't stopping. Not in the slightest. His teeth rakes across my neck as he circles around my clit, flicking it up before flicking down. I arch against him. Shivers radiate up and down my spine as I move against his fingers, moaning when another finger enters inside me, plunging in and out.

I don't know if I can take it anymore. I feel like I'm flying. I open my eyes, staring up at the clouds and the snowflakes lightly falling around us. His other hand cups my breast, pinching my nipple in-between his fingers.

My moans heighten as I thrust into his hand, wiggling my ass against his cock. I want him deep in me. I want him pounding that thing so hard I can't walk for days, but I also don't want him to stop touching me. I don't want him to stop this exquisite torture.

"Seth," I cry, his fingers moving faster against me. His thumb circling around my clit in such a wondrous rhythm. I grab his arms, digging my nails into his flesh, earning a hiss in response. "Don't stop," I whimper.

"Are you getting close, Rachel?" Seth whispers against my ear and I shiver, feeling like a string pulled so taut I think I'll snap.

I nod, but my movements are lazy.

"Come for me, Rachel," he says while thrusting his dick against my ass. "Come for my hard."

I cry out, feeling myself getting so close. I buck against him, not able to stop my movements. The water splashes against us, and I feel myself nearing the edge, about to dive off.

"We're back!"

Seth stills and I gasp, whirling around and seeing Lucas and Hunter coming into the kitchen. I'm so turned on, I don't even care if they join or not. I grab Seth's hand, pressing it against my clit, but he pulls himself out of my grasp and drags his body out of the pool, running back inside and grabbing a blanket off the couch.

"That was quick. Were you able to get any beer?" I hear him ask.

My hands fist as I watch them, feeling as if I'm about to explode into a million tiny pieces. *How am I blue balled again? What is going on here? Are they doing this on purpose? How is a girl supposed to get off around her?*

Lucas shakes his head. "The store was closed, but I know there's a pizza in the freezer and I think there might be a couple bottles of vodka too."

Hunter waves to me, smiling brightly. "You coming inside, Rachel?" He calls.

My hands grip the pool's edge, my nails digging into the brick. "I don't know," I mumble, knowing they can't hear me.

"Yeah, why don't you come inside?" asks Lucas, grabbing another thick blanket from the couch and striding out of the house, towards me. He smiles, holding the blanket wide and waiting patiently for me to enter. "We don't want you staying out here all night."

I grind my teeth before I force a smile. My insides feel so wet I wonder if I will leak all over his beautiful veranda. I decide I don't care and quickly shove my body out of the water, shivering when the air bites me once more. Lucas wraps the blanket around my body and I am thankful for him being so considerate, seeing how we had a very different kind of relationship at the beginning of the school year.

Although, now with both Seth and Hunter teasing my womanly goods, I'm not so sure if they had decided in the car they were going to continue bullying me.

Just in other ways.

I don't know if this is worse or not. Before, it was a bunch of betting and making me do annoying chores such as cleaning up after them and dealing with their house parties and asshole ways. Now they are torturing me with desire.

Currently, it definitely feels worse.

I pad inside the house while Lucas picks up my and Seth's discarded clothes. I watch Hunter put a log into the fireplace as I sit down next to Seth, tightening my hold on the blanket as I feel shivers rack my body. Seth leans against me, resting his head on my shoulder. I don't know if I want to nuzzle my head against mine or smack him away.

I decide nuzzling is nice, but it doesn't stop me from grinding my teeth as I feel my clit twinge, desperate for release.

Did I suddenly become a man? Why am I thinking with my clit and not my head? All this is very nice. The "cottage" is amazing. The bros are being sweet. I don't need to get off. I smile at the fire, watching Hunter sit back and feeling Seth nuzzle against my body. Yes, this is all extremely nice. Although, it would be even better if someone would get my rocks off.

I groan inwardly, disgusted with myself. I push Seth away, rising from the couch and padding towards the staircase.

"Where are you going?" asks Lucas, a pizza box in his hands.

"Bathroom," I say with a forced smile.

If the men aren't going to do it, then I'm going to do it. It'll probably take me five minutes. Ten max.

"Oh, you don't have to go upstairs," says Lucas, dropping the pizza box on the counter and grabbing my hand. He practically drags me down the hall and I frown, wishing I hadn't said anything at all. "We have a bathroom on this floor." He opens a door leading into a huge bathroom with a long sideways mirror, a bidet, and a large tub on the side.

"Thank you," I say awkwardly, my body tingling with need. I wait for Lucas to go, yet he hovers, shifting his weight from foot to foot. "Yes?" I ask, growing very impatient.

Lucas steps quickly towards me, placing a chaste kiss on my lips before stepping back. "I missed you," he says, his gaze on the floor. "A lot."

I smile. His sweetness is endearing and I feel joy bloom within me. And here I was worried things would be awkward, and they were, but it wasn't a bad sort of awkward. It's nice being with the bros again, having their energy around me.

I step towards Lucas, nuzzling my nose against his. "I missed you, too," I say with a giggle before pressing my lips against his.

He grabs my ass, hauling me up against him and I moan, feeling so tight inside I might implode. I lift my leg and he captures it, holding it against my hip and rubbing his cock against me through the fabric. I wrap my arms around him and he lifts me, carrying me towards the sink counter and placing me on it.

Lucas breaks the kiss, grabbing the blankets and wrenching them open. He moans, grabbing my breasts before seizing my lips once more, deepening the kiss while sliding his fingers into me. I gasp, grinding against him. I'm so close to coming. I'm so close.

He slides his mouth away, kissing a path down the length of my body until he's crouched in front of me, sliding his tongue against my clit.

"Yes," I breathe, my hands in his hair and holding him there. "Yes."

His tongue circles around my nub. My legs tremble. I bite my lip, thrusting myself against his face and not caring. "Lucas," I breathe.

The door bursts open and Lucas lifts his head as Hunter and Seth come inside.

"Oh my God!" I shout, not even bothering to hide my body as anger takes over.

"What the hell?" Shouts Lucas while rising. "What do you think you're doing?"

I sigh, crossing my arms while the bros scowl at each other. "What do you mean, what are we doing?" Shouts Seth. "You cock blocked us!" He points a finger at Lucas, digging it into his chest.

Lucas scoffs. "What do you mean I cock blocked you? We all drew numbers and I kept to-"

"No, no, no, no," says Hunter. "You interrupted my time with Rachel. You can't say you kept to anything if you interrupted."

"And then the both of you interrupted my time with Rachel," says Seth.

"Yeah, but my time wasn't even finished," says Hunter.

"Is the store even closed?" Asks Seth. Both Lucas and Hunter look away. "Oh my God!" shouts Seth. "I can't believe you two!"

I don't know what comes over me, but I begin giggling. I stop as their gazes turn to me, clamping my mouth shut, but I'm unable to help myself from bursting into a fit of laughter. I clutch my stomach as I stare at my lovers, feeling so much joy at finally being with them once more.

"Did I miss something?" asks Hunter while looking at Seth and Lucas. "What's so funny?"

"Nothing," I giggle. "It's just that," I pause, inhaling deeply to calm myself, "I thought you three were back to bullying me. To think you were actually bullying each other."

Lucas frowns while crossing his arms, his eyes narrowing on me. "We weren't necessarily bullying each other."

"Yeah," says Seth. "It was just a little miscommunication."

I scoff, jumping down from the counter. "Oh, really," I say while smiling at the boys coyly.

I leave the bathroom, striding through the halls naked and returning to the fireplace. I hear the bros following behind me, smiling even more to myself, knowing I have each and every one of them wrapped tightly around my little finger.

"What's going on?" I hear Hunter whisper behind me.

"I have no clue," I hear Seth.

I lay down on the carpet in front of the fireplace and spread my legs wide, watching each and every one of them go slack jaw.

"What's going on is that I want all three of you to make love to me," I say, opening my legs wider. "Right now. In your attempt to cock block each other, you have effectively blue balled me." I darken my gaze when neither of them begin stripping. "I am so fucking horny. Do I really need to beg?"

Seth looks over at Hunter and Lucas and I swear I'm so close to smacking him, especially when he turns to me and with a coy, mischievous grin, says, "That would be a good start."

I sigh, feeling absolutely frustrating as I roll onto my knees and gaze up at the bros. "Please," I say, my voice just above a whisper. "Please, shove your dicks so deep inside me I can't walk, let alone ski tomorrow."

Lucas's nostrils flare and Hunter strips off his shirt, throwing it on the couch behind him. "You don't have to tell me twice," says Hunter as he begins unbuttoning and unzipping his jeans.

Seth tosses his blanket from his naked body, his cock already hard and pulsing. I crawl towards him, licking my lips while he watches me, his blue eyes dilating while I slowly lick the top of his dripping head.

"Yessss," he hisses while his fingers dig into my scalp, bringing my head closer so I can take his tip into my mouth.

He tries to thrust deeper, but I'm in control. I hold the base of his cock with one hand while I cradle his balls in the other and I suck on his tip as if it's a tasty lollipop, my gaze lifting and watching his head fall back. A moan escapes his lips and I smile against his flesh, taking him deeper into my throat.

Lucas sits at my right while Hunter takes my left, both stroking my arms and my legs while mouthing my neck. Hunter nuzzles my cheek, breathing in my hair while his hands cup my breasts, playing with my nipples while Lucas positions himself behind me. Lucas fondles my ass, spreading my cheeks, a finger circling at my entrance there.

I lift my butt, wanting more of his touch while I take each and every thrust Seth gives me in my mouth.

Seth moans, his movements becoming more erratic while Hunter tries to position himself under me. I release Seth with a pop, chuckling at his frustrated cry.

"What the hell?" he shouts, his cock twitching with need.

"Patience is a virtue," I say while I straddle Hunter.

Lucas moans as he slides his cock against my ass, and a hiss escapes my lips as his finger slides into my other hole. I shiver as Hunter flicks his thumb over my clit. Grabbing his hand, I move him away from that area and angle myself just above his cock.

"If you do that," I breathe, my tongue feeling limp in my mouth, "I will come immediately."

Hunter chuckles, but stops, sucking in air as I slowly lower myself onto his dick. A shiver ripples down my spine as I feel him fill me. Lucas moans, his forehead nuzzling my shoulder while his cock leaks precum on my ass. He inserts another finger as Hunter thrusts into me deep and hard. I cry out, tilting my head back and grinding against him.

Seth grabs my hair and jerks me back into him, but I'm ready and want him. I take his cock deep into my mouth, my tongue twisting around his length while I feel Lucas leveling his dick at my entrance, slowly sliding it into my tight hole.

"Damn, it's so fucking good," Lucas groans.

I moan, feeling Hunter and Lucas time their thrusts, creating a slow and hard rhythm I can barely keep track of. My mind feels like it's melting. The only thing I can think of is the need to release. My whole body is quivering with desire. I can barely remain balanced on top of Hunter, who thankfully grabs my hips and holds me steady. With each thrust he sends into me, I grind myself against him.

Lucas shoves his dick harder into my ass. His hands come around, fondling with my nipples as he mouths and rakes his teeth against my neck. I moan against Seth's dick, hear him hiss above me. I lift my gaze, watching his face seem to crack, looking desperate and needing as he grinds himself into me.

"Don't you dare pull away," he cries, thrusting harder into me.

I gag, but I push it back, focusing on Lucas thrusting into my ass, pinching my nipples. I feel so full. I don't think I can take it anymore. I feel like I'm soaring up high into the sky, about to reach the very tip and fall into oblivion.

"Fuck, Rachel," Seth cries, his hands digging painfully into me as his cock twitches and pulses before finally I feel the salty taste of his cum and see his slack jawed expression. He holds me there for a moment while he continues emptying himself, sighing in bliss and stroking my face.

"God, that was so fucking good, Rachel," he whispers, his knuckles caressing my cheeks before pushing my hair away from my face.

I swallow his cum before his dick slides out, and he lowers himself next to me, nuzzling my shoulder while I continue being stuffed from both ends. Lucas's hands on my breasts tighten and he's no longer meeting Hunter's methodic thrusts. I cry out as I feel his teeth sinking into my neck, grinding my ass against him while Hunter strokes my hips.

"Rachel," Lucas breathes against my neck.

I moan in response, feeling Hunter circle a finger around my clit once, twice. "I'm going to come," I cried out, shivering and unable to control my body movements as I thrust against Hunter and then back into Lucas.

Lucas moans, grinding his dick into me and shivering. I slam my hips back into him and he stills, his body twitching. He moans and I feel him emptying himself in me. His body goes limp, and he slides away from me, taking his warmth with him.

Hunter rolls us over until I'm on my back. I feel him slide away from me, looking around for something. "Fuck," he mutters. "Where are my fucking jeans?"

I whimper, reaching to him. I'm so close. "Please don't stop," I cry, my hand finding his hard, slick dick and giving it a few pumps.

I watch him shiver, his gaze turning predatory on me. "Need a condom, babe," he says, hovering over me while I continue stroking the sensitive part of his tip. He shivers again and I arch my back, sliding my clit against his cock.

"Got it," says Seth, handing Hunter the small package.

Hunter quickly shifts away from me and rips the package open with his teeth. He slides it onto his dick and then shoves himself deep inside me, making me cry out as he hits something deep inside me.

Hunter tosses my legs over his shoulders as he continues pushing in and out of me. Lucas sits above me, grabbing my arms and holding them down on the ground. He lowers himself, taking a nipple into his mouth and I whimper, feeling his velvety tongue slide against the little nub. My body stills as I feel fingers circling against my clit and I arch my back, crying out as intense pleasure courses through me as the bros worship my body.

"I'm going to come!" I shout, feeling Hunter thrust deeper and harder into me.

My arms lift, but Lucas keeps me pinned down, his mouth switching from one breast to the other. Seth's fingers add pressure on my clit. I shriek, my body climbing higher and higher and there is nothing to stop me. It's like I'm on a rollercoaster ride, going so high up into the sky with each and every touch and kiss until finally, I am screaming so loud it must be echoing throughout the mountains for the whole of Colorado to hear. I can't stop myself. My nails rake against Lucas's arms. My hips buck against Seth's fingers and Hunter's dick until finally my body lies limp on the floor and the only sound I can hear is the crackling of the fire and Hunter's whimper as he releases himself in me.

Hunter releases my legs and they fall with a thump on the ground. Lucas lifts himself up, leaving my arms free to do what they want, yet I honestly can't move. I feel absolutely satisfied, exhausted, and famished.

Lucas stands while Seth cuddles next to me, putting his arm under my hand and wrapping the other around his waist. Hunter sidles up next to me on the other side, stroking my hair and nuzzling my shoulder.

"So, I take it I'm making dinner," said Lucas from the kitchen.

I chuckle, yet it sounds more like a grunt.

"You're the one who decided not to skip out on the store," calls Hunter, not bothering to look at Lucas as he gazes into my eyes with a soft smile on his face.

"And you're the one who cock blocked us," adds Seth, who strokes my arm and kisses my shoulder.

Lucas sighs. "Fine. But it's going to be shit. I have no clue how long this pizza has been here."

Hunter, Seth, and I shrug in unison before breaking out into a fit of giggles.

"No more cock blocking," I say after we finish laughing, lacing my fingers with Seth and nuzzling against Hunter's shoulder.

"Fine with me," says Seth, his voice muffled by my hair.

Hunter nods.

I lift my head, wondering if Lucas has heard me, but I see him there, naked in the kitchen, smiling with crossed arms as he watches us, his usual neat gentleman crew-cut in disarray.

"Ok," he says, looking a bit sheepish.

"We're all in this together," I say while slowly rising and looking between the three bros. "And I know we still have a bunch to figure out since we haven't been in a relationship like this. Especially me," I add, twiddling my fingers awkwardly. "But we don't need to feel jealous of each other. I care for all of you equally." I take Seth and Hunter's hands, placing a kiss on each while Lucas strides towards us.

Lucas caresses my cheek and I lean into the touch. "Together," he says.

I nod, feeling so happy and content to finally be back with my boys; to finally feel like I have returned home.

2

RACHEL

It's the next day and we are at the ski slopes. Well, I should say, Hunter and Seth are at the ski slopes whereas I… well I'm at the bunny hill. Which I am totally okay with. I have never been skiing in my life and already I'm thinking this will be the very last time I go. I would have been completely fine if they had left me at home with the pool and Netflix, but Lucas had insisted he would teach me.

"It'll be fine," I remembered him telling me.

It doesn't feel like it's fine, I think as I fall once again on my super bruised butt.

I hear Lucas sigh and grimace, knowing he's probably getting a bit frustrated. He probably thought this would be easy and I would pick this up with a snap of his fingers like Seth or Hunter or any of their other jock-minded friends. *Well, guess again.*

I groan and try to lean into my ski sticks, or whatever they're called. I'm nearly up on my feet when, of course, one of my skis slide and I'm down again. I groan and lay down, totally over it. We had been at this for at least two hours and all I could do was fall down.

Honestly, I'm not surprised in the slightest.

"Alright," says Lucas while walking towards me. He had taken off his skis a while ago after realizing we were never getting on the big slopes today. Possibly not for the whole trip. "I think we are going about this all wrong. Let's just work on your balance for now."

I groan as I take his hand and he hauls me up. I wobble for a bit, holding onto him to steady myself. "I think tomorrow you boys should go on your own," I say, frowning down at my skis.

"Nonsense," says Lucas while grabbing my collar and sliding me up one of the tiny hills. I scowl at a five-year-old whizzing past me.

A freaking five-year-old can ski better than me.

"Really, Lucas, you don't have to do this," I say as he turns me around and angles me at a clearing. "So I suck at skiing."

"You don't suck." Lucas sighs and points at the clearing. "Just try to make it there without falling. Remember-"

"Serve the pizza," I say mournfully, rolling my eyes as I hear him chuckle.

"Yes. Exactly. This is your first time. Don't be so hard on yourself."

I sigh. "I just know this isn't fun for you, Lucas. I'm sorry I'm holding you up."

Seth scoffs. "I've been skiing hundreds of times and I will probably at least a hundred more. Spending three days teaching my girlfriend to ski is not the end of the world."

My heart practically leaps into my throat as I hear "girlfriend" and nothing more. I can't stop the dopey grin taking over my face and I lean into him, no longer afraid about falling onto my butt or making a complete ass out of myself.

"Girlfriend, huh?" I tease, poking him in the chest.

I don't know if it's the chilled air or if he's embarrassed, but his cheeks go a bit pinker and his eyes dart away from me. "Yeah," he murmurs. "That's what you are."

I giggle, feeling my strength restored and ready to take on this puny hill with all my might. I mean, I know Lucas and the bros are in a relationship with me, but I never in a million years would think they'd actually admit or say "girlfriend".

Especially, knowing their whole jock attitude.

I pat him on the shoulder. "Well, it's nice having such a kind boyfriend look after me." I giggle, watching him roll his eyes.

"Alright, enough already." he points at the clearing again. "Focus on not falling and maybe we can go for some hot cocoa after this."

I nod and lower my goggles, feeling all business. Hot cocoa is no laughing matter and I take it very seriously. I just hope I don't fall flat on my big, bruised butt again.

"Are you ready?"

I nod.

"Alright, get set." Lucas grabs my shoulders, readying for a push.

"I'm set." My hands tighten on my sticks.

"And... go!"

Lucas pushes me and I grit my teeth, wobbling as I go down the teeny tiny hill. I'm moving at a turtle's pace compared to all the other kids around me. I angle my feet to slow, making a pizza like Lucas taught me. My legs wobble, but I bend my knees, trying to make myself as small as possible so I don't fall.

My sliding stops and I hover there, waiting for something terrible to happen. When it doesn't, I rise and look over my shoulder, finding Lucas running towards me with a big smile on his face. I wave at him, feeling like I have won a billion dollars.

"I did it!" I shout while trying to turn around, my body sways and I stick my arms out, trying to balance. "Ah, crap!"

Lucas catches me before I fall and he chuckles, holding onto me while I wobble. "That was very good," he says, poking my nose with his gloved finger.

"Can we get hot cocoa now?" I don't even wait. I'm already kicking at my skis, releasing my boots which Lucas helped me rent from the store.

"Yes, we can get hot cocoa." He grabs my skis and throws them over his shoulder before leading the way to the small wooden house in the distance piping smoking into the air. My skin tingles as I look forward to feeling warmth in my bones again. I have to fight off the need to skip in joy, so happy that this time I didn't fall.

Never mind Lucas's help.

I moan, feeling the hot chocolaty liquid assault my taste buds. Lucas chuckles and shakes his head as I lick the whipped cream from my nose. He holds his phone to his ear, calling Seth and wondering where they were and if they wanted to take a lunch break. I am definitely keen on eating. *Who knew squatting for two hours and just trying to balance on two boards attached to your feet could be such a workout?*

"Hey," says Lucas into his phone. "Where are you?"

I take another sip from my drink, looking over my shoulder at the girls giggling at the counter while talking to a group of boys around our age. The girls look beautiful with their hair neatly braided into two pigtails. One wearing a completely pink outfit while the other two are wearing something similar but in white and purple.

I look down at my mismatched ski attire. The black coat is large, which makes sense since I borrowed it from Seth, who is closest to my size. Lucas had given me the bright blue snow pants from his mom's stash as well as the goggles and helmet. I didn't even bother with hair and makeup, knowing it would eventually get destroyed from the wind and snow.

I frown, turning around and stuffing my face with more whipped cream and coffee. I shouldn't compare myself to others. Seth, Lucas, and Hunter think I'm cute. I think I'm cute. That's all that really matters.

Although, I could have prepared more for this trip.

"Alright," says Lucas, shoving his cellphone into his coat. "Seth and Hunter will be here soon. They just want to go down one more slope. Seth wants steak."

I chuckle, shaking my head. "Is there even a steak restaurant around here?"

Lucas nods, rising from the couch across and dumping himself next to me, wrapping his arm around my shoulders. "There's one just a ten-minute walk from here," he says while nuzzling my cheek.

I giggle and bat him away. "Lucas," I whisper as his other hand massages my thigh.

"Until then, I guess it's just you and me."

My giggles are stifled by his lips against mine, his hand digging into my leg while his other pulls me closer to him.

"Lucas Brent, is that you?"

Lucas and I break our kiss, turning to one of the red-headed men coming our way. He smiles, looking curiously between us while his clique follows behind, including the beautiful ski girls.

Lucas smiles, yet it looks more like a wince. Obviously, he doesn't want to be around this guy, which is only annunciated when he doesn't make a move to stand or say hello.

I wonder why.

"It is you," says the red head. "I guess I should've known you'd come up here for break."

"Hey, Marcus," Lucas practically groans. "Fancy seeing you here."

"You should have a look at this guy's place," says Marcus to a blonde girl. "It's like a mansion. Lucas comes from old money and shit."

I feel Lucas tense next to me and take his hand, giving it a gentle squeeze. "So, what's up with you?" Asks Lucas through his teeth. I notice now, his smile seems to be fading. Fast.

"Nothing much," Marcus shrugs. "Just having some fun." His eyes brighten and he jerks his head back and forth to look at the people surrounding him. "Actually, we're having a party tonight. You and your chick should join."

So, I'm a chick now? I raise an eyebrow and look at Lucas, but he isn't looking at me. I want to tell him no way in hell are we going over to his place.

"Maybe we can stop by later," says Lucas. "Depending on our schedule."

Marcus leers at me, obviously taking Lucas's words way too far. I can practically see him undressing me and all I want to do is turn around and will him away. "Oooh!" Marcus laughs. "I see."

I narrow my eyes. *Ugh. Just go away already.*

"Well, you know where I'm at," says Marcus while turning around, tossing an arm around the blonde's shoulder. "Just come around when you feel like it."

"Ok, will do."

I watch the group leave, feeling irritated that in just a matter of minutes I had been reduced from a woman to a "chick," but I don't have all that much time to feel offended when I see Seth and Hunter stride through the door. I brighten, rising from the couch, clutching my hot cocoa to my chest and happy to see my boys.

"That was fast," says Lucas while coming to stand next to me.

Seth shrugs while throwing off his gloves on a nearby table and taking off his hat. His gravity defying hair tufts up and he cracks his neck with a groan. "We decided not to go down the slope."

I frown. "Why not? Did something happen?"

I notice Seth glancing at Hunter, who has left our group to return the skis and the sticks. "Nothing happened."

My frown deepens. It's his shoulder. It has to be. I stride towards Hunter, but he's already leaving to the restroom and I feel that worry gnawing at the back of my head again. I follow him anyway, finding him leaning against the wall while shaking a bottle of pills into his hand, throwing them into his mouth and swallowing without any water.

"Hey," I say softly, watching him still.

He shoves the bottle into his coat without bothering to look at me. "Hey," he murmurs.

"Are you doing ok?" I ask while walking towards him, stopping when I'm directly in front of him.

"I'm fine," Hunter says harshly, yet he doesn't seem fine at all.

He has his hair tied up into a man bun. Loose strands fall against his pallid face. He still seems so small, too thin compared to when I last saw him before the holidays. "Has something happened?" I ask, choosing my words carefully.

Hunter shakes his head. "I'm fine, Rachel. Really." He smiles at me, yet I can tell it's forced. There's no glimmer in his eyes and shadows seem to haunt his face. "You don't need to worry about me."

I take his hand, lacing his fingers with mine. He inhales deeply while I press my head against his good shoulder, hoping just by my warmth and my presence I can offer him a bit of my strength. "I'm always here for you, Hunter."

I feel him nod. "I know."

"You can talk to me."

He doesn't say anything and I decide to let it go. I can't force the man to do anything he doesn't want to do. If he doesn't want to talk, then he doesn't want to talk.

I follow him out of the hall, watching him straighten his back and paste on a big smile. "So, what's the plan?" He asks, his jovial booming voice obviously fake.

Lucas groans. "Marcus invited us to a party."

"Marcus?" Asks Seth with a face. "Who the hell is that?"

"No one of importance." Lucas shakes his head. "I'm totally fine not going, by the way. The guy is a fucking asshole."

Seth chuckles. "I'm a fucking asshole and you love me."

"No. This guy is really a fucking asshole. Cares about looks and money. That's it."

Seth crosses his arms. "You care about looks and money, too, Lucas."

Lucas tilts his head up, looking at the ceiling while sliding a hand over his face. "Whatever. You guys want to go or not?"

"I'm confused," I say, plopping myself in the middle of the group on a couch. "I thought we were going for steak."

"Oh, we most definitely still are," says Seth, jumping into the couch next to me.

I hiss as my mug dips, splashing hot cocoa on my bare hand. "Seth," I groan.

Seth takes my hand, licking up the liquid in a way that stirs my insides. "Sorry," he murmurs against my hand, before placing a kiss on my reddening skin.

I can't help, but smile, leaning into the arm he wraps around my shoulder. "All forgiven."

"Well, I'm down to party," says Hunter, leaning against the couch. "Might be nice to socialize a bit before the semester starts."

The three of us stare at Hunter as if he has completely lost his mind. "Socialize?" Lucas repeats. "You call going to Marcus's party socializing?"

Seth sighs. "Cut the man a break, Lucas. He hasn't even met this Marcus. Neither have I, for that matter."

"Oh, trust me, you're not missing much," I say, rolling my eyes. "Apparently, I don't even have a name. I'm just a chick."

Seth gasps mockingly. "No, you? Just a chick? That bastard." He smacks his leg for emphasis while I shake my head. "You're not just a chick, you're the number one chick."

I smack his shoulder teasingly which he grabs before I can get away. He pulls me to him and I gasp, holding my mug up high so I don't spill it on the couch. "Seriously, Seth."

Seth scoffs. "Oh, you know you like it."

"Well, I for one would like to go to the party," I hear Hunter say. I turn to him, watching him cross his arms and glare at us as if we were two rowdy teenagers.

I guess that isn't really too far from the truth.

Lucas groans. "I guess we can go."

Seth shrugs. "I'm fine with it. I'm kinda interested in meeting this Marcus character." Seth kisses my forehead. "What about you, Chickadee?"

I groan. "Fine. We can go, but I want another hot cocoa."

Hunter smiles and I'm happy and worried at the joy I see glimmering in his gaze. "On it!" He calls while turning back to the counter.

***

Well, Lucas definitely wasn't lying when he said Marcus cared about looks and money, I think while looking around the cottage, holding a glass of champagne in my hand. The place is packed full of beautiful, big-breasted women and jock studs. A chandelier hangs from the ceiling, smaller than Lucas's yet extremely gaudy with blue and green crystals hanging from gold chains. The whole place is smaller than Lucas's cottage-mansion, yet extravagantly decorated in mismatched colors. As if Marcus and his family are actually trying to show off how much money they have.

Girls laugh, tripping over themselves and splashing wine all over the wooden floor while a man picks one of them up, throwing her over his shoulder and running away with her. I lean into Seth, my hand tightening on his and praying he doesn't leave me alone in this mess. I see Lucas leaning against a wall, listening to Marcus go on and on, looking extremely bored while Hunter pours himself another beer.

That's already his fourth beer. I pull my phone out of my back pocket, groaning at the time. We've only been here for an hour. I look up, finding Hunter down his drink, gulping down every last drop before pouring yet another.

I lean into Seth. "Is Hunter okay?"

Seth follows my gaze and I feel him still next to me as he watches Hunter sway and nearly trip over his feet. "I honestly don't know."

I frown. That's not the answer I wanted at all. I can't take my eyes off Hunter as he swerves, looking around himself. His face is filled with confusion, as if he doesn't even know where he is. *What exactly was in those pills he took?* I wonder. My whole body inches to go towards him, help him, maybe even take him home.

He smiles at a group of girls, holding up a hand and twiddling his fingers at them and my gaze darkens. Jealousy brims within me as I watch the girls giggle and wave back.

Oh, hells no.

I take a step forward, about to smack him over the head, but I'm stopped by Seth. "You go save Lucas from Marcus and I will grab Hunter."

I give him a curt nod before forcing myself to turn around, yet I can't help, but think about those girls and how wasted Hunter is.

Just what the hell is going on with him?

Tomorrow, I tell myself, *tomorrow I am definitely talking to him and getting to the bottom of all this.* There is no way I am going to let this fester for the whole second semester, especially after we've already resolved our issues from the last.

I lift my head, push back my shoulders, and straighten my spine before striding towards Lucas, sliding a hand up his arm. He glances at me, yet Marcus doesn't even seem to notice.

"So, I told her," says Marcus, "Bitch, you ain't nothing to me. I got a whole house filled with better looking women. Younger even."

Lucas sighs and I can see he is truly fighting the need to roll his eyes. "And what did she say, Marcus?"

Marcus chuckles before taking a long swig of his beer. "She screams. In the middle of the fucking restaurant. She just screams and throws her drink at me."

I grind my teeth, not even wanting to know how or why this conversation was even taking place. Not all that long ago, Seth and his bros were pretty similar to Marcus. Screwing girls here and there and not caring about relationships or attachments.

Yet, now, looking at Lucas, I feel like that's completely changed.

Hopefully.

"Funny," says Lucas, downing the rest of his drink and slamming it down on the shelf next to him. He turns to me, sliding an arm over my shoulders and drags me to him. "What's up?"

Smiling, I set my empty champagne glass next to his beer cup on the shelf and wrap my arms around his neck. "Dance with me?"

His brows rise, disappearing behind his bangs hanging loosely over his forehead. "Dance with you?" He chuckles and looks around. "Where?"

I guess I didn't quite think my little ploy through, given most people were either drinking, talking, or playing drinking games, but the champagne was getting to my head and I knew Marcus wouldn't follow us.

"Anywhere?" I shrug and Lucas laughs, his hand sliding down to my waist.

"Well, you heard the lady," says Lucas, not bothering to look at Marcus as he guides me towards a space in the middle of the room.

I hear Marcus's laughter behind us. "Yeah, yeah. Bitches right?"

Lucas's smile slips and I see his expression darken into a deep scowl. He looks over his shoulder and I follow his gaze, watching Marcus's form seem to shrink under Lucas's look. "Her name is Rachel," says Lucas.

Marcus shifts awkwardly from foot to foot, his eyes dropping to his drink in his hand. "Yeah. Right. Rachel." He chuckles, which sounds more like he's releasing air to ensure he's still breathing before quickly turning around and dragging some other poor victim into another boring conversation.

Lucas sighs and shakes his head before turning back to me, his expression softening as our eyes meet. My heart warms as I gaze up at him, feeling like we had just achieved some wonderful milestone in our relationship.

"Now, where were we?" He asks, his hand stroking my hair behind my ear in a gentle caress I lean into.

"You don't actually have to dance with me. I just wanted to save you from Marcus."

"Oh?" Lucas's smile brightens, making my heart skip a beat. "How shall I ever repay you?"

I giggle and go up onto my tiptoes, whispering into his ear, "I can think of a few things."

Something twists inside me as I feel him shudder under my fingertips. His hands tighten on my waist, pulling me flush against him until my lips are just centimeters away from his. I watch his eyes flicker down to my lips, lingering there. His breath hitches and I feel our faces closing in on each other. I can practically taste the beer in his breath and excitement brims within me, wanting to feel his velvety tongue dance with mine.

"I'm not trashed!"

Lucas and I still, realization dawning in his eyes which I am sure I mirrored. We whirl around, watching Hunter bat Seth's hands away from him before stumbling backwards. I watch in horror as Hunter trips over his feet, nearly stumbling into a group of women who scramble away from him.

"What the hell is wrong with you?" Shouts a girl, her mascara smeared underneath her eyes, giving her a raccoon look.

Hunter's eyes aren't focusing. Something is wrong. I know it can't just be the beer, although drinking five large cups surely didn't help. It must be the combination with the pills. I watch Seth hesitantly step towards Hunter, as if he were an injured doe in the middle of the street. He holds up his hands, his back bent to appear small and innocent.

"Hunter, I'm just trying to help," says Seth with a worried smile. "Lucas, Rachel, and I were thinking about getting out of here. Going swimming. Wanna join?"

"No," says Hunter bitterly. Seth takes his hand, but Hunter smacks him away. "Get off me," he slurs. "You can go. I'm staying."

Seth sighs. "I don't think that's a good idea, Hunter."

Hunter scoffs and turns on his heel. He stops in front of the table filled with beer and liquor and pours himself another drink. "Well, you're not the boss of me, Seth."

Seth frowns and I can see he's about to say something rude or insulting. I quickly step in, putting my hand on Hunter's shoulder. He hisses and whirls around, scowling down at me before his expression softens, realizing it's me and not Seth.

"Rachel," he breathes and I can see in his eyes he's having problems knowing what to see. His face looks droopy, as if he has no control over his body.

I take the cup from his hand, setting it down on the table before he drops it. His grasp is loose and easy to maneuver. "Hunter, I think it's time to go home."

Hunter frowns and for a moment he looks like a toddler about to throw a huge temper tantrum. "But I don't want to go." He sniffs. "I'm not trashed."

"Oh, I know," I say while grasping his hand, lacing my fingers with his and tugging him towards me. "But I am. I need some help home."

"Can't Lucas or Seth help-" Hunter stops as I flutter my eyelashes up at him and lean into his touch.

"I want you to help me, Hunter." I nuzzle my head into his shoulder, hoping he would fall for the bait and finally leave.

I hear him sigh, feel his grip tighten on my hand and allow myself a little victorious smile as he says, "Alright, Rachel. Let's go."

I glance over at Seth and Lucas, who stare at me like I'm some sort of talented enchantress. Yet, they don't question it and both follow along behind us towards the door. We're nearly there, nearly home free when Marcus shouts, "Hey, Lucas! Maybe don't invite Mr. Lightweight over there next time."

Hunter stills next to me and I feel impending doom pierce through me, knowing none of this is going to end well.

"Hunter-" Seth begins.

"What did that asshole call me?" Hunter asks, his voice so low I barely recognize it.

"Nothing," I say, letting him go and placing myself between Hunter and the party. "Let's just go." I usher him towards the door, but he swerves around me. When I turn around, I see him stalking towards Marcus, his feet taking him in a zigzagged path.

"Alright, let's go," says Lucas, grabbing Hunter's arm before he can make it to Marcus.

Marcus laughs, throwing an arm over a tall brunette who's wearing a tight black dress that barely covers her ass. "Thanks Lucas," Marcus calls while Lucas drags Hunter away. "I would hate making a mess of your friend. He's so drunk, just a little flick in the nose would knock him over."

Hunter lunges for him, but Seth grabs his bad shoulder, earning a shout. I reach for Seth as he stumbles backwards, but not in time. Seth stumbles into a small table with a gaudy vase holding several fake flowers, knocking everything onto the floor and sending the vase crashing into several tiny pieces.

"My mother's antique flamingo vase!" Marcus shouts, kneeling in front of the tiny pieces, picking each one up and cradling them in his palms. He shoots a glare at Hunter while Seth rubs his head, stumbling to stand. "This is all your fault!" Marcus points a finger at Hunter, who's mouth hangs open in both shock and confusion.

In Hunter's defense, it's just a vase. An ugly vase. And one that should have been put elsewhere if Marcus was going to have a huge party. I take Hunter's hand, pulling him towards me and beelining for the door.

Lucas sighs, taking out his wallet and a huge bundle of cash. "How much was it?" He asks, his voice filled with irritation.

"At least $500,000, if not more. There is no way-"

I pause at the door, watching Lucas stuff a thick wad of cash into Marcus's hands, effectively shutting him up. Marcus counts the money as Lucas turns around, lifting his head to the ceiling and shaking it in annoyance.

"It's always a pleasure!" Marcus calls as we finally leave.

"Wish I could say the same," Lucas mutters as Seth slams the door and Hunter stumbles into the snow.

"Why the hell did you push me?" shouts Seth while Hunter leans over.

Before Hunter can answer, he vomits. He groans, wiping his mouth and holding his middle before heaving more of his stomach remains in the snowy path to Marcus's house. Seth gags, stepping to my side while Lucas smacks Hunter on the back.

"Better here than at my place," says Lucas.

Seth wraps an arm around my shoulder and the both of us walk around the two bros, leading the way back to Lucas's cottage. "Alright, next time I save Lucas and you deal with Hunter," Seth whispers into my ear.

I smile, pulling Seth closer to me. I'm happy to finally be heading home, yet tomorrow brings new worries.

I am going to have to talk to Hunter.

I need to know what the hell is going on.

3

HUNTER

I groan as I roll over, nuzzling my head into something soft. My head aches. Actually, everything aches. I feel like my skin is about to crawl off my body in search of a more worthy canvas. My mouth feels like it has spent the enter night either swallowing spiders creeping inside to weave spiderwebs or licking a dog's asshole. Possibly both.

I wince as my eyes flutter open, finding a window with its curtains drawn back allowing bright light to seep into my room and enhance the pounding in my head. Groaning, I roll over, hugging the blanket to my body. My frown deepens when I find a huge glass of water on the bedside table and an empty bucket.

Just what happened last night?

I rise, and instantly regret that decision, plummeting back into the soft bed and throwing the blanket over my face. Well, it's obvious. I drank way too much last night. Hopefully, I didn't make a complete ass of myself.

I squint my eyes, staring daggers into the red comforter above me and try to remember what happened. I had been drinking beer, feeling sorry for myself. Honestly, I shouldn't have been drinking, especially since I had been taking my pain meds before, but at the time, I didn't give a shit about my health.

I just needed to numb the pain.

I still need to numb the pain.

I hear laughter from somewhere and shrivel even deeper into my blanket sanctuary. My shoulder pains from the slight movement and I bite my lip, stifling a groan as I feel something akin to daggers piercing through my flesh. I punch the mattress, grinding my teeth and riding out the storm. I would need my drugs soon, but I don't think I have the energy right now to go digging through my stuff to find the bottle.

Closing my eyes, I will myself to sleep, wanting to just spend the whole day in bed rather than face another situation where I would have to pretend everything in my life is just perfect. It's becoming draining and I don't know if I can do it any longer.

Instead of falling asleep, my mind dives into memories from winter break, which I try to force away. They taunt me, easing me back into discussions with dad at the hospital. Discussions about Mom that I'm just not ready for.

I remember sitting in the hallway, waiting for Mom to come out of the doctor's office. When the door had opened, it was Dad, who came out first. Dad, who pretty much just left us after Mom had her double mastectomy; spending his days in the office working, working as late as possible and sometimes spending the night at the office. Whereas I had been there for her as much as I possibly could with school and practice.

He had done absolutely nothing for her. Other than pay the bills of course.

I still don't know why Mom allowed him to get away with so much. Christmas was fucking awkward as hell with Dad and I pretty much walking on eggshells around each other. And then he wanted to go to join in on her appointments, making me sit outside when it was I who had attended each and everyone for the several years.

I remembered standing, remembered wondering why it was Dad coming out and not Mom. *Why didn't they come out together?* I had questioned myself, my skin prickling in alarm.

"Where's Mom?" I had asked.

"She's going to have to spend the next few days in the hospital." Dad hadn't been looking me in the eye. He was so intent on everything else around us; the white walls, the uncomfortable chairs, the pristine white floors. Pretty much everything was so much more interesting to look at rather than me.

"Why?" I had asked, annoyed that she couldn't go home.

"Son, why don't you sit down?"

"Because I'm quite fine with standing."

Dad sighed, sitting down in the chair next to me, his hands running over his face while focusing his attention once more on the floor.

"The cancer has returned."

"What?" I remembered breathing, as if someone had just punched me in my gut. "How?"

He shook his head.

"But she had a fucking bilateral mastectomy! How the fuck can she have it again?"

"Language!" Dad shouted, as if my word choice was somehow more important than Mom's life. "I don't know, Hunter. These things just happen."

"I want to see Mom," I had said, going for the door.

I remembered Dad standing, grabbing my hand before I could grab the handle. "She's still speaking with the doctor. Hunter, please don't make this any harder on her. She's going through a lot."

"I know," I had whispered angrily. "Because unlike you, I've been with her as much as I possibly can. Unlike you, I actually go to all her appointments, visit her in the hospital, help her get in and out of bed when she's too weak due to chemo. Where the fuck have you been?"

I sniff, blinking back tears and forcing the memories away. I should get up. If I can't sleep I don't want to be alone, especially when I feel like such shit. I throw the blankets off me and force myself out of bed, finding I'm topless and in my jeans from yesterday. I find my shirt from last night discarded on the wood floor. Picking it up I gag as a rancid smell assaults my nose, finding dried vomit going down its front.

Well, that's just great.

I throw it on the ground and find my backpack in a chair resting in the corner of the room. I sift through the wrinkled socks and pants to find a reasonably clean shirt and stiff my arms into the sleeves, wincing as pain radiates through my shoulder and down my back. Looking around, I find my ski coat in a pile with my boots, sweaty socks, and snow pants. I dig through the pockets, pulling out the bottle of Vicodin and quickly swallowing a pill. The bitter taste sits on my tongue, making me cringe and wish I had taken it with some juice or water. I peak inside the bottle counting the five remaining pills, which would hardly last me today and tomorrow.

I need to find someone who sells on campus or ask coach if he knows a doctor who can give me a prescription. Honestly, with how fucked up my shoulder is, I probably should've canceled on the ski trip. I could barely ski yesterday with Seth. But I wanted to see Rachel. I wanted to spend time with her before the semester began.

I really missed her over vacation.

Laughter sounds waft inside my room and I realize everyone is probably gathered in the living room. Looking at the clock, my eyes widen as I see it's nearly two o'clock in the afternoon.

Why the hell are they here? Shouldn't they be at the slopes?

I really hope they haven't been waiting on me this whole time. It will be dark soon. The day is pretty much wasted if they wanted to go skiing. Guilt stabs through my heart as I trudge through the hall and step lightly down the stairs, not wanting to draw too much attention to myself. If I hadn't gotten so trashed the night before, they would've been on the slopes, having fun skiing.

But instead they spent the day here.

All because of me.

"There he is!" shouts Seth, glancing over his shoulder while I meekly enter the kitchen.

"Did you sleep okay?" asks Rachel while I pour myself a fresh glass of cold water.

I nod, taking a long drink from my glass before saying, "Like the dead."

"We were going to wake you, but Rachel thought it best to let you rest," says Lucas.

I lean against the counter, looking down at them sitting in a small circle on the floor, holding cards with a stack in the middle. "What happened last night?" I ask, knowing I probably didn't want the answer, but unable to fight the curiosity taking over.

Seth groans while Lucas purses his lips. I look between them, wondering who is going to answer first. None of them look very happy. Even Rachel is making a face and I worry I truly made a huge ass of myself.

"What?" I ask when no one answers.

"Well, you got shit faced," says Seth. Good old Seth, never one to hold back when the truth is involved.

"You broke a vase," adds Lucas.

I blink. "I broke a vase?"

Seth nods. "An expensive one."

"How expensive?" I look around, but no one answers.

Rachel stands and strides towards me, taking my hand in hers and giving it a gentle squeeze. "It doesn't matter now," she says with a sad smile. "We're just happy we got you home safely."

Her words don't make me feel any better. In fact, they make me feel much worse. My mind reels, wondering why she seems so concerned now, wondering what I did to make her look at me with such sadness, with such pity.

I hate it.

I wrench my hand from her grip, wanting to go back upstairs and hide in bed, but knowing it would look strange. I know I shouldn't feel angry, especially since they helped me get home, but I do. I feel angry with myself for being such an idiot, for letting others see how broken I feel.

"Hunter-" I hear Rachel begin as I turn around, but I don't hear anything else.

"I'm going for a swim," I say before quickly striding away.

My shoulders are shaking as I walk to the double glass doors, opening one and striding out onto the frosted veranda, barefoot. I focus on the stinging sensation of the snow piercing my flesh rather than the memories of my mother in the hospital and Rachel looking sadly upon me.

I don't want to feel. All I want to do is act. I can't bear allowing those memories overtake me. I can't bear feeling so weak and powerless.

I hardly remember throwing off my clothes and jumping into the pool. The hot water seeps into my skin, loosening the tightness in my shoulders. I try to swim laps, but raising my arm over my shoulder hurts too much so I just lie there, staring up at the low grey clouds, threatening to snow, floating and welcoming the silence.

Water splashes and I turn, watching Rachel's head pop up from the water, her hair clinging to her face. She tilts her head back, moving the soaked locks away from her eyes before turning towards me, our gazes locking. She smiles as she swims towards me, stopping and running her hands along my shoulders and arms.

"I thought you could use some company," she says, stroking my hair away from my chin. She strokes the side of my face and I lean into her touch, closing my eyes and wishing she could always be there, wishing she would never let me go.

But I know, that's not the case.

People say they will be there, but it's always a lie. Eventually they leave one way or another.

"You don't have to be embarrassed," she says and my eyes snap open, narrowing on her.

"I'm not embarrassed," I say, which is pretty much a lie. I do feel embarrassed about my actions, yet admitting it makes me feel weak, inferior. I'm Hunter. I'm a football star for Aurora University. I don't get embarrassed. Getting trashed and acting like an idiot just came with the job.

She frowns, her fingers sliding away from my hair and stroking my shoulders. Her fingers focus on my bad side, stroking and pressing against the muscle. I grab her fingers before she presses any deeper and place them against my chest.

"How has physical therapy been?" She asks to my chest.

I close my eyes, knowing she already knew the answer. "I haven't been going."

"Why?"

I shrug, hoping I seem casual and unfazed. "I don't need it."

I lean forward until I feel her head against mine, pressing my forehead against her wet hair and nuzzling her. My hands wrap around her, pulling her closer to me and my cock twitches when her legs wrap around me and I feel her womanhood pressing against my tip.

Yes. This is exactly what I need. I don't need to talk about my feelings. I don't need to worry about the painkillers and the physical therapy appointments I haven't been going to. I don't need to worry about my useless father or my dying mother.

I just need a good, hard fuck.

My eyes flutter open and I see she's looking up at me, her eyebrows furrowed in worry. She opens her mouth as if to say something, but before she can I seize her lips, instantly deepening the kiss by pressing my tongue against hers. I hear her little gasp in shock, feel her legs tighten around me. My hands stroke her back, her arms, before cupping her ass and grinding myself against her.

Her head tilts back and I break the kiss, mouthing a path down her neck and grazing my teeth against her nape. She shudders and her nails dig into my shoulders.

"Hunter," she breathes and I growl, sliding my dick against her clit as I search for her entrance. "Hunter." She taps my shoulders, her legs tightening for a moment before moving away from my hips.

I groan, trying to bring her back to me, my hips thrusting and jabbing into her thigh. "Rachel, please," I whisper against her lips.

"Hunter, wait," she says, patting my shoulder and pushing me away.

I lean against the pool wall, my arms lying on the edge. I don't know why but my eyes brim with unshed tears. My heart twinges, as if it's shattering into a million pieces. Doesn't she know I need her right now? I need to feel something. I feel so unbelievably alone and broken and I feel like I'm stuck in limbo, not knowing where to go, what to do.

I'm a man. I shouldn't be feeling this way. I shouldn't be on the verge of tears, about to explode in front of a girl.

"Hunter, why don't you talk to me?" Rachel slowly swims towards me. "Tell me what's going on. Obviously something's wrong."

I sniff, wiping away the unshed tears. I grind my teeth against a sob, threatening to escape, instead forcing myself to laugh. "Nothing's wrong," I say, my voice cracking.

"I don't believe you."

I roll my eyes. "Fine."

Rachel sighs. "Stop fighting me. Tell me what's wrong, Hunter. Maybe I can help."

I scoff, shaking my head. "Like you could help me."

Rachel touches my shoulder and I turn to her, meeting her pitiful gaze. "Is it your shoulder?" She asks, her voice barely above a whisper.

I splash water in her face and quickly shove my body out of the pool, running through the veranda. "No it's not my fucking shoulder!" I shout, not bother to look back as I slam the door open.

I grab a blanket lying on the couch and throw it over me, ignoring the wide gazes of Lucas and Seth.

"What's going-" Seth starts, but I ignore him as I storm up the stairs back to my room.

This whole trip was a mistake. It was supposed to be fun. I was supposed to be skiing, drinking beer while watching the fire, fucking Rachel and enjoying some relaxing time before the new semester, but no. Rachel just had to go and be so fucking annoying. My shoulder this, are you okay that.

Can't she just leave me alone?

I throw upon the door to my room and rummage through my things, finding my pills and quickly popping open the bottle. My shoulder hasn't been aggravating me all that much today, but I just want to numb the pain. Any pain.

I down a pill and shove the rest in my backpack, determined not to take anymore until tomorrow.

Until I find someone who can get me more.

"Hunter, please talk to me," I hear Rachel say from behind. "What's going on? You're not acting yourself."

I scoff, glancing over my shoulder, seeing her dripping wet in the threshold wearing a long t-shirt ending mid thigh. "And how exactly do you know that?" I say, prowling towards her. "You barely know me, Rachel."

"I know you're sweet and you're kind."

I laugh bitterly. "Oh, really? It wasn't all that long ago Rachel that you hated us. That you hated me."

"I don't hate you, Hunter. I care about you. A lot."

I press a hand against the doorframe, towering over her. She's so small compared to me, yet she's standing with her chin jutting out, her eyes filled with fire. She's so freaking hot. My body is completely attuned to her and all I want to do is throw her over my shoulder, slam her down on the bed, and fuck her until she's screaming my name, begging for release.

"Why are you still taking painkillers?" she asks, her question taking me by surprise.

I blink, not knowing how to answer.

"I thought you said you were going to stop. I thought you were going to see the physical therapist instead."

I was going to, I think. *But then… things got in the way. And the painkillers make everything so easy.*

"That's none of your business," I say instead.

"It is my business." She stabs a finger into my chest. "Hunter, I'm so worried about you. You were a complete mess last night and you look unwell. Something must have happened. Please, just-"

"Leave me alone!" I shout, pressing my hands against my ears and whirling around, striding as far away from her as possible. "I told you already, everything's fine."

"No, it's not."

"Then take a hint. I don't want to talk about it."

"Why not?"

"Because I don't!" I shout, slamming my hands down on the windowsill, scowling outside at the beautiful snow-covered mountains in the distance. "Not everything has to be about you, or include you, Rachel. You're not my girlfriend. You don't just get to bark orders at me and insist I do everything at your beck and call."

There is silence behind me, followed by several sniffs. I toss my head back, groaning, knowing she's crying. A part of me wants to turn around, apologize for being a jerk, but the other part of me just wants to be alone.

"Okay," I hear her say, a slight tremble in her voice. "I understand."

I hear footsteps walking away, going down the stairs. I hear some muffled voices, most likely coming from Seth and Lucas, probably talking about what an ass I am. I don't care. I'm too exhausted. I return to my bed, throwing the blankets over me and willing myself back to sleep, this time happy when the shadows finally grant me my wish.

***

I pack my things, stuffing everything into my backpack, not bothering to fold anything. I try not to think while I do, which is easy since it's six in the morning. After sleeping most of the day away yesterday, I spent my next waking hours searching for a way out of this hellhole, finding a bus about a fifteen-minute walk away, probably more like thirty in all this snow and ice, which would take me to the outskirts of Aurora University. Then I could walk the rest of the way home.

I should've probably discussed this with the bros and Rachel. It probably looks like I'm running away, and I suppose I am, but I don't want to be fighting this whole trip. I don't want to deal with Rachel worrying about me all the time, pestering me with questions.

I think it's just for the best that we resume all this after we've all had a break from each other. Especially me and Rachel.

I just can't right now.

It's probably my fault. Actually, I think it's most definitely my fault. If I could just get over this hump, or whatever it is that is holding me back, and tell Rachel what's going on then maybe we wouldn't be fighting. But speaking to her about my mom, about what my family is going through, makes me feel like then it's true. My mom is actually dying.

And honestly, I'm not ready for the truth right now. I'm only twenty-one years old. I want to stay in my little Lala Land of pretend. I don't want to lose my mom. It's too soon for her to be going away.

I groan and wipe my face, hating myself for being so emotional. I feel so drained, yet I've hardly done anything. And it doesn't help that today is Saturday and I only have a day or so left until school resumes.

So much for a relaxing trip.

I tiptoe through the hall, grimacing when a creak sounds and pausing, waiting for Lucas or Rachel to throw open the door and demand to know where I'm going. I'm actually surprised Lucas and Seth didn't come upstairs yesterday and demand to know why we were fighting. I was actually thankful for that bit of privacy, although I had a feeling they would probably demand to know when we were back at the apartment.

Ugh. This whole situation is messy. Maybe this relationship or whatever I have with Rachel isn't working. Maybe it's time to call a quits on... us.

I sigh, standing in front of the door, my hand hesitating in front of the handle. If I leave now, what does that mean? Does that mean it's truly over between me and Rachel? Or does that mean our fight is on pause? Will this also be the end to my relationship with Lucas and Seth?

I drop my hand and look up the staircase, tempted to stay and resolve everything. I really missed Rachel. I really, really care for her. More than I have cared for any other woman other than my mother.

If this relationship fails, it's not on Rachel.

It's on me. It's my fault. I'm the one who's being the asshole. I'm the one who's not opening up to her.

She deserves so much better than me.

With that last thought, I take a breath and force myself to open the door, stepping outside into the snow and walking down the long path towards the bus stop.

4

SETH

Running in the snow is always a bit tricky. There's ice to watch out for and it's always best to have the grippiest shoes to ensure traction. Then there's the whole thing with outerwear. Do you wear everything you have because it's freezing outside, only to become a sweaty mess fifteen minutes in, wanting to rip every layer of fabric off your body? Or do you wear hardly anything and nearly freeze to death at the beginning of your run with the hope you become a reasonably happy runner about twenty minutes into your run?

Well, either way I was kinda screwed when I set out at five this morning. One with the ice. There are patches here and there and sometimes it's difficult to tell with the black ice. And then with the clothes, because, of course, I'm terrible at packing for myself so of course I ran in my old flimsy running joggers with the hole in the crotch.

Idiot me.

However, that isn't on my mind when I see Hunter in the distance, walking towards me and away from Lucas's mansion. His head is slumped down, not paying attention to me approaching him and he seems to be, once again, in a very foul mood.

I look down at my runner's watch, seeing that it's a little after six in the morning; a time I didn't think Hunter experienced unless he was coming in from a party. I frown, noticing his backpack hanging from his good shoulder.

Is the asshole really leaving?

I run for him, running as fast as possible. He can't leave now. Rachel is probably still upset. She was crying so hard last night. I had never seen her so upset. Not since four eyes tried to take advantage of her.

They had a fight so what. He can't just leave. Not without making things right.

"Where are you going?" I gasp, stopping in front of him and planting my hands on my knees.

Hunter stops, meeting my gaze with bloodshot eyes. They guy has been looking like shit these days. His face looks a bit thin and pale and his hair has been greasier than usual. Normally, Hunter is pretty narcissistic about his looks like the rest of us, yet the guy seems to have completely gone off the deep end.

"I'm heading back to the apartment early," says Hunter, his eyes sliding away from me and focusing on the snow.

"Does this have to do with Rachel?"

Hunter shrugs, but gives no answer and I sigh, lifting my head and trying to appear taller, bigger in front of this Thor look-alike. "You should talk to her," I say, watching his gaze turn into a scowl. "I know you care about her. If you leave now, she's only going to worry more."

Hunter shakes his head. "I need a break."

"A break from what?"

I don't even understand why they fought. Rachel wanted to know why Hunter is acting so weird, which is exactly what Lucas and I want to know. But apparently, Hunter wants to remain all secretive.

What exactly happened over winter break?

Hunter sighs and pulls his backpack further up his shoulder. "It's nothing you would understand."

I raise an eyebrow. "Try me. I'm a good listener."

Hunter scoffs.

"Ok, I'm sometimes a good listener. Especially with best friends."

Hunter shakes his head and steps around me. "I really don't want to talk about it, Seth. Especially now."

I follow him, not ready to let this go. "Okay, then you don't have to talk about it. Just stay. Hang out with us.

We'll be driving back tomorrow. You can stay one more day, right?"

Hunter sighs. "I'll just bring the group down. I think it's just best if I go home now. Get things ready for the semester."

I raise an eyebrow.. "Get things ready- who are you and what did you do to Hunter?"

Hunter chuckles, but his gaze doesn't meet my eyes.

I touch his shoulder, shaking it lightly. "I don't think you should be alone right now. You won't bring down the group. Not at all. We're a family. We stick together."

He nods, yet I can tell I'm not getting through to him. It's like he built a huge wall around him, refusing to let anyone inside. Like Sleepy Beauty's castle or whatever. If he really doesn't want to hang with us, what more can I do? I don't even know what else I can say.

"Okay, well, we'll be back tomorrow afternoon," I say when Hunter continues standing in front of me, looking down at the snow. "Just promise to take care of yourself. Get some rest and order some burritos or a pizza or something."

He nods and turns around without a word. I watch him go, frowning and feeling like I made the wrong choice. I should make him stay, drag his ass back and demand he at least just be in the same house as us. He can lock himself away in his bedroom so long as we're there if something bad happens.

I step forward, tempting to run and catch up with him, grab his ear and yank it back to Lucas's cottage, but I stop myself. Hunter is a big boy. He's always made his own choices and done his own thing. Nothing is going to change that.

I sigh and turn around, running back to the cottage and trying not to think about Hunter's pale, thin face or his bloodshot eyes.

***

When I arrive, I try not to think about Rachel's reaction to when I tell her Hunter had left. Instead, I guzzle down several glasses of water and set myself to work, sifting through the pots and pans in the cabinets below. After finding a skillet and scrounge around the refrigerator, finding some eggs, milk, and butter Lucas had bought yesterday before the party. I also find some flour and baking soda and set to work.

"What are you doing?" I hear Lucas ask from the living room.

I nearly jump, but I stop myself in time, not bothering to look up while I mix the baking soda and flour together. "What's it look like I'm doing?" I crack the eggs and pour in the milk. "I'm making pancakes."

"Why?"

I roll my eyes while stirring. "Because Rachel will need a big breakfast before we go skiing."

"So," I hear him rise from the couch, hear his footsteps on the floor while I turn on the stove and heat the pan. "This isn't about Hunter leaving?"

I sigh, my shoulders slumping while I wait for the butter to melt. "How did you know?"

"Heard something in the hallway. Saw Hunter leaving from my window."

I frown. "You didn't stop him?"

"I didn't think he would stay even if I tried. You saw him on your way back?"

I nod and pour in the mixture. "Yeah, I tried to talk him out of it. But he had his mind made up."

I glance over my shoulder and see Lucas leaning against the counter, staring at a crumb. "I think something happened over break," he says, his dark eyes lifting to mine. "I'm wondering if it has something to do with his mom."

I nod. "It would make sense. I just don't understand why he doesn't want to talk about it."

Lucas shrugs. "It's probably too hard for him to talk about. I think-" Lucas sighs and scratches the back of his head, his lips set into a hard line. "Ah! Nevermind. Those pancakes smell good."

I open my mouth, about to ask what Lucas was going to say when I hear footsteps on the stairs heading our way, which could only belong to one person. Excitement and anxiety tears through me, happy to see Rachel here, amongst us after these weeks apart, but at the same time really worried about how she's going to take the news.

She peaks around the corner, smiles at the both of us. Lucas straightens while I return to flipping the pancakes.

"That smells absolutely delicious," she says before placing a kiss on my cheek.

"Good, cuz they're for you," I say, handing her a plate with two pancakes.

"Hey, what about me?" I hear Lucas ask behind me and chuckle, placing more batter onto the skillet.

"Yeah, yeah, yeah. I'll make some for you, too."

"Where's Hunter?"

I grimace and wait for Lucas to say something, yet there's only silence. I flip Lucas's pancake, trying to focus on cooking rather than the drama that's about to break out.

"Well?" Asks Rachel when neither of us say anything.

"Lucas, do you want to do the honors?" I ask while dumping one pancake on a plate and adding more batter.

"Why don't you?"

I groan. "Because I'm cooking, asshole."

I can feel his scowl digging daggers into my scalp, but I don't care. I'm making breakfast. He can be the one to relay the bad news.

"Well, Hunter went back to the apartment."

"Why?"

Lucas sighs and I glance over my shoulder, watching him take Rachel's hand and hold it between them. "I think he needed some space to think."

"But I thought we were going to go back together."

I sigh, turning off the stove and placing the last pancake on Lucas's plate. I slide it over the counter towards him. I should probably make something for myself, but I'm no longer hungry. Something in my stomach twists at the whole situation, especially now, seeing tears in Rachel's eyes.

"Well, we'll see him tomorrow," says Lucas and I can see him trying desperately to find some sort of positive in this awkward situation.

Rachel sniffs and I watch her bite her bottom lip. "Did I do something wrong?"

"No," I say quickly, walking around the counter and throwing my arm over her shoulder, pulling her into a hug. "You did nothing wrong."

"Then why did he leave? Why doesn't he want to talk to me? I don't understand."

"I don't think you're supposed to understand," I say into her hair.

She pulls away from me, wiping at her eyes before stabbing a fork into her breakfast, shoving a large bite into her mouth.

"Let's have fun today," says Lucas. "We can go skiing first and then do some ice skating."

"Yeah," I say as cheerfully as I can muster. "It's our last day. Let's try to enjoy it as much as possible."

She nods curtly, shoving another bite into her mouth before offering a small, sad smile to us both.

After grabbing our gear and driving to the resort, I spent most of the day helping Lucas teach Rachel how to ski. She was absolutely pathetic. Like mind-blowingly pathetic. I had never seen anyone be so terrible at skiing. Every time she stood up, she would fall right back down. Even the five-year-olds were way better than her, zipping and laughing while they flew by.

I look down at the clock now, seeing that it's way past lunch. I look longingly at the larger slopes, wondering if I'll ever be able to ski down them, but at this rate, I know I should just give up. I'll go next time. There's always a next time when Lucas is your friend.

I glance over at the tall dark man now, who hasn't even touched his skis the whole day, unlike me. He helps Rachel up the small bunny hill, holding her hands and pulling her up, smiling at her affectionately as if none of this bothers him.

He's a very good faker.

I mean, I can believe he's having fun with Rachel. I think he likes taking others under his wing, but I know he's more upset about Hunter than he's letting on. I can't believe the bastard is smiling. The whole day I have been fighting the need to pout, to demand we head back and see how Hunter is doing.

Rachel looks over my shoulder, her goggles blocking my view of her eyes. She raises a hand at me and I force a smile, waving back. At least all this is taking her mind off Hunter. That fight last night was tough to listen to, and even more tough afterwards, when she came down crying. I was even more shocked when Hunter remained in his room for the rest of the day and the entire night. He didn't even come down for steaks we were grilling. Like… what the hell was up with that?

I watch Lucas push Rachel down the slope as if she's four years old and fight the need to roll my eyes. She wobbles downwards, moving her skis into a triangle, slowing her slide down the puny hill. She ends up right in front of me, a large smile on her face as she tries to keep her balance.

"I did it!"

"You sure did," I say sarcastically.

"Oh, you're so mean!" Rachel shouts, smacking my shoulders with her gloved hands.

"No! Stop!" I laugh, holding my hands up, but she doesn't stop. She wobbles on her skis before stumbling forward into my arms. I lose my balance and fall backwards, groaning as I feel the cold snow against my naked neck and her body pressing me into the chill.

She slides up her goggles while I lift my head and my heart seems to flutter as our gazes meet. I chuckle, poking her nose with my gloved finger, a smile growing on my face as she wrinkles her cute little nose.

And I feel myself needing to take her home immediately.

I lift us both up, help her kick her skis off while Lucas strides towards us. "Are we done, yet?" I ask.

"But you didn't get to go down the bigger slopes," says Rachel, slowly rising.

I smile. "I have other things on my mind."

Lucas raises an eyebrow while I waggle mine.

***

I don't quite remember how we got home, since I was so intent on pounding Rachel. I do remember ditching the whole ice skating plan and while Lucas drove, I could barely keep my hands to myself as I kissed and sucked on Rachel's lips. I remember the doors slamming and running inside, trying to get in as quick as possible.

I feel absolutely insatiable as soon as we get inside. Stripping off gloves and my coat, I toss them around the living room not caring where they land. I slip on the wet floor in an attempt to get to Rachel, feeling my cock harden as I watch her writhe against Lucas, currently mouthing her neck. His eyes are glued to mine and I feel my cheeks flush, my cock twitching and leaking precum.

    Lucas unzips Rachel's coat, gently pulling her arms out from the thick fabric and tossing it on the couch. Rachel shoves her boots off while I yank my sweater off my body, turning my attention to my snow pants.

    Lucas unzips his coat, his fingers moving frantically and I can see the outline of his hardened bulge through his tight pants. Rachel seems to notice as well and strides towards him, pulling off her shirt until she's standing in only her bra and her snow pants. Her hand cups his bulge, stroking it and earning a moan from Lucas, who bucks against her.

    I stride towards them, wrapping my arms around her and cupping her breasts. Pulling them out of their constraints, I pinch and pull at her nipples, smiling as her head lulls against my shoulder. She gasps when I pinch the right especially hard and I groan, feeling her ass squirm against my hard length. Lucas takes the left into his mouth, sucking on it and earning a cry from her lips. Quickly, he slides off his shirt and I watch Rachel reach for his pants, pulling them and his underwear down, which he kicks to the side.

    We take turns kissing her, touching her. My cock slides against her ass while I mouth her neck and Lucas seizes her lips. I want her wanting and begging like before. I want to slip my dick into her wet oasis and lose myself in her. I don't want to think about Hunter; don't want to worry about if he actually made it home and if his family is well.

    All I want is the bliss of being with Rachel and feeling her body pressed against mine.

    I pull away from her neck, finding an armchair behind us and I stumble backwards, pulling us there together as a group. I sit Rachel down in the chair, ignoring her curious gaze as I position myself behind her. I unclasp her bra, pulling it away while Lucas does the same with her pants.

"What are you two up to?" She asks coyly. She smiles up at me, yet I notice there's no gleam in her eye. It's unusual and I worry she's still thinking about Hunter.

I press her back into the chair, my hands sliding down her front to grasp her breasts once more. She arches while I continue to pinch and prod. I watch Lucas spread her legs, his fingers sliding against her womanhood. Rachel moans, her legs going over Lucas's shoulders while he pushes a finger inside her.

"We're going to torture you so good you won't even remember your name," I whisper into her ear, enjoying the shudders racking her body.

Her breasts heave with each breath she takes. It's like watching a porno, watching Lucas slide a finger inside her, listening to Rachel's moans and cries as she thrusts her hips into him. I bite my lip, feeling precum once again leak from the tip of my cock as Rachel's voice heightens, her moans becoming louder and longer as Lucas tongues her clit, circling around her little pleasure nub while sliding another finger inside her.

I want his fingers to be my cock so bad. I want to feel her on my dick. I don't even know if I can outlast this torture session long enough to feel it. My fingers pull and pinch at her breasts frantically while I try to calm myself, but it only seems to make me grow even hornier as she bucks against me and Lucas.

Her hand laces with mine while her other clutches at Lucas's hair. Her head jerks from side to side as she clings to us. "Don't stop!" she shouts and I hear Lucas's slurping becoming louder, watch as he inserts another finger into her.

I watch him push in and out of her several times before pulling away, his gaze locking with mine. A predatory smile on his face as he gazes up at me, "She's pretty wet."

    My cock twitches and I release her, scrambling towards her front and pressing my fingers against her entrance. I moan, feeling her wet walls tighten around my fingers, wishing I could just forgo the condom and ram my cock deep inside her.

    "I told you not to stop," Rachel whimpers, thrusting her hips against me.

    She smiles wickedly and then with one foot, she kicks me away. I allow myself to fall backwards, allow her to straddle me. She grabs my cock with both hands, pumping me up and down. My eyes roll to the back of my head, moaning as she jerks me.

    "Condom!" I shout, my hands trying to grab something.

    My nails dig into the wood, clawing at it. I reach for the couch leg, yet it's too far away. I need something to ground me. I feel like my body is floating too high, like I will explode if I don't hang on to something. I hear tearing and open my eyes, watching Lucas hand Rachel a condom. She wraps it around my twitching and pulsing cock and my hands reach for her, landing on her hips as she rises above me.

    "I don't know how long I can last," I say, my words coming out as a breath and turning into one long moan as she slowly lowers herself on me.

    I watch her balance on top of me before taking Lucas's cock in her mouth, sucking at his tip and then taking him deep in her throat. I lick my lips, my hips thrusting up and into her. Rachel gasps against Lucas's cock and I do it again, trying to shove myself so deep inside she screams.

    I steady her with my hands, holding onto her hips while I continue moving. I don't think I can even stop at this point. My hips have a mind of their own and all I want is that sweet release. I watch Rachel meet each and everyone of my thrusts and my heart flutters as she moans and writhes above me.

I hear Lucas above us, his thrusts smacking into Rachel's mouth. She cups his balls, tugging at them lightly and eliciting more gasps from Lucas. "Fuck, Rachel," I hear him whisper, watch him stroke her cheek and gaze lovingly down at her. "You're so fucking good."

"Yes," I hiss, thrusting even harder into her, hearing her moans turn to cries. "So fucking good. Amazingly good." I groan while my hand slips from her hip and my thumb rubs against her clit. She leans into the touch and I feel my cock pulse, knowing I am getting so close to that sweet release.

"Please, tell me you're close," I whimper, my head thrashing back and forth.

I hear a moan from Lucas and a cry from Rachel and finally I let myself go. I allow my primitive side to take over, thrusting into her hard and fast while my thumb circles around her. I hear Lucas's thrusts picking up, hearing the steady smack of him while Rachel cries above me, her hips moving fervently against me.

"I'm going to come," I hear Lucas breathe above me, hear him shout. I watch him clutch Rachel's head, holding her there as he pours himself into her. I slow my pace, not wanting to move so violently that she ends up choking on his cum. Although, it takes every power within me to slow down.

As soon as she swallows I grab her hips and slam her onto me, thrusting upwards as hard as I possibly can. "Yes!" Rachel shouts, her hands clinging to my shoulders, her nails digging into my flesh and probably leaving marks I will find tomorrow.

I feel my cock pulsing, feel myself spiking, nearing the end of the race. I can't stop myself from throwing back my head, shouting my release as I slam myself into her one more time, my cock twitching before pouring myself inside. Rachel twitches above me, my thumb still massaging her clit until finally her jaw slackens and I hear her cry out in bliss.

Her body slumps against mine and I rub her back while sliding my cock out from her. I hear my heart pounding, feel Lucas's breath on my shoulder as he nuzzles against us. He strokes Rachel's hair, moving it away from her face. Both of us watch her. Her eyes are closed, her lashes kissing her freckled skin, her lips slightly parted.

And then her eyes are blinking open, looking sadly between us and I already know the words she's going to say before she says them.

"I'm still worried about Hunter."

5

HUNTER

I open the door and throw my backpack inside, watching it slide across the floor. The place looks the same, although pretty quiet without Lucas and Seth's bickering and Rachel's laughter. I frown, leaning against the wall and wondering for the thousandth time today if I made the right choice. I was being a big bump on the log. I didn't want to ruin their vacation anymore than I already had. And I certainly didn't want to talk about what was going on.

What other choice did I have?

I sigh, sliding my body down the wall and staring at the empty kitchen and the empty living room. What should I do next? I guess I could make myself something to eat. I hadn't eaten the whole day, and it was already four.

I push myself off the floor and walk towards the refrigerator. When I open it, I frown, finding a carton of orange juice, half drunk and probably fermenting given the expiration date was from last year. There's also a pizza box, although I don't think I want to open the lid and see what's underneath given the smell wreaking out of the door.

I slam it shut and sigh, scratching my head and wondering if I should just go to the grocery store.

Or maybe I could go home. It's not that far away. Dad would probably be there and I could go visit Mom. I grimace just thinking of my father, recalling the last time I saw him, which was at the doctor's appointment. I don't think he would want to see me after that little discussion. I did pretty much call him useless.

Why did I say that?

If anyone's useless, I am. I'm the one who's been with her throughout her disease and even after having both breasts removed, she's still ill, she's still fighting death.

And I don't think she can win this battle. Not this time.

I feel my bottom lip tremble, feel my heart swell at the thought and I lean against the refrigerator, allowing myself to be weak this one time, now that I'm alone. I sob into my hands, allowing the tears to flow out of me, allowing myself to feel the guilt wrack through me. I haven't been to visit my mother since I discovered the truth. I haven't seen her since they diagnosed her again. What kind of son am I?

Terrible.
Exhausted.
Nothing.
Nothing. That's exactly what I am.

I gasp, wiping the tears from my eyes as I try to regain some level of control. I can't go to the grocery store looking like this. I need to look somewhat decent.

My phone beeps and vibrates and I reach into my jean pocket, grabbing it and seeing that I have two text messages. One is from Rachel, the other is from Millie.

I frown, not knowing which one to open first. The text from Rachel is about twenty minutes old. She's had some time to think and reflect on why I was gone and about our fight. Maybe it wouldn't be so bad if I read it.

But at the same time, I don't want to deal with it. I want a break. I don't want another screaming match and her demanding me to open up when all I want is a hug.

Instead, I open Millie's text message, seeing that she just sent it: *Hey, party tonight handsome! Want to get freaky? ;)*

Millie is fun. Also, an exceptional lay. It might be fun to get out, hang out with some different people for a change. My gaze goes to Rachel's message, lingering there for a moment before finally making up my mind.

I text: *Where's the party at?*

***

The house is only a short twenty-minute walk away and easy to find due to the banging music and the clusters of jocks and scantily clad women hanging out on the lawn and porch. I nod my head at those I recognize while stuffing my hands into my pockets to keep them from fidgeting. I don't know why, but I feel nervous. Anxiety tenses my shoulders and I can't help but feel guilty, knowing that I should be with Rachel and the bros enjoying our last night at the cottage and sliding my dick in and out of Rachel's mouth.

The image makes me hard and I nearly turn around as I reach the top step up the porch, wondering what the hell am I doing. I haven't talked to Millie in the last few months and she had blown me off before.

I should go home.

Despite that, I don't want to be alone and I reach for the door, throwing it open and stepping inside. As soon as I enter the bass of the music hits me, making sound nearly impossible. Smoke and something else permeates the air.

Pot?

I dodge several jocks heading towards me. The whole place is crowded, sweltering. I'm tempted to throw off my coat, but I'm afraid I might lose it in this mess. I pass by a kitchen filled with bros holding a guy's legs as he does a keg stand.

"Chug! Chug! Chug! Chug!" They shout while the guy's legs sway in the air.

I look around for a moment, finding girls laughing while sitting on the countertops, but I don't see Millie.

Maybe this is a bad idea.

"Hey handsome," I hear someone say from behind, feel arms reaching around me and a chin nuzzling into my shoulder.

I turn and see Millie, her blonde hair curled and framing her face. Bright eyes gleam up at me while she presses her breasts against my arm. Her hand laces with mine and she pulls me deeper into the chaos with not another word.

I follow her into a small room with several raggedy couches resting against wooden walls. It's quieter here with only a few guys sitting in a corner, talking quietly to themselves. They don't even glance our way as Millie pushes me onto the couch. I watch them for a moment, wondering why they seem so vacant. I don't recognize them from classes or from any sports, but then again the campus is big.

"It's been awhile," says Millie while unzipping my coat.

She hovers above me for a moment, her gaze raking over me like I'm some sort of juicy steak she's about to sink her teeth in. I feel another twinge of guilt sting my heart and sit up, trying to focus on my surroundings and not on the beautiful girl lifting her leg up to straddle my lap.

I cringe as I see her naked thigh, realizing just now that she's wearing a very short skirt, and it's currently riding up, nearly exposing her underwear. I can feel her warmth against my lap and my cock twitches, wanting to sink deep inside her. I grind my teeth, hating myself for being here and feeling this way when I should be with Rachel.

I clear my throat, focusing on the smoke smudged walls on the guys in the corner nodding off. One is wearing a baseball cap pushed over his forehead and covering his face. His brown curls are tangled and hang limply on his shoulders. The other sitting next to him has his black

hoody up with his chin to his chest, appearing like he's sleeping with his eyes closed.
Well, they're the life of the party, now aren't they? I think while my eyes slide to the door.
"Yeah, it has been awhile," I say, not knowing what else to tell her. It's not like Millie and I were ever known for our lengthy, deep, all-nighter discussions. Usually we spoke through our bodies, not with our lips, unless our lips were on each other's bodies.
"I've missed you," Millie pouts while stroking my face, leaning in close to me.
I slide my tongue over my teeth as her cleavage is practically thrown into my face. I'm so close to throwing her off me and running away or throwing her on the couch and having my way with her in front of these losers.
I close my eyes and take a deep breath. I need to go. I need to return home and call Rachel and apologize for being an ass.
Lips meet my jaw and I flinch, my fingers digging into the couch to keep from touching Millie. Her tongue traces the shell of my ear and I feel guilt and desire pull and push at me, as if I have a demon and an angel on each shoulder pulling me back and forth.
"Have you missed me?" she breathes into my ear.
I open my eyes and turn towards her. Licking my lips, I open my mouth, not knowing what I'm about to say or do. Millie leans into me, her lips slowly lowering onto mine until-
The door slams open and we both jump. "Jesus!" Millie shouts, sliding off me and pulling down her skirt. I see a flash of black panties and quickly look away, finding two men standing at the door. They look between us, their eyes narrowing on the guys passed out across from us.
"There they are," said one, a tall and thin looking man who has to be at least ten years older than me. He sways towards the guys, shaking one's shoulder violently.

"Wake the fuck up!" he shouts, but the guy only slides further into the couch, groaning but his eyes remaining firmly close.

"Millie," says the other man, closer to my age with a pudgy face and a thick gut. He's wearing a thick Aurora sweater with the hood up. He grabs Millie's arm and pulls her into him, giving her a big bear hug and making her giggle.

"Oh, Drew!" she laughs while smacking his shoulder. "Put me down!"

Drew sets her down, his eyes sliding to mine. He steps towards me while I stand, eagerly making my way for the door. "I should get going," I murmur, keeping my head downcast. I cringe as I watch the other man out of the corner of my eye grab one of the sleepers, dragging him off from the couch before shoving him back down.

"No, stay," says Drew, placing a hand on my chest before I can make it to the door. "I interrupted you two. I apologize."

I shook my head. "It's nothing. I was about to leave anyway." I turn to Millie, giving her an apologetic look while she frowns at me and crosses her arms.

"You look like you could use some fun," says Drew while walking around me. He pats Millie's shoulder before sitting down into the sofa. "Jerry, will you stop it already?" he says to his accomplice with a sigh. "They're obviously out of it. Just give it a break. We'll get them in the morning." He pats his lap and Millie smiles, hopping onto his leg and wrapping her arms around his neck.

Jerry sighs and sits down next to the sleepers, taking out a plastic bag of some sort of white powder. I frown, my feet shifting from side to side. I don't want to be rude and up and leave, worried Millie will spread around to the frats and sororities I behaved like a little bitch at a party she invited me to. But, whatever is in that bag, it can't be good. I could lose my football scholarship. Hell, scratch that, if the cops were to bust this place, I could say goodbye to a football career.

"Don't worry," says Drew with a large smile. "Come, talk with us. We won't bite."

I shake my head. "I really should probably get going."

Drew sighs. "It's just, you look like you saw a ghost or something."

I shrug. "I'm just... having an off night."

Drew nods, looking understanding. "Fair enough. Say no more. Millie, why don't you grab us some beer."

Millie nods, placing a kiss on Drew's cheek before standing. Drew smacks her ass as she stands and she giggles, rubbing her cheek while sliding by me.

"And some shots!" Drew calls after her before the door closes.

"Hey," says Jerry, pointing a finger at me. "Don't I recognize you from somewhere?"

I shrug. "I don't know." I walk around the couch and sit on the far corner, ensuring there's a seat between me and Drew.

"Aren't you the quarterback or something?"

I smile and nod. "Yes, I play football."

Jerry smacks his hands together. "I knew it! You're like, good and stuff."

I twiddle my fingers together, feeling antsy and wishing I could have something to hold or do with my fingers. My leg bounces up and down and I feel something in the back of my head itch. That gnawing need is clawing at me. I don't have my pills on me. I only have a few left. I need to save them.

But still, I can't stop that yearning from taking over. I wring my hands, trying to pay attention to the rhythmic booming of the bass in the background rather than my need for the pills. Drew's eyes are on me, watching my every move while Jerry plays with one of the sleepers' hats.

The door opens and Millie reappears with two large bottles in her hands. "Guess who brought vodka?" she calls in a singsong tune before sauntering inside.

She plops herself between me and Drew and hands one bottle to Jerry and the other to Drew. I watch as each takes a long swig, trying to ignore Millie's hands sliding against my arm. Drew hands me the bottle and I take it urgently, chugging down several long swigs of vodka, enjoying the burn in the back of my throat and the fuzziness drowning out that itch in the back of my head.

"Man, you can drink," says Drew when I hand the bottle back. "But I bet famous jocks like you get invited to all the cool parties."

"Oh, Hunter isn't just a footballer," says Millie, grabbing the bottle from Jerry and taking a long swig. "He lives in a house with beautiful men. They're like Gods."

Drew chuckles. "As Godlike as me, Millie-bean?" he asks while gesturing to himself.

Millie slides her hands off me and leans into Drew. "No, you're the best, Drew-bear."

"Well are we going to get this party started or what?" asks Jerry, dangling the bag of white powder up for all eyes to see.

I grab the bottle from Millie and take another swig. "No," I say between each long swig, the alcohol making words feel funny on my tongue. "I don't do drugs," I slur.

Millie giggles while Jerry scoffs.

Drew straightens on the couch and nods at me, once again staring at me with those understanding eyes I have been longing for so long. I wish my dad would look at me like that. I wish he would just recognize how painful it is for me to care for mom, when he should have been there for the both of us.

I wish Rachel would just let me be sad; just hug me and be there for me rather than pressing me for answers I don't even know if I have and judging me for letting myself go. I wish the bros would at least keep the pity from their eyes when they looked at me. I could read them like an open book. I knew they felt pity for me; knew they whispered about my shoulder and my dead career when my back was turned.

"You know, alcohol is a drug," says Drew.

I chuckle. "Yeah, yeah, everyone says that, but it's legal."

"It still kills, just like drugs. You use it to have fun, just like we use a bit of powder here and there for fun." Drew shrugs before taking the bag from Jerry's hands. "Just one is regulated whereas the other isn't."

I shake my head and take another long swig. "I'm quite fine with my vodka," I slur while shaking the bottle, grimacing when I notice it's nearly empty.

Drew nods. "Totally fine," he says before sprinkling some powder on his tongue before moving to Millie. "No peer pressure here."

"I want to go dancing," says Millie while bounding out of the couch. "Can we go dancing?" She grabs Drew's hand and drags him out of the couch.

I stand, but waver, my balance completely thrown off. Groaning, I shake my head, yet it only makes my dizziness worse. Everything is coming to me in two's and I laugh, stumbling backwards and nearly falling into the couch.

Drew takes my hand and steadies me. "Better stay with us until you sober up a bit," he says while pulling me out of the room and through the halls.

The music seems louder, the bass blasting and making the walls reverberate. I follow them into the living room, feeling like I'm walking through a dream. So many faces stare back at me, some laughing, others crying. Their faces merge together and become a blur, and all I can concentrate on is the beat of the music and the chattering around me.

I sway back and forth in the living room, feeling Millie slide her hands up and down my body. I groan, trying to keep myself upright, but I think I might vomit. My stomach wretches and I stumble out of the room, pushing my way through the crowd until I'm running inside the kitchen, vomiting my insides into a sink.

Gasping, I wash it down the sink before chugging several gulps of water. I feel hands at my back, and assuming it's Millie, I bat the hands away, not wanting her to touch me any longer.

"Stop," I murmur, turning to the person and finding Drew.

"You are all sorts of messed up," he says with a smile.

"I should get home," I say, already looking for an exit.

"Here," says Drew while handing a beer to me. "Just have another drink with us." He gives me a wink and taps his cup against mine.

I sigh, and quickly down the contents before following him back into the living room. The music has changed into something pop-y and several girls are on the floor with their hands in the air. I sway to the beat, closing my eyes and feeling like I'm in my own little world. I try not to think about Rachel, about the bros, and my mom in the hospital. I try to be present and enjoy the now.

As I move something comes over me, something soothing and my heart flutters, feeling as if I am one with this song. I feel as if I am flying, or orgasming. My skin tingles with a strange sensation, like I'm hot and cold at the same time. Everything feels so wonderful.

My lips twitch upwards and I raise my hands up, feeling incredible joy spreading through me. Someone is grinding against me and I open my eyes, seeing Millie grabbing my hands and placing them on her hips. We move as one with the beat. My head lulls from side to side and I feel like I'm swimming. Drew hands me another beer and I chug it. I'm losing control of time, of my body. I feel giddy, wanting to dance and talk and sit all at once. I ride the waves, sitting on the couch and petting it, allowing the smooth fabric soothe me.

"Hunter, let's go," says Millie while trying to drag me away.

I shake my head. "I don't want to," I say quickly. Each breath I take it feels as if I am plunging myself into ecstasy. I feel wonderful. Life is wonderful, beautiful, and I never want to be rid of this sensation.

"Hunter, please," says Millie while tugging on me again.

"Millie, I don't want to fuck you." I tug her back to the couch. My teeth grind together. I can't stop myself from smiling. "Do you want to talk? I can tell you so much. Like about Rachel and how beautiful she is, or about Seth and how much of an idiot he can be."

Millie glares at me, tears brimming her eyes. "No, I don't want to talk about Rachel, you idiot! I want to fuck you."

I shake my head, the sensation feeling absolutely wonderful. "No, let's not," I say simply. "Let's dance!" I bound from the sofa and sprint to the middle of the living room where five people are still dancing.

Millie smacks the couch and stalks away, but I'm too happy to care. All I want to do is dance. My mother flashes into my mind and I groan, rubbing my eyes and frowning. I shake it away and listening to the music, jumping up and down in time with the beat. The music has changed into rock music. I laugh while shoving my shoulders against someone. Someone shoves themselves against me and we continue moshing for I don't know how long.

I don't know where I get more beer, but within a blink of an eye it's in my hand. It disappears just as quickly. Things happen in flashes, my mind no longer able to process everything. My heart beats rapidly and I press my hand against it, worried I'm going to have a heart attack.

Nevertheless, when Drew and Jerry go to the bathroom, I follow them.

And I sniff everything they give me.

There is more dancing and more drinking and I don't know how long it's been since Millie left me.

I blink, feeling sharp rays burst in from the window.

Why is it so sunny? I wonder while staring at my hands.

I blink again and we're in the bathroom, snorting powder off the toilet.

I stumble onto a couch and pass out. When I open my eyes Drew is saying something to me while Jerry is beating someone into a pulp.

I can't make sense of Drew's words.

I can't make sense of anything.

I slowly slip on the couch, resting my head against the cushions while Drew continues to say something to me, his voice sounding distant.

I blink, but this time my eyes don't open.

The shadows suck me deep inside their embrace.

6

RACHEL

I smile as we approach the apartment and nearly throw myself out of the SUV when Lucas finishes parking. I don't even bother to grab my suitcase, choosing to run across the street and bolt up the stairs, taking two steps at a time. Digging in my coat pockets for the keys I jam them into the keyhole, wondering if Hunter is lounging in the living room or playing Mario Kart.

He must still be angry with me.

He hasn't answered any of my texts.

"Rachel!" I hear Seth call from below. "A little help here would be nice."

I ignore him as I throw open the door. "Hunter," I call, but frown when I see the couch empty and the lights off. The door to his room is slightly ajar and I pad towards it, knocking on it slightly while murmuring, "Hunter."

His backpack is in the corner. Clothes are strewn all over the floor, but the bed is empty. I sigh, my shoulders slumping while I turn around, striding out of his room and listening for the sound of the shower running. However, I hear nothing and when I push the bathroom door open, I find it empty.

He's not here.

I blink back the tears and take a deep breath. It's four in the afternoon. *He's probably in the gym or at football practice,* I tell myself. However, I can't help but feel like something is wrong. I can't help but wonder why he isn't here. Is he really still mad at me?

I don't even know what I did wrong.

"Alright, you're shit's here," gasps Seth while throwing my suitcase inside. His shoulders heave while he wipes the sweat from his brow. "What the hell did you pack in that thing?"

I smile and walk towards him. "Just everything I need." I wrap my arms around his neck and place a chaste kiss on his lips. "Thanks for hauling it up."

Seth scowls at me, but I know he's just teasing. "Next time, you do it. I'm not your bell boy."

I giggle while patting his cheek. "Nope, you definitely are not."

"Is Hunter here?" asks Lucas while he shoves his body inside the door, carrying several bags and a large suitcase behind him.

I shake my head. "No. I think he's at the gym."

At least I hope so.

Lucas nods. "It's probably for the best. He just needs to blow off some steam."

Seth nods in agreement. "Yeah, I wouldn't worry about it."

Lucas kicks the door close and I grab my suitcase, dragging it behind me to my old room. I push the door open, smiling at the dingy place I now call home. Fairy lights are strung up around my desk with a cork board propped up against the wall. Different photos of me and the bros, the campus, and me and the girls are pinned to it. The chair wobbles as I drop my body in it, spinning myself around and near tumbling out of it. I still need to either replace the leg or buy a new chair altogether. Little light enters from the tiny window. The sun is beginning to set, but I still have so much to do.

I grab my cell from my coat pocket and send a text to my group chat with Lauren and Charlie: *Hey ladies!!! I'm back!! Let's say coffee tomorrow at the Coffee Shop?*

Not even a minute goes by and I receive at text from Charlie: *I'm game, gurl! 2pm sharp!*

I chuckle and read the next message from Lauren: *Ooooh! Coffee. Sounds great :)*

It will be nice to chitchat with the girls again. I have so much to tell them about New York and the ski trip. I lay my cellphone on my desk before turning to my mighty suitcase, wanting to search for my charger.

As I unzip it I wonder if I should bring up Hunter to my girlfriends. Maybe they could give me some advice on what to do. I can't decide if I should give him some space, or throw myself at him. Although, the latter idea is something I have pretty much decided on, a part of me knows neediness tends to drive men away.

Maybe just letting him be is the best for now.

My head perks up as I hear the door slam close and I drop whatever garments I have in my hands and quickly stumble out of my room. I don't know why, but I'm practically running for the door. "Hunter?" I call, a large smile on my face.

I stop when I see someone in the kitchen, his head hanging over the sink while he guzzles down several gulps of water. He looks like Hunter. He definitely acts like Hunter. Yet, is he Hunter? His hands tremble as he turns off the water and wipes the liquid from his mouth. His long blonde hair looks greasy and lusterless and hangs over his eyes, which turn to me, looking shadowed and bloodshot.

"Hey, Rachel," he says awkwardly, turning his gaze to the floor while leaning against the countertop. "What's up?"

He doesn't look like he's been to the gym at all. And he's only wearing a t-shirt and jeans. *Did he just get in?* I wonder before asking myself, *where's his coat?*

As if he reads my mind, his hands move up and down his exposed arms, his skin prickled with chill. I watch his jaw clench and unclench while I answer, "Nothing. We just got back."

Seth pops his head out of his room and I watch him stride into the kitchen, looking Hunter up and down. "Where did you come from?" He sniffs and groans, taking a step back while covering his mouth. "Shit man, where the hell have you been? You smell like a fucking bar."

Hunter chuckles while scratching his head. "Yeah, I should probably go take a shower."

Lucas strides in from behind, crossing his arms and leaning against the wall. "Hey man, you're back." He looks Hunter up and down before crinkling his nose and making a face. "Where have you been?"

I cross my arms, mirroring Lucas's stance while I mutter, "Obviously not at the gym."

Hunter groans, his head rolling from side to side as he straightens away from the counter and towards his room. "Nowhere important."

"We were worried about you," says Lucas as Hunter strode past him.

Hunter pauses, his hand on the doorknob to his room. "Yeah, well, you didn't need to be."

Seth sighs and takes a step towards Hunter. "You can tell us, Hunter. We-"

"Oh my fucking god!" shouts Hunter while throwing open his door. "Will you leave me the fuck alone!"

He slams it shut in our faces and all three of us stare at it. I don't know what the boys are thinking, but my mouth gapes open, wondering why he went from zero to one hundred in the blink of an eye.

We just want to know if he's okay.

He's obviously not.

I step towards Hunter's door, wanting to knock on it, wanting to give him a hug and tell him whatever it is he doesn't have to tell me. I just want to be there for him. I want to beg him not to push me and the others away.

But Lucas grabs my shoulder, stopping me.

I turn around, seeing Lucas's and Seth's glares and deep frowns. They glance at each other for a moment before giving me a shake of their head in unison, as if they are able to read each other's minds.

"Don't, Rachel," says Lucas while pulling me into his arms. I sniff, wrapping my arms around Lucas's waist before nuzzling my forehead into his shoulder. "Just give him his space for now, alright?" he whispers into my ear.

Seth comes to stand next to me, nuzzling his forehead against my cheek while running a hand up and down my back. "You don't deserve to be treated that way," he murmurs and I sniff again, blinking back tears.

Oh, why is this so difficult? Why can't Hunter just talk to me? All I want to do is be there for him. But I guess...

That's not what he wants.

I force a smile and push the two away, wiping the tears from my eyes and hoping I've put on a brave face. They both stare back at me solemnly, and I force a chuckle, taking their arms and leading them to the couch.

"Let's do something fun!" I say, trying to sound as cheerful as possible, but my voice comes out thick, slightly trembling as I try to swallow a sob. "It's our last night."

Thankfully, Lucas and Seth decide to ignore the quivering in my voice and both smile at me. Lucas grabs his phone and holds it up while announcing, "I'll order the pizza."

Seth leads me to the couch. "And I'll prepare the entertainment." He waggles his eyebrows while lowering himself on the floor, picking up two games and holding them in front of my face. "Halo or Mario Kart?"

I grab Mario Kart, giggling when Seth rolls his eyes with a mocking groan. "Knew it!"

He shoves it into the player while Lucas speaks with the pizza place. Seth sidles next to me on the couch, handing me a controller while wrapping an arm around my shoulders, pulling me close. I chance a glance behind me, at Hunter's door, silently wishing he would come out of his room and join us.

Yet, his door remains shut.

7

LUCAS

I blink my exhausted, weary eyes as I walk through campus, trying to avoid falling on my ass with all the ice covering the sidewalks. I'm practically ice skating my way to class, which is pretty dangerous considering I barely got any sleep last night. Between Hunter being a fucking asshole to us and Seth and I trying to cheer Rachel up, all while operating on a completely different sleep schedule, this first day of class is really going to blow. Which sucks, because I've been looking forward to it all vacation long.

    I stop in front of the liberal arts building, taking a moment to gaze up at the marble stone, its windowsills covered in pristine white snow with naked trees surrounding the area. I inhale deeply, allowing the fresh air to seep into my body while I look around at the area. It's completely different from the Political Science building I'm usually accustomed to going to, where the building is more brutalist and there's no greenery around. It's like I've walked into a completely different world, surrounded by students shuffling past, who are dressed in black beanies and rumpled coats.

    The art building isn't far from here, probably about a five-minute walk, and I briefly wonder if I can meet with Rachel after class some day for a quick coffee. While looking around I imagine the place in spring; imagining the trees covered in leaves and blossoming flowers. There's even a patch of grass in front of the building with benches overlooking the campus. I imagine myself sitting with Rachel, her talking about photography, me talking about my poetry all while drinking coffee and looking at the beauty of Aurora University.

I sigh, feeling overwhelmed with excitement and nervousness. This is my second writing class this year, this time focusing on poetry. I don't know how I did it, but I was able to talk my councilor into skipping Writing 201 after showing a flimsy portfolio of my work to several English professors. I guess they liked what they saw, which surprised me. A part of me wonders if they somehow made a mistake, but I don't plan on asking them.

I frown, wondering how this is going to go over in the Brent household. It was already hard enough explaining the first writing class to my father. I originally told him it was good for future lawyers to be able to craft an eloquent speech.

I doubt he would be so reasonable with me taking another writing class.

But I don't want to be a lawyer. I never wanted to be. It's something he wanted for me; to follow in the footsteps of all the Brents before me. Become a lawyer, make tons of money, settle down with a perfect wife and have perfect children I barely know. And repeat.

I shake my head as I enter the building, the warmth hitting me immediately. I smile up at the long hall in front of me, a staircase to my right. I'm finally here, about to pursue my dream in becoming a poet. And fuck my father. I'm not him. And I don't ever want to be him. One of these days, I'm going to become a writer.

He just doesn't know it yet.

I feel my cellphone buzz in my back pocket as soon as I take a step towards the hall. Grabbing it, I move away from the entrance as students push past me, finding a corner out of everyone's way. I frown at the time before I groan. Not only is my class starting in about five minutes, but my caller ID reads: *Rich Bastard.*

It's my dad.

Speak of the devil.

I inhale deeply, counting to ten and reminding myself the asshole pays for my bills so I shouldn't be a complete jerk. And I want him to keep paying for my luxurious lifestyle. I haven't worked a day in my life and I plan on keeping it that way for just a bit longer.

Forcing a smile, I answer, "Hey Dad."

"Why are you taking another writing class?"

Ugh.

I knew he was going to find out eventually, but why now? It's like the guy stalks each and every one of my moves.

"Can we talk about this later?" I ask, trying to sound calm and reasonable, which is easier said than done. "Class is about to start."

How did the guy even access my school account?

I close my eyes as I recall saving my password on my laptop at home. He probably found a tech guy to break into the computer and accessed it that way.

Great.

"I know it's about to start," I hear him say on the other side. He sounds like he's trying very hard not to shout at me. I realize he's probably known for a while. Maybe Mom talked him out of calling me and he finally reached his breaking point. "That's why I'm calling."

I grind my teeth to keep myself from saying anything, knowing it will only make things worse. I hear Mom in the background saying, "You should have waited until tonight."

Ah, Mom. Always the mediator.

"I thought we agreed you'd be taking that American Foreign Policy class."

I wince. He is still on that whole thing. That class looks, and probably is, absolutely boring. "Yeah, I remember us talking about it." *However, I didn't say anything about actually taking it.*

"It will look better on your transcript rather than-"

I frown, noticing the students quickly dispersing to their classes. I look at my watch, noticing I have about thirty seconds before being marked tardy. "I'm sorry, Dad. I really must go. Can't we talk about this later?"

"No, we can't talk about this later!"

I grimace, pulling the phone away from my ear while striding down the hall, looking at the numbers and searching for Room 113.

"This is a complete waste of your time. You should be focusing on what will help you in grad school."

"Uh-huh," I say, stopping in front of my room. I look at the time, stifling a groan as I see I'm already two minutes late. I hear Dad going on and on, but I'm not paying attention.

I grab a gum wrapper from my coat pocket and rub it against the receiver on my phone. "Dad?" I shout. "Dad?"

I hear him shouting, but I continue rubbing my phone with the wrapper, a twisted smile taking hold of my lips. "Ah crap! I think something's wrong with my phone. I can't hear you. Dad? Dad?"

I quickly hang up and frown as I see him call back. I press the off button, waiting for my screen to go black before shoving my phone back into my pocket.

I should have thought of that sooner.

I knock lightly at the door, cracking it open and cringing at the irritated look the professor shoots me. *Not the greatest first impression,* I think while pushing the door further open and stepping inside. The professor straightens her spectacles on her nose, her eyes narrowing on me. I look around the room, my face heating as all eyes turn to me. Some irritated, others curious. I drop my gaze to the floor, feeling instantly self-conscious.

"Sorry for being late," I murmur, shoving my hands into my coat pockets to keep myself from fidgeting. I stand there, not moving. A part of me wonders if she will kick me out and all my father's hopes and dreams will come true. Instead, I hear her heave an exasperated sigh. "Just take a seat," she says and I lift my head, watching her while she gestures to the seats in front of her.

I quickly grab a chair in the front, dropping my bag on the floor. There are only about fifteen other students in the small class and looking at the girls I'm sitting between, I notice a syllabus on everyone's desk.

I look to the right, looking over a girl's shoulder while trying to read what we will be going through when I hear the professor's heels clacking on the floor. She hands me a packet, her eyes assessing me once more as she says, "Don't make a habit of being late."

I force a smile and nod. "Of course," I breathe, taking the packet earnestly and flipping through its pages.

"Now, for those of you who were late-"

I grimace. *She's really not going to let this go, now is she?*

"My name is Professor Wood, and this is Writing 301 with a focus on poetry."

I nod while reading through the syllabus, taking note that we will have a project due each month. We'll be learning about different styles of poetry. Most of our homework assignments will entail reading Robert Frost, William Blake, Emily Dickinson, and, of course Edgar Allan Poe. I notice a few other author names, yet I don't recognize them.

"I also want to announce a writing contest taking place between now and April."

My head perks up as I watch the smart board change, showing a simple caption of the Berkshire Prize. I scramble for my bag, quickly unzipping it and searching for a pen. I grab one and attempt to write the due date on my syllabus, but the pen isn't working. I shake it, but no ink comes out. I scribble, but nothing.

"Here."

I peak my head up, finding the professor standing in front of me again, offering me a pencil and my cheeks heat so much I fear I have caught fire. There are giggles behind me, which does nothing to ease my embarrassment.

"Thank you," I murmur, taking the pencil and keeping my head down.

Ugh. In just five minutes I've turned myself into the class loser.

Stupid Dad calling me and throwing me off my game.

I write down the due date, happy to see I have until mid-April to send in my pieces. The contest is for a poetry book with a grand prize of $3,000. I have a notebook filled with little blurbs and writing exercises, but nothing I would call worthy of being in a book. I could probably use a few of the works I sent in to the English professors. But they aren't perfect, and for something like this, I would need my best work.

As soon as I finish writing the information down, I frown, knowing there is no way I could ever win something this huge. I'm barely a writer. Just a wannabe. Eventually Dad will have his way and I will have to forget I ever tried to make a writer out of myself.

I lean back into my seat and try to focus on Professor Wood and not the ache in my heart, knowing this is all useless. I'm not a writer. This is just something I'm doing to piss my dad off.

I sigh and rub my head, feeling an ache sprouting near my temple as I think to myself, *What am I doing with my life?*

8

RACHEL

There's a spring in my step as I slide my way to class, which is pretty much the only way I can get there. Salt is on the ground, yet it doesn't seem like the ice is melting any time soon. I hold my coffee out to the side, careful not to spill anything on me as I continue to skate my way to the art building.

Watch me slip and spill everything on myself.

Thankfully, I'm not wearing anything white, choosing to don a thick black coat that reaches my ankles and a black sock hat. My thick blonde curls stick out of it and is tangled in the mess that is my black-and-white striped scarf, which is pretty much a blanket. I plan on wearing it in class, as well. It's totally freezing today. I can feel the chill biting through my fingers even though I'm wearing thick black mittens. It doesn't matter. It's so cold I can barely feel my toes. It's like I'm not wearing anything, but it seems that my winter clothes are practically useless.

I stomp my feet on the rug as I enter the building, which does nothing since the floors are coated in dark slush. I carefully side-step a student who nearly bulldozes through me, not aware of their surroundings at all as they shout into their phone. Carefully, I step on the floor and gasp as I slip and catch myself from falling on my rump.

That was definitely a close one.

But nothing is going to get me down today. It's the first day of classes and I'm starting my day with Drawing 101. I'll be learning the delightful craft of drawing still life drawing, which I'm taking as an elective. Photography is my art, but it's good to expand my horizons.

And sure, Hunter remained in his room and didn't say goodbye to me or anything in the morning. It's fine.

He's his own man. It's not like it hurt anything. I sniff, feeling a little ache in my heart and finding it difficult to breathe.

Lying to myself hurt. It hurt a lot.

And I really miss Hunter.

I shake my head and take a quick swig of my coffee, enjoying the sugary vanilla taste and allowing it to wash away all the doom and gloom. *Yes, just think of how wonderful coffee is,* I tell myself while taking another swig. *And how wonderful it will be to see Charlie and Lauren again.*

I open the door to my drawing class, looking around at the large bright windows letting in natural sunlight and the easels sitting in a circle around a small table. There are a few girls sitting in a corner. One even has the same idea as me with her coat lying against the back of her chair and her mustard colored scarf wrapped around her shoulders like a blanket.

Great minds think alike.

I sit next to her, sliding off my coat and wrapping my scarf around my shoulders. "Hey," I say to the girls, interrupting whatever quiet conversation they're having. "First time taking this class?"

They turn to me and Miss Mustard Scarf gives me the up down look while her curly haired friend makes a face. "Yeah," they say in unison, their tones varying from snooty to 'don't-talk-to-us'.

I nod and turn away, releasing a sigh and muttering, "Guess not everyone wants to make friends. Duly noted."

I peak over the easel, looking at the items on the table and finding a basket with all the cliché items inside such as an apple, a pear, and some grapes. It's too bad Charlie and Lauren aren't taking this class. At least I would have someone to talk to.

The door opens and I perk up, wondering if anyone nice would enter, but my eyes widen, finding a very familiar, glasses wearing boy standing in the threshold. His blue eyes meet mine and I feel my heart stop, fear snaking around it like chains pinning me down while his lips twist into a sweet smile.

One I had fallen for before.

I quickly look away and bow my head, hoping somehow the small action would make me invisible. I cling to my scarf, clamping my eyes close while chanting inside my head: *go away, go away, go away.*

"Hey, Rachel," I hear Josh say.

My hands shake uncontrollably while I open my eyes, peaking up at him like I'm some sort of mouse having been found by a very fat tabby cat. I watch in horror as he sits down next to me, dropping his bag next to mine while sliding his coat off.

How can he pretend like nothing happened?

"How was your break? I know mine was busy." He chuckles while shaking his head. "My parents had me pretty busy, driving me all over the place and visiting cousins and aunts. I got loads of presents, but all of them-"

I stand, grabbing my bag and coat in one big heap.

"Hey, where are you going?" I hear him ask while I make my way to the other side of the room, hoping to find a spot where I don't have to see his stupid face.

"Don't talk to me," I say harshly before continuing towards an empty chair. I drop my things down, frowning when I see his pathetic face staring at me all wide eyed and innocent looking. He seriously thinks he's done nothing wrong and we can just be friends. What the hell. How can he possibly think that? What the hell is going on inside that stupid little head?

I grind my teeth, my eyes clamping close as memories return of him pushing me down on the couch. Of him grabbing my leg as I tried to get away. The bruises on my arms. A shudder ripples down my spine as I chant once again: *go away, go away, go away.*

"Alright, shall we start," I hear the professor say as the door clicks close.

My eyes open and I see Josh still staring at me. I grab my easel and move it, blocking my view of him before turning my gaze up at the professor, who is currently leaning against his little table of clichés.

His bald head shines under the natural light shining through the windows and I try to concentrate on that rather than Josh sitting in the room. The professor smiles while he straightens his rumpled tie, made from a yellow and purple polka dotted fabric. His gaze lands on me and I immediately straighten in my chair.

"Welcome to Drawing 101," he announces to the small class composed of just seven students including myself. "My name is Mr. Brown and this term you will be learning how to create art from the deepest, darkest chasms of your soul."

I nod, letting his words wash over me, yet I still can't get Josh's blue eyes out of my head, nor my screams from last I was alone with him.

***

It's nearly two and after my photography class I briskly walk through the quad, walking past Fleet Feet Sports on my way to the Coffee Shop. I briefly look inside, finding Seth busy with a customer, and I make a note to come back later to check my work schedule. And maybe get a much needed kiss.

I bolted out of my drawing class as soon as it ended and attended my last two classes before meeting with the girls. Unfortunately my classes had barely kept my mind off Josh. I don't know why he was contacting me after so long of steering clear. *Did he think a few words of kindness would erase all the bad that happened between us?*

The guy needs a reality check if that's what he's thinking.

I enter the Coffee Shop, hearing the bell ding as I step inside before slamming close. The place is busy, bustling with crowds of students studying in corners and waiting in line for coffee. Looking around the place, I find Charlie and Lauren sitting at a corner seat near the window, with two chairs with a dark backpack in one and a black leather purse in the other. Charlie stands and waves at me and I quickly walk toward them, stepping over duffel bags and book bags sitting in the small path to them.

"Rachel!" Shouts Charlie whole throwing her arms around me, giving me a tight hug. "It's been too long."

I chuckle while pulling away from her, turning towards Lauren who also gives me a hug. "Long time no see," she says before grabbing her backpack and sitting down.

"Yes, it's been way too long."

"Did you order?" asks Charlie while nodding towards the counter, where the long line continues to grow.

I shook my head. "I'll order later. If I go now, I'll probably be standing there for the next hour."

"How was your vacation?" asks Lauren.

I force a smile as I think of Hunter leaving in the middle of the ski trip. "It was good." I'm still not sure about talking to the girls about this. I'm dating three guys at the same time, well, maybe two now. It's not like many girls my age are in my situation.

And they'll probably tell me to say so long to Hunter, which I really don't want to do.

"Oh, it was good, was it?" Charlie waggles her eyebrows. "You went on that trip with the bros, didn't you?"

My face heats as I realize what she's implying. It's embarrassing enough speaking about sex, but about sex with three men? I'm sure Lauren and Charlie had their suspicions about what me and the bros got up to when no one was or around. *Or more like how we did it...*

"Yes, I went on a ski trip with the boys."

Charlie giggles while Lauren shakes her head. "Well, details, girl!" shouts Charlie while smacking the table. "Tell us everything. I gotta know."

Lauren pats my shoulder reassuringly. "You don't have to tell us everything, Rachel," she says.

Charlie scoffs. "Says you. My dating pool has been deader than a doormat. I need someone to live vicariously through."

I raise an eyebrow and look Charlie up and down. The girl is absolutely beautiful with her perfect blond bobbed hair and her pristine makeup. She reminds me of a doll with her perfect body and her perfect fashion sense. "I highly doubt your dating life would ever be considered dead."

Charlie sighs, sounding exasperated. "Enough about me. Let's hear it. I'm desperate-"

"Hey guys."

My eyes widen as I recognize that tenor voice. I don't turn around. I just got him out of my head. Why is he here now?

"Josh-y!" shouts Charlie while bounding out of her chair and throwing her arms around the hipster asshole who seems to be following me all around campus.

Lauren smiles as she stands, giving Josh a hug. "It's been awhile," I hear her sigh.

My hands grip each other, my leg bouncing up and down. Terror seizes me as I watch Charlie move her bag. Josh steps around the table and sits down across from me. He offers me a small smile, but I can't do anything. All I can see his him grabbing me, not letting me go.

Charlie says something and I hear Lauren laugh next to me, watch Josh chuckle while he lowers his gaze to the table. Their voices sound distant. My heart is hammering in my chest and I'm finding it difficult to breathe. I need to get out of here before I make a scene.

I quickly stand, shoving my chair back. Three pairs of eyes turn to me, wide and curious. "I'm sorry," I say, my voice sounding funny to my ears. The words stick on my tongue as I force them out, my voice slightly trembling as I continue with, "I just remembered I was supposed to work today."

I shakily pick up my bag, throwing it over my shoulder. "I'm so sorry," I say, hoping the girls think my fear is akin to me losing my job. I'm still not ready to talk to them about Josh or what happened.

But now I'm realizing I probably should.

What if he does something to them?

"Oh, ok," says Charlie. "I'm sorry to hear that."

"I really need to go," I say, turning on my heel and trying to make it to the door without running.

"Don't be a stranger!" shouts Josh as I throw open the door.

The wind blows threw me, biting against my exposed skin. I have no clue where I'm going. My feet are just taking me somewhere; somewhere far away where I don't have to deal with Josh and his charming smile and his stupid glasses. Somewhere safe, where he will never go.

I step inside Fleet Feet Sports, looking around and finding Seth leaning against the counter. He straightens a smile on his face meant for customers, but it lowers as he takes my shivering form in. I blink back tears while striding towards him, my arms reaching for him, needing his warmth.

"What happened?" he asks while walking around the counter, wrapping his arms around my waist and pulling me close.

I nuzzle my face into his shoulder, gasping while I continue to blink back my tears. It's not working. I'm crying like a big baby. "I had a bad day," I croak before sobbing into his arms, letting everything out. His hands tighten around me and he strokes my head, shushing me while I continue to cry.

"It's alright," he says. "Tell me who I need to beat up."

I giggle and push him away, wiping my eyes with my scarf and sniffing the snot back into my nose to the best of my ability. I probably look like a complete mess, but Seth strokes the side of my face, pulling me in for a sweet, gentle kiss. I close my eyes, relishing in the feel of him. He caresses the side of my face as his tongue slips inside, stroking me gently. My shivers subside and he ends the kiss. His forehead presses against mine while his fingers lace with my hands.

"Tell me what happened," he says while tugging me to the counter and sitting me in the chair.

I sigh, rubbing my head while trying to put words together into my head. "It's Josh."

Seth's gaze darkens, and he straightens. I notice his hands fisting at his sides, but he doesn't move as he asks, "What about him?"

"He's in my drawing class."

"Drop the class."

I frown. "I don't want to," I whisper. "I was really excited to take that class. The professor is really nice."

"Did he say anything to you?"

I nod.

Seth rolls up his sleeves. "I'll kill him."

I roll my eyes. Typical jock, solving problems with their fists rather than working it out logically. "That's not going to help anything, Seth."

"It'll definitely make me feel better," he mutters.

I smile at him, placing a hand on his shoulder and squeezing it gently. "It's sweet though. Knowing you care so much about me."

Seth perks up, his chest puffing out and reminding me of a rooster. "I'm sweet, huh?"

I giggle and shake my head, feeling a brief minute of joy, before recalling how Josh sat next to Charlie, talking with the girls as if nothing had happened. "That's not all." I sigh, my gaze going to my knees. "I can sit away from Josh during class. And with the professor there, I know nothing will happen. But the girls…" I shake my head.

"You still haven't told them?"

I try to ignore the anger in his voice and the guilt clinging to my heart. "No. I haven't."

"You need to tell them, Rachel."

I nod.

"It's for their own good. What if-"

"I know. I know!" I shout while throwing my hands up into the air. I can't look at him right now. I will only feel guiltier. "He was there. At the coffee shop. They invited him."

"Well, you got to put an end to that."

I nod, knowing he's right.

"They're your friends, Rachel. They'll understand." He grabs my chin and lifts my eyes. As soon as I meet his gaze, I feel tears welling up again, threatening to stream down my cheeks and mess up my makeup even more than before. "Tell them what happened with Josh. I think it will do you some good to speak about it. You haven't said a word since it happened and I don't think it does you any good just shoving it under a rug and pretending nothing happened."

I sniff and nod again. Words seem difficult today and all I can do is listen to Seth. What he speaks is true. I should talk about it more. I should at least tell my girlfriends what happened.

It's just so hard.

Every time I think about telling someone, the memories return.

"And you should tell the school board about what he did."

My eyes widen and I lean away from him, nearly falling out of my seat. "No."

"Yes," Seth says sternly. "You know I'm right."

"They won't do anything, Seth."

"At least they will know something happened. Just in case he attacks another girl."

I shake my head. "It was my fault in the first place."

"How the hell was it your fault?" Seth shouts, making me grimace.

"I shouldn't have been over there in the first place."

Seth scoffs. "By that kind of logic, it should be my fault. I was the one who kicked you out. Is it my fault you got assaulted?"

My brows furrow together and I stare back at Seth, seeing his shoulders slumped and his eyes glittering with unshed tears of his own. I reach for him, grabbing his hands and pressing them against my heart. "No," I breathe and Seth sighs, pressing his forehead against mine.

"It's not your fault that guy is an asshole, Rachel."

I nod, but I don't say anything.

I might tell my friends eventually about Josh, but there is no way I am going to the school board.

"Do you want to work today?" asks Seth. "Get your mind off things? I can stay and walk you home after?"

I shake my head while sliding off the chair. "No, I should get a head start on my school work. I have a pretty heavy load this semester." I groan and rub my head, feeling a headache coming on from all the crying. "Can you just tell me when I work next?"

"Wednesday," Seth answers almost immediately. He smiles as my gaze narrows on him and gives me a shrug. "What can I say, I had a look as soon as I got in. We'll be working together." He waggles his eyebrows and I shake my head. "Maybe we can… do some other work while we're here."

I chuckle and swat at him, but he dodges me easily. With one final kiss goodbye, I walk out the door, shrugging my backpack further up my shoulder while I attempt to keep my balance on the ice covered sidewalks.

I can barely keep my eyes open as I walk. They feel so heavy from crying, exhausted from trying to focus on school rather than on Josh. And Hunter. I sigh, looking upwards at the cloud filled sky and wondering what the hell is wrong with this term. Sure, the workload is harder, but my personal life is supposed to be easy. I already have met amazing girlfriends and I'm dating three hot, sex Gods.

This term is supposed to be fun, yet I've already spent most of it either crying or obsessing about boys. I sigh as I trudge up the steps towards the apartment, shoving my hand into my bag to search for the keys. I briefly wonder if Hunter is home, but he's most likely at football practice, or maybe at the gym.

Or somewhere far away from me, I think sadly.

I unlock the door and throw my backpack onto the couch, sliding my coat off and throwing it on the coat rack near the front door. I kick it close and stretch my arms over my head, hearing them pop and grimacing at the sound. Maybe I can put on some peppy music. That should get my mood up.

Hunter's door opens and my eyes widen as he steps into the living room, bare chested and wearing low hanging sweatpants and slippers. His hair is tangled and hangs limply over his shoulders. He looks like he hasn't bathed in a week. There is stubble along his jaw and he looks oddly thin.

I run my hands through my hair, feeling nervous as his bloodshot eyes meet mine. "Hey, Hunter," I say, trying to force a smile, but it probably looks more like a grimace.

Hunter smiles. "Hey."

9

HUNTER

Blinking my eyes open, I groan, feeling the thudding ache pounding through my head and the nausea twisting my stomach. My room is unusually dark and I roll over to check the time. My eyes snap open and I throw off the blankets as soon as I see it's nearly four in the afternoon. I stumble out of bed and jerk my head around in search for my football gear, which is a terrible mistake. I fall to my knees, clutching my stomach and biting back the bile coming up my throat.

I shiver as I swallow, hating myself for feeling this way; hating myself for all my stupid mistakes from the other night. Slumping forward, my forehead hits the mattress, nuzzling it for a moment in an attempt to gain some sort of comfort. I close my eyes, trying to remember what happened at the party, yet everything comes in flashes, nothing quite making sense. I remember Millie coming onto me, remember her being pissed.

I recall meeting Drew and Jerry thinking the duo was strange.

Drew had given me a beer and then everything from that point on was hazy.

I groan. Drew obviously put something in my beer. That has to be it. I have never been that out of control. Sure, I drink a lot and have gotten carried away before. But this had been different. For the first time in a very long while, I had been able to let go. I had felt happy.

There is no way I can ever do it again.

I hear something buzz and open my eyes, looking around and finding my phone on the nightstand. I reach for it, groaning when my fingers slightly brush it from my place on the floor. Movement is difficult and I don't know if I can lean over without feeling nausea again. I remain like that, my hand reaching out, willing my phone to magically appear in my hand. It buzzes again and finally I get up the courage to move, grinding my teeth as my head spins while I grab my phone.

My eyes widen when I unlock the screen and look at all the missed messages. Several are from the coach, wondering why I haven't gone to practice. Some are from Dad insisting I return his calls. I see a missed call from Mom and frown, wondering if she's okay. I quickly dial her, hoping it's nothing more than a simple check in. I never know these days with her being so ill. A simple call could mean she's dying.

I sniff and close my eyes against the tears threatening to fall, telling myself everything is fine.

"Hello," I hear her on the phone, her voice cracking, sounding weak.

I force a smile. "Hey, Mom," I say, trying to sound cheerful. "Sorry I missed your call."

"Oh, it's fine. I assumed you were at practice."

I nod as if she can see me. "Is everything alright?" My heart hammers as I wait for her answer.

I hear her chuckle on the other line. "You and your father. Constantly worrying over me." I roll my eyes. It's like she's forgotten that Dad has been MIA for the past several months now that he has suddenly taken an interest. "I just wanted to check in. See how you're doing."

My jaw clenches as I recall sitting at the doctor's office, waiting for her to come out from her appointment. My hand grips my phone and I don't know how much longer I can listen to her pretending that everything is fine when it's not. "Well, everything's fine here," I say shakily. My shoulder is killing me. I look around for my bag, finding it far away in the corner of my room. There should be a couple pills left.

"The doctor says I might be able to go home in the next few days."

I crawl towards my bag as I say, "That's great, Mom. So, they were able to... fix it?" I pop open the top and frown at the two pills staring back at me.

Fuck.

I really need to get some more.

"Not necessarily."

The pills are in my hand, but I stop myself from throwing them into my mouth. "What do you mean 'not necessarily'?"

I hear her sigh and heart plummets, knowing what she is going to say. But I don't want to hear it. I don't want her to stop fighting. She's so close to being free from this disease. How can she just give up?

"Hunter, I just want to be home, with my family."

The tears are coming back. I don't think I can listen anymore. I know I'm being a bad son, I know I'm acting like a child. But I am the child. "Mom-"

"I want to live my life while I still can and even if we continue to fight this thing," she sighs again. "I don't want to die in a hospital surrounded by doctors."

I shove the pills into my mouth, needing something to drown out this pain tearing at my heart. I feel like the world just split and I'm falling with no one to catch me. Swallowing, I choke down my sobs, cursing myself for feeling so powerless. "Well, if you think that's best," I say, grimacing at the trembling in my voice.

"Hunter-"

"I gotta go," I say quickly, my tongue heavy as I force the words out. I can't listen to this now. I need to get out of here. I need to do something.

"Ok, honey." Her voice is so soft. I know I've upset her. I know she wants to talk with me about this, but I just can't. Not now. "I love you."

I nod. "Love you, too, Mom."

I quickly click the phone off and release a breath while leaning back against the wall. I bang my head softly against it and close my eyes. She's been in and out of hospitals for the past two years. I should have expected this to happen. Of course she's tired and wants some normalcy in her life. But why can't she just fight a little longer for me?

I force myself up and stumble through my room while I look for something clean to wear, which is harder than it looks since everything is pretty much rumpled and on the floor. Throwing off my shirt, which reeks of sweat and smoke, I find some comfortable sweatpants to throw on over my boxers and decide I can do without a shirt. It's not like I plan on going anywhere today anyway. I will just tell coach tomorrow that I had a stomach bug. He should buy it. It's not like I miss football practice all the time.

Throwing open my door, I make a beeline for the kitchen in desperate need of some water where I find Rachel standing, obviously just now returning home from classes.

She grimaces while forcing her lips upwards in some sort of half-assed smile while saying, "Hey, Hunter." She fidgets in front of me, lowering her gaze a bit and I feel like a complete asshole for the way I've treated her.

She's just trying to help and yet I keep pushing her away. It's not her fault I injured my shoulder. It's not her fault that my dad is an ass and my mom is dying. I smile while stepping towards her. "Hey," I say simply, knowing I should say more, but my head is killing me.

"You're done with football practice already?"

I try to keep it cool. I don't want to worry her. She doesn't need to know what happened at the party. Hell, I don't even know what happened. "Yeah," I say with an easy shrug. "Coach decided to take it easy."

Rachel nods, but doesn't say anything else, which is upsetting. When have we never had anything to say anything to each other? We used to joke around, talk about our worries and our lives. It's my fault, I realize. I'm the one who pushed her away, therefore she doesn't know what to say or do around me.

    I take another step towards her, erasing the space between us. "Hey," I begin while stroking her hair behind her ear. "I'm sorry. I've been a jerk."

    She nods and sniffs, but doesn't meet my gaze.

    "I'm sorry for worrying you. I just," I sigh and rub my aching head, "I'm going through some things right now."

    Rachel lifts her gaze to me, glittering with tears which makes my heart break knowing I'm responsible for making her feel this way. "You know I care about you," she breathes. "You can always talk to me."

    I shake my head, knowing she's right. I can talk to her, but something is holding me back. I don't want to be judged. I already have issues with my shoulder, my career is on the line, and I don't want to talk about my family troubles.

    It just makes it all too real to me.

    "I know," I say instead.

    She waits for a moment, watching me as if she expects me to break down and tell her my deepest and darkest secrets, but my lips remain sealed. "Hunter," she begins, but I capture her lips with mine, stopping her from saying whatever she's about to say.

    My hands slide around her, pulling her close. One hand goes up her back, tangling in her hair while I suck and tease her mouth. Her lips open beneath mine while her hands wrap around me and I deepen the kiss. As my tongue strokes hers, I hear her moan. My hand slides down the length of her back to cup her ass and I grind my hardening cock against her, enjoying the soft gasps escaping her lips.

I know this solves nothing. I know when I'm done I will feel the same mourning and pain tearing through me, but for a moment I just want to forget. I want to feel Rachel's body pressed against mine, hear her screams as she orgasms; my name on her lips.

I disentangle my hand from her hair and, cupping her ass with both hands, I pick her up. Her legs wrap around me while I stumble backwards. My arms shake as I carry her back to my room. I haven't had anything to eat and the water I so desperately needed before has been forgone in my attempts for sex.

I dump her body onto my bed and ignore the pounding in my head as I crawl on top of her. She parts her legs for me while her hands reach for me. I take one and mouth her palm while my other hand unbuttons her jeans. Her mouth parts as her gaze locks with mine, watching me while I unzip her pants and shove my hands deep inside her panties. She arches her back when I find her clit, stroking it while I bite and suck on her hand. My cock is twitching while I watch her squirm in my bed. My sweatpants are tented and she reaches a hand down between us and presses her palm against my clothed tip.

I moan and thrust against her, wanting more of her touch. She reaches for my pants, her fingers playing with the waistband. "Hunter," she breathes, her fingers pulling away from me. I stare down at her while my fingers continue to press and circle around her clit. "Do you still want me?"

The question makes my heart twinge, knowing that I've been cruel to her recently and making her doubt us. Hell, even I had been doubting us when I left the ski trip. But I still want her. It's me who is messed up, not her.

It's me who should let her go. But I don't want to.

I lean in close until I'm hovering just above her. Her green eyes watch me with a mixture of desire and worry. "Of course I still want you," I whisper, smiling as her lips twitch upwards. "I'll always want you." I press my lips against hers and moan as I allow my body to rest neatly between her legs.

I grind myself against her core, my cock leaking at her whimpers and gasps. I suck on her bottom lip, my teeth grazing slightly against it before releasing. I'm desperate to feel her flesh against mine. Grabbing her shirt, I pull it up, throwing it behind me and watching her reaching around to unclasp her bra.

As soon as her breasts are released from their prison, my hands are cupping them, my thumbs circling her nipples until they are taut. She squirms underneath me, grinding herself against my tip. Need and desire makes my body shake and soon I am shoving my pants and boxers down until they are at my ankles.

Rachel follows my lead, shoving her jeans and panties down until they are at her ankles. Before she can kick them off, I grab one leg and mouth her knee. She shudders as my other hand presses against her thigh, massaging the muscle as I slowly make my way up to her core. I push her jeans down as I slowly continue my path upwards, until her jeans are lying on the bed and my tongue is licking her juices.

"Hunter," she breathes as I push her pussy lips away and ravish her clit. Her fingernails dig into my scalp, holding me there while I suck and prod. She whimpers and squirms until her legs wrap around me and press me closer to her. "Don't stop."

I chuckle, feeling mischievous while I lift my head away from her to meet her shocked and needy look. "What?" I ask coyly.

"Hunter," she whines while wiggling to get closer to me. "Don't be mean."

I lift my head higher and look innocently up at her. "Me? Mean?" I point to myself. "How am I being mean?"

"Hunter," Rachel hisses, her hands clawing at my bed. "Come on."

I chuckle before lowering my mouth and sliding my tongue against her clit. She shivers and I draw back. "Do you like that?"

"Yes," she whimpers, her face jerking from side to side.

I lick her again and she gasps. "Tell me you want it."

"I want it," she says desperately.

"No," I say while sliding my thumb around her clit. "Tell me exactly what you want, Rachel."

She groans in both frustration and want and I can see her cheeks flushing in embarrassment. I watch her as I wait and my fingers continue torturing her; sliding up and down her little pleasure nib, pinching it slightly before circling around until it's as taut as her nipples. Rachel gasps and moans. Her fingernails scrape at my shoulders, then cling at my bedsheets, before switching back to my shoulders, not knowing what or who to hang onto as I continue stroking her.

"I want you," she breathes finally.

I push a finger inside her, feeling just how much she wants me. I bite back a moan as I feel how wet she is. I imagine plunging my dick deep inside her, feeling her moist and hot insides tightening as I continue thrusting into her. The image is enough to send me over the edge and I climb over her, biting back a cry as I feel a tear in my shoulder. I'm not going to let anything ruin this.

I reach towards my nightstand and throw open the drawer, finding several condoms. Ripping off the packaging, I shove my hard cock inside and then angle myself at her entrance. I press my tip into her while my hands lace with hers, pinning her beneath me. She slides her body against mine, moaning as my tip strokes her clit. I lower myself on her, claiming her lips as she continues

moving her hips. With one thrust, I enter her and moan as her body tightens around me, sucking me deeper inside. Rachel gasps, her nails digging into my shoulders and once again I bite back another cry as I feel my shoulder seize at the touch.
Don't think about it, I tell myself. I thrust harder into Rachel and she cries out. Her hands wrap around me and I do it again and again; thrusting harder and deeper as I try to drown out the pain in my shoulder.

"Hunter!" She cries while clinging to me.

A shudder ripples down my spine and I thrust harder. Her hips grind against mine. A moan escapes my lips as she thrusts against my hard length and I can feel myself leaking. I stare down at her, meeting her lustful expression. I release one of her hands to stroke the side of her hair, her face, her neck.

God, she's so beautiful.
Why is she with an asshole like me?

I grimace as another pull pierces through my injured shoulder. Stupidly, I put all my weight on that side. "Are you okay?" Rachel whispers while caressing my cheek.

I roll us over until she's on top of me, straddling my hips. "I'm fine," I say between clenched teeth before thrusting deeper inside.

Her breasts bounce with movement and Rachel gasps. Her hands press against my chest as she tries to balance herself on top of me. I barely give her any time before thrusting into her again, making each movement harder, earning a cry each time.

Rachel's head rolls as I continue with my pace, moving faster as I feel myself climbing higher. I'm closing in. I can feel my balls tightening. I'm almost to the breaking point and with each high-pitched cry pouring out from Rachel's lips, I know she's near her breaking point. I grab her hips and slam them down against me, earning a scream which makes me twitch all over. I do it again and again, feeling her tighten around me.

"You like that?" I ask while slamming her against me again.

Rachel doesn't respond. Her nails dig into my chest as she screams, as her body continues sucking me in. "Hunter!" She cries, her voice sounding desperate to my ears and making me move harder, faster. "Hunter!"

I move my body upwards until I'm almost in a sitting position. Grabbing her hair, I yank her towards me, claiming her lips. Rachel moans against me while my hands reach between us, my thumb strumming her clit as I thrust inside. She stills while her lips break away from mine. Her tilts back and she emits a high-pitched moan as her body quivers with release. With one last thrust my cock twitches and I feel myself coming inside.

Her head hits my shoulder and she gasps while her hands slide over me. I nuzzle my head against hers, feeling limp and worn. I feel peace coming over me as I hold her to me, not ever wanting to let her go, but knowing eventually we'll have to return to reality.

She moves away from me all too soon and she smiles, placing a chaste kiss on my lips before whispering in my ear, "That was amazing."

I chuckle, stroking her back and keeping her to me. I'm not ready for her to leave. I'm not ready for this to end, but already she's beginning to pull from me. Already, the shadows are returning.

I hear the door to the apartment slam and I sigh, letting Rachel go as I hear Lucas shout, "Hello! Anyone home?"

Rachel moves her legs from me and quickly crawls off the bed. "Yes!" She calls while picking up her panties and sliding them over her pale legs.

The door opens and I watch Lucas come in, watch him lean against the wall and look mischievously between us. "Looks like I returned too late," he says while his eyes rake over Rachel's half naked form. "Care for round two?"

Rachel clasps her bra and shakes her head with a chuckle. "You boys will be the death of me," she says while grabbing her shirt. "I have so much homework to do. It's not even funny."

I watch Lucas stride towards Rachel and swallow the bitter taste of jealousy as he takes her hand and kisses her knuckles, as if he is her handsome prince. "Rain check?"

Rachel giggles. "Of course."

I frown, watching as she nuzzles her nose against his. I don't know why I feel so jealous. We are all in a relationship with Rachel. She treats us equally and fairly, but I can't help but feel like I'm a third wheel. Maybe it's because I left the ski trip? It's probably that. Or it could be we got into a fight and I refuse to talk about it. Honestly, it could be loads of things.

I still as Rachel glances over her shoulder and smiles at me. "You want to study with me, Hunter? I can order some Chinese."

I blink, knowing it would do me some good, but I shake my head. "No, I need to get some rest." *Liar,* I hear a dark voice whisper in the back of my head. "Today was pretty exhausting with football practice and all." *Fucking liar.*

Rachel frowns, but nods. "Oh, okay."

I watch them leave. Even after the door has clicked closed, I continue watching the place Rachel and Lucas once stood while loneliness overcomes me.

***

It isn't until I get a text from Millie that I finally decide to dress and leave my room. I have no clue why she is messaging me after the way I treated her last time, but I guess the girl wanted to try again.

I don't understand women.

Actually, these days, I don't even understand myself. I shouldn't be going. Last time I was at a party, I got so messed up I didn't return home until late yesterday afternoon and then I spent all of today in bed, feeling like absolute shit. I should be resting, drinking water, talking to Rachel about why I've been such a jerk these days.

But going to a party sounds much better than thinking about my problems.

I try to ignore the eyes on me when I leave my room. The whole gang is hanging out in the living room with boxes filled with noodles, rice, Kung Pow Chicken, and Sweet and Sour Chicken surrounding them on the floor.

"Hey, man!" calls Seth while slowly standing.

"'Sup," I say. I head for the kitchen, not bothering to meet their curious and possibly annoyed gazes. I lean over the sink and guzzle down several gulps of water, which immediately helps the ache in my head. My hands shake as I hold onto the counter. The smell of food is making my stomach gurgle.

I still haven't had anything to eat.

"You look pretty," continues Seth while smacking my shoulder.

I know I don't. I haven't shaved in days nor have I showered. I just haven't felt like it. Everything seems so difficult these days. Everything, that is, but sleeping. I pretty much tied my hair into a man bun, sprayed some axe, and called it a day. Although, I should probably make some time for a shower at some point. My hair is so greasy it's starting to look brown.

"Where you off to?" I hear Lucas ask.

I wipe my mouth and turn around, finding Lucas standing next to Seth with his arms crossed.

I shrug. "Millie messaged me about a party. Thought I would go."

Lucas and Seth look at each other and I hold back an irritated sigh.

"Millie?" asks Lucas while raising an eyebrow at me.

"I didn't know you're still hanging out with her," says Seth.

I nod. "We hang out occasionally."

"Why?" asks Lucas, glancing over his shoulder at Rachel, who's still sitting on the floor, pretending not to listen while she pokes her chicken with her chopsticks.

"I don't know." I stalk past them towards the door, my shoulder bumping into Seth's. I grind my teeth, holding back a hiss of pain while my fists clench and unclench. Why are they asking me so many fucking questions? I'm a grown ass man. I can do what I want. "It's just a party," I say while shrugging on my only coat, reminding myself to find the other one I had left behind.

"Well, can we come?" Asks Seth while gesturing towards himself and Lucas.

I stifle a groan, knowing it would seem weird to them. A part of me wants to meet up with Drew and Jerry again.

And not for the right reasons.

If Lucas and Seth join, they'll just keep me from having fun. Fun I don't even know if I want, but it beats the way I've been feeling recently.

"Can I come, too?" I hear Rachel ask from behind the bros.

I watch her stand and stride towards me with a forced smile. "It could be fun," she says while stopping in front of me.

I nod and smile, yet inside I'm boiling. I force the word out anyway, not wanting to be questioned further on why I want to go on my own.

"Sure."

I will just have to be quick and efficient.

10

RACHEL

I frown while looking around at the house filled with drunk jocks pounding back shots and beers while Millie's girlfriends continued watching me with glares and scrutinizing looks. This is truly the last thing I wanted to do on my first Monday back at school. However, once Hunter mentioned "Millie" I couldn't let him go on his own.

Honestly, I was, and I am, very jealous.

I spent the whole walk here analyzing my fight with Hunter and the reason why he showed up in the middle of the afternoon on Sunday; knowing now he was most likely at a party with Millie and definitely not at the gym. And honestly, I did not buy the whole 'football practice was let out early' crap Hunter had told me earlier today.

Something is up.

I can feel it in my bones.

I glance at Hunter, watching him pound back his beer before grabbing another. Lucas and Seth are supposed to be around here somewhere, but I think they got sucked into a Flip Cup Tournament. I was hoping they would keep an eye on Hunter, but I guess they decided to have their own fun. Which is what I should be doing now.

Looking at Hunter now, I frown. He looks like shit and I can tell he's lost weight. His face looks more angular even under the scruff marring his usually smooth-shaven face. And sure, I think Hunter looks handsome no matter what he does with his body, but this is not a good look for him.

And I'm finding myself despising this new Hunter.

Where is the man I developed feelings for last year? I want to ask him, but he won't answer so what's the point.

The best I can do now is just go to these parties with him and make sure he doesn't get into trouble.

Which is easier said than done.

"Hey!" Hunter shouts and I turn, seeing two strange-looking men approaching him.

One is tall and thin, looking in his mid-thirties with straggly brown hair and a scowl on his face while the other is thicker around the gut with a heavyset face and short blonde hair. The pudgy man smiles at Hunter while clapping him on the back, his eyes sliding towards me.

"Who is this?" He asks while gesturing towards me.

I already don't like him.

I can't quite place my finger on it, but there's something wrong about the man. It's not his face, not his smile or the clothes he wears, which are simple sweatpants with an Aurora hoodie. The guy must be dying with all these bodies swirling between us.

No, it has nothing to do with that.

Something about his aura has me on guard and I don't like the way the fat man's friend keeps scowling at every passerby.

"Drew, this is Rachel," says Hunter while setting a hand on my shoulder. His voice is cheerful, yet I can tell Hunter is pushing himself. He looks absolutely exhausted. I have no clue why he felt the need to come out and party when it's obvious he feels like shit.

I would have said something earlier, but I don't want to get my head bitten off, which seems to be happening more and more when it comes to Hunter.

"Ah, the famous Rachel," says Drew while taking my hand and kissing my knuckles.

I suppress a shudder and the need to gag while I force a smile. "You've heard about me?"

"Hunter couldn't stop talking about you," says Drew while shoving his shoulder playfully against Hunter's. I watch Hunter inhale deeply, keeping his cool while he slowly turns around and touches his shoulder with a shaking hand. He can pretend all he wants that he's fine, but I can tell he's in pain.

I'm about to ask how the two know each other when I see Millie saunter through the crowded hallway, her eyes locked on Hunter before they slide over to me. She smiles wickedly before moving around Drew. My gaze narrows on her while her hands slide up Hunter's shoulders before wedging herself between us.

"Hey, Hunter," she says sweetly. "I'm so happy you made it." She glances at me, her eyes flicking over my jeans and my simple green shirt. Sure, I could have dressed in a tight dress or a short skirt, but it's cold and after a day like today, all I want to wear is something cozy.

I scowl at Millie as she presses her breasts against Hunter's arm, which are barely covered in her lilac sweater with an extremely low neckline. She's wearing a denim skirt and knee-high boots, looking absolutely perfect with her perfect make up and her perfect hair. Then here I am, probably looking like an absolute mess.

I try to calm myself down. I don't need to try. I'm beautiful the way I am. And besides, Hunter cares about me. He pretty much said that when we were doing it. *Well, he said he wants me. I shake my head. That's pretty much the same thing in bro language. Right?*

"I see Rachel tagged along," says Millie while offering me a fake smile. "I guess you got bored of your whole picture thing. Can't say I blame you."

I smile my best fake smile while stepping towards her. "No, I'm still doing photography, Millie. I just wanted to have a night out."

Millie nods while her brows furrow. Her bottom lip sticks out into a pout. I'm seriously two seconds away from ripping her arms off my boyfriend. "I see. You're that type of girl." She looks up at Hunter, who's busy talking with Drew and not even paying attention to her. "You can't let Hunter out to play. Gotta follow along wherever he goes."

"No, Millie. I don't. Although, maybe you're that type of girl. Tossing a toy to the side once you get bored, then getting jealous when someone else decides to pick it up and play with it."

Millie blinks at me. "I have no clue what you're talking about."

I sigh while crossing my arms. "Now that. I can definitely believe."

Millie releases Hunter and steps towards me, but I refuse to back down. I jut out my chin as she stands in my face, waiting and ready for whatever she has to throw at me. "You do realize, Hunter will dump you eventually," she says, her voice low just for me to hear.

"I highly doubt that."

"Oh, really?" she asks with a mocking bright smile. "Then why was he here on Saturday? Why was he with me and not with you?"

I open my mouth, about to yell at her to keep her slimy hands off my man when I feel something on my shoulder. I whirl around, tempted to yell at whomever it is to leave me alone, when I stop and practically deflate as my gaze locks with Seth, who looks worried.

"Hey, is everything okay?" He asks while wrapping his arms around me. "You look upset," he whispers in my ear.

"Just Millie being Millie."

"Hey, Seth!" I hear Millie call behind me.

Seth rolls his eyes, not bothering to reply to her as he takes my hand and pulls me into the kitchen. "Join us," says Seth with a smile. "You can be on my team."

I smile back at him and nod. I take my place between Seth and Lucas at the table while beers are being refilled for Flip Cup. I try to have fun. I try to keep my mind off Hunter as we continue to play and take shots. My mind is growing fuzzy, but I can't deny after a few drinks, I'm feeling quite buzzed and happy. After the fourth game of Flip Cup, Seth goes to stand in line at the toilet while Lucas and I wait for him in the living room. The couches are covered with girls and jocks making out while the middle of the floor is filled with people grinding against each other. Lucas and I lean against the wall, holding each other's hands as we wait for Seth, which I suspect will take at least an hour at this rate since there's only one bathroom in the whole place.

"So," I start, trying to form words in my sluggish brain. "How was your poetry class? It's near the art department, isn't it?"

Lucas nods vigorously, but then grimaces. "I was late."

I chuckle. "On the first day."

"Yeah, my dad called and tried to get me to drop the class."

I scoff. "Like that will ever happen."

Lucas sighs. "I don't know. Maybe he's right." His gaze slides to the floor.

"Why do you say that?" I grab his chin and lift his face up so I can look into his dark eyes. "I thought you were excited for that class?"

"I am or," Lucas makes a face, "was. I don't know. I just feel like I'm wasting time. It's just a stupid hobby anyway. It's not like I can make a career of it."

I shrug. "You never know. There are lots of famous writers out there."

Lucas levels a look at me. "And how many are rich?"

I nod while making a face. "Not many." I place a hand on Lucas's shoulder. "But being wealthy isn't everything."

Lucas chuckles. "You say that, because you've never had money."

I scowl and stab a long nail into his shoulder, earning a hiss. "True," I say while he bats my hand away. "But still. You should shoot for your dreams." I watch Lucas nod, yet I can tell something else is eating away at him. "Why are you having all this self doubt now?"

He sighs and runs a hand through his dark hair. "I don't know. I guess... there's a writing contest going on and I just don't think I'm any good."

"Well, how do you know? You've never shared your work with anyone but me." I stroke the side of his face as I say, "I think your poetry is brilliant."

Lucas rolls his eyes. "That's because you like me."

I shake my head. "Nah. That's not it."

Lucas laughs. "It so totally is."

"Well, why don't you try reading your work at a poetry slam. The Coffee Shop has one every Thursday I think. We can go this week!"

Lucas frowns. "I don't know, Rachel."

"Ok, maybe not this week. But we can go the week after. Or the week after that."

Lucas laughs.

"Have either of you seen Hunter?"

I turn, finding a worried Seth standing near us. He's not looking at us though. His gaze is fixed to the dancers in the middle of the room, but I don't see Hunter there. In fact, I haven't seen him in what seems like hours.

I grab my phone from my back pocket. My eyes snap open at the time, seeing that it's nearly two in the morning and I have an early class to get my butt to in about seven hours. We've been here for at least four hours and during that time, I haven't seen Hunter show his face at all.

"No," I say while pulling away from the wall, worry spreading through me.

"We should find him," says Seth. "I know he has football practice early in the morning tomorrow."

Lucas nods while leading the way out of the living room. "Have you looked in the kitchen?"

"Yeah, he's not there. He's not in the line for the bathroom. I know he isn't in the bathroom." Seth nods towards the staircase. "I'm wondering-"

I scowl and clench my jaw, not wanting to think why Hunter is upstairs in one of the bedrooms. I haven't seen Millie in forever, as well. Stomping up the stairs I try to push my anger away, which is proving to be quite difficult. I can't help but imagining the two of them together. *We just made love earlier today. Does he really need to get his rocks off again?*

I open one of the doors, finding a couple I have never met in my life making out while pulling at each other's clothes. They quickly turn to me, the girl's eyes widening while the guy shouts, "Can't we get some privacy?"

I slam the door shut. Well, Hunter isn't in there.

I turn to the next door, opening it and finding an empty office with stacks of papers on the desk and books stacked on shelves.

"Found him!" I hear Seth shout and turn around to the room across from me.

I stalk inside, expecting to find a naked Hunter and Millie, but instead discover Hunter completely passed out on a couch with Millie hovering above him, like a cougar about to pounce.

"Get away from him!" I shout while stalking towards Millie. I shove her away and caress Hunter's face. His eyes are closed, but there's an eerie smile on his lips.

"I wasn't doing anything," I hear Millie say, but at this point I don't care.

"We need to get him home," I say.

I watch as Lucas and Seth grab his arms and pull him up from the couch. I pat Hunter's cheeks, hoping to jar him awake. He giggles while his head slumps forward.

His chin digs into his chest and drool dribbles down to his shirt.

"Hunter, are you alright?" I whisper while stroking his jaw.

"I'm fine," he giggles with his eyes still shut.

I look up at Seth and Lucas. Their expressions mirror mine; filled with worry and concern. "We're taking you home," I say while Lucas and Seth help him up.

"He said he's fine," says Millie.

I scowl at her, about to smack her, but knowing it would solve nothing. "He is not fine," I say lowly. "He's the opposite of fine."

Millie scoffs and rolls her eyes. "Whatever."

I want to yell at her but what good would it do? Millie's selfish and only cares about one thing: herself.

"Yeah, whatever, Millie," I mutter while holding the door open for the boys.

Hunter's feet aren't able to balance and keep sliding against the floor. His head lolls from side to side while Seth and Lucas struggle to carry him down the stairs. Stares follow us as we help Hunter out of the house, but even when we are on our way towards our apartment, I can't help the worry tensing my shoulders.

"Is he going to be okay?" I ask as we walk through the freezing cold.

"He'll be fine," says Seth easily. He glances at me and gives me a bright smile, but I can see the fear in his eyes. "He just drank too much."

"Again," Lucas mutters.

"He just needs a bit of sleep and he should be good to go," says Seth.

Hunter bursts into a fit of laughter. "Sleep," he says and then continues laughing.

I sniff and try to keep myself from crying.

What happened to the Hunter I know?

11

HUNTER

A siren blares and I jump, my heart leaping all the way into my throat. I look around, trying to make sense of where I am. There's an alarm clock buzzing at me and I'm in a bed fully clothed.

Wait.

I'm in my bed.

I slam my hand on the clock, feeling tempted to go back to bed since it's seven in the morning, but I need to go to football practice. Coach is probably already pissed I blew off yesterday. I shakily get out of bed. My body feels like it's been run over by a semi-truck, then eaten by vultures, and finally regurgitated into a pile of guts. My stomach twists with each and every step I take towards the door.

I lean against the wall on my good shoulder as I slowly trudge towards the bathroom. My teeth feel mossy from not brushing them, my mouth feels like the tooth fairy up and died inside and probably smells like it, too. I shiver as I enter the bathroom. Not because I'm cold. I just can't seem to stop shaking.

Shrugging off my clothes, I step inside and turn on the water, allowing the liquid to wash away the sweat and smoke permeating off me. Today is a new day. I'll make better decisions. Different decisions.

I bite back a cry as I lift my arm to shampoo my hair, reminding me I need to find someone to get me more painkillers. Anything really. I just need to numb the pain. That's it. And then I can play football like I'm supposed to.

I lean my head against the tiled wall, closing my eyes and remembering the night before. Millie had been at the party, yet I barely remember saying more than two words to her. Drew and Jerry had found me. I remember following them upstairs, asking them about what we had taken the night before.

"We don't have any of that," Drew had said. *"But we have something else. Something better."*

And it had been better.

Way better.

My hands press against the wall as I remember the feeling flowing through me, taking away all the pain, all the worries that seem to be slowly driving me crazy. *In one minute nothing mattered anymore.* And I hate to admit it, but it's better than the painkillers.

And I want more.

I shake my head, telling myself there is no way I can have anymore. Football stars don't do crap like that. If I want a career in the NFL, I need to stop whatever it is I am doing.

I turn off the water and grab a towel, dabbing it against my skin, which feels like it's about to crawl off my body. I wrap it around my waist and stalk back down the hallway, stopping when I see Lucas and Seth in the kitchen. Seth leans against the refrigerator, eyeing me with worry while Lucas crosses his arms and looks like a pissed bouncer dealing with some annoying hooligans.

I don't have time for this.

I open my door and stride inside, about to slam it when Lucas catches it and forces it open. "We need to talk," he says, his voice low and venomous.

I sigh and shake my head. "Fine, whatever." I turn around and throw off my towel. "Make it quick. I'm already running late."

I search for my boxers, finding some that don't smell like complete ass and pull them up before searching for my football gear.

"Where the fuck were you last night?" asks Lucas.

I shrug. "Around."

"I was fucking worried," I hear Seth say. "I was looking for you everywhere. You just up and disappeared." I scoff. "Like I haven't done that shit before." I pull on my track pants and a t-shirt before grabbing my duffel bag and sliding it over my shoulders. "You guys," I say with a forced smile as I slowly turn around to face them, "nothing is going on."

"No," says Seth while slamming a hand against the wall. "We do have to talk about it. You've been acting like a fucking asshole since the ski trip and I want to know why." He scowls at me. "Is it your shoulder?"

I shake my head. "I don't want to talk about it." I step towards the door, but Lucas and Seth block my way. I roll my eyes. "Guys, I need to get-"

"Is it your mom?" asks Seth.

"Can't you get it into your thick fucking skull?" I shout, feeling something snap within me at the mere mention of my mother. Sure, the guys know a bit, but they don't know everything. And they don't need to know everything. "I don't want to talk about it."

"You need to talk about it," says Lucas. "I'm not living like this anymore."

"Like what, Lucas?" I ask while shoving him away from me.

His eyes widen and he looks like he's about to punch me. I wait for it, but he remains still, his fists clenched at his sides. I laugh as I watch his chest heave, not because it's funny, but because I don't know what else to do. I need them gone. I don't want to deal with… this.

"Seriously," says Seth, his voice barely above a whisper. "Tell us what's going on. Rachel has been worried. We've been worried."

I close my eyes. "I don't want to talk about it. I just want to go to football practice."

"Ok, fine," I hear Lucas say. "We'll let it go, if you just tell us what the hell you were on last night."

My eyes snap open and I wonder for a brief second if they saw me do anything. "What?" I breathe, fear racking through me.

"There's no way you were just drunk," says Lucas while pointing a finger at me. "You did something. What was it?"

I chuckle bitterly. "I have no clue what you are talking about."

"Liar!" Seth and Lucas shout in unison.

I shake my head. I've had enough of this. I don't deserve any of this. "I'm late for football practice," I say while stepping forward, but the bros refuse to move. "Get out of my way."

"No," says Seth while Lucas shakes his head.

I ram Seth with my shoulder while I shove Lucas away from me. Lucas grabs me, wrenching my bad shoulder backwards and I scream, grabbing onto his hand and throwing him off me. I gasp, holding the place that burns and trying to calm my breath. I blink away the tears, but a few escape, streaming down my face and dripping onto the floor.

"I'm sorry," says Lucas while reaching towards me.

I wrench away from him. "Stay away from me."

I stalk away from Seth and Lucas, ignoring their shocked looks while I walk towards the apartment door, slamming it close behind me.

***

"Where the hell have you been?" shouts Coach as soon as he sees me enter the field. "I called you five times yesterday."

"Sorry, Coach," I say while shoving on my helmet. "Stomach bug."

Coach looks me up and down and shakes his head. "Yeah, you look like shit."

I wait for him to either send me to the sidelines or yell at me some more, yet he only shakes his head and turns on his heel. *Lucky me,* I think while breaking into a run. I catch up easily to my teammates, but my body feels unusually weak and I find it difficult keeping up.

"What's up with you, Hunter?" Logan asks while smacking my shoulder. A shudder ripples through as I grind my teeth through the pain. "Not like you to miss practice."

"Nothing," I gasp, already out of breath and I've hardly moved.

"Stacey saw you at that house party last Saturday," says Matt. "Says you were pretty fucked up."

Logan laughs. "Yeah, I bet. Hunter always gets fucked up."

"Although, it's still not like you to miss practice," says Matt.

He glances at me and when I meet his gaze, I realize he knows. He knows I've done something really bad. I try to shake the worry away, knowing he wouldn't do anything with the information, but I can't help but wonder if this is going to ruin my football career.

Your football career hasn't even started, numb nuts, says a dark voice in the back of my head. *You can hardly call yourself a football star now with your fucked up shoulder and your fucked up life.*

"Whatever," I gasp. "I'm here now."

Logan scoffs. "Hardly. I've never seen you so out of breath, Hunter." He laughs and the noise grates on my nerves.

"I'm not surprised," says Matt.

"Oh, really? Why not? Hunter doing harder-"

I smash my shoulder against Logan, tackling him against the fence. "Shut it, Logan!" I shout while grabbing his throat and keeping him there. "Just shut the fuck up!"

Logan smacks my hand as he gasps for breath. I feel people pulling at me and my eyes widen, realizing what I've just done. I release him and step away, watching him

cru
on i
the

Loga
off m

as I wa
can bar
am I act
better. M
me feels
onto to k
 I c
to control   ...iu I hear a
buzz comii   ....acn inside, grabbing my cell
phone and .....uing Mom's name on the screen.

I shove it back in my bag.
I can't.
Not now.
Whatever she has to say, it can wait until tomorrow. I know it can't be good and I already feel terrible. What am I going to do? I can't talk to my mom, because we'll just wind up talking about her dying and I can't imagine going through all that right now. I can't go home and face my friends, because they will just continue to pester me and I will continue being a fucking asshole to them. I can't play football, because otherwise I will just turn into a crazy jerk.

I just want something to take all this pain away.

I grab my phone and flip through my contacts until I stop, clicking on the name I need.

I text: *Hey Millie, is there a party going on tonight?*

...ket filled with fruit on the table in ... catching Josh watching me before ... to my drawing. The jerk keeps trying to ...tion and I am way too hungover to be ... his antics. It's only the second day of this class ...ady I am contemplating dropping it. I just can't ...t. I can't focus with Josh in the room. And maybe it's ...st the hangover talking, but I also suck at drawing. I really, really do. There's no way I can pass this class with the way things are going.

"Alright," says Mr. Brown while clapping his hands twice, making the ache in my head press against my temples. I stifle a groan while I shove my pencil back into its bright pink case. "That's enough for today. I will see you all tomorrow."

I slide my sunglasses back over my face and pack up my things, moving at an incredibly slow pace in order to avoid Josh. Yesterday I noticed he ran out of here, so most likely he has a class right after this. I mean, I do too, but at this point I think I'm going to skip it.

I swallow a gag, feeling bile rise. Yep, I'm totally going to skip it. I straighten myself while sliding my backpack over one shoulder. I muster up the strength to walk towards the door, feeling like my body is going to snap at the slightest little breeze the rustles through the room.

"Rachel, is it?"

I turn to Mr. Brown, who is currently sitting with a very bright smile on his face as he watches me.

I nod curtly and then curse myself for moving so violently. I press my fingers against my temple as the pounding in my head continues. "Yes, Mr. Brown?"

"May I have a word?"

All air leaves my lungs as I turn to the door and all the beauty it holds. I know what this is about. Mr. Brown is irritated I came to his class reeking of beer. I shouldn't be hungover in his class. Coming was a mistake.

I shakily grab a chair and drag it in front of his desk. Standing is just not possible for me and now that Mr. Brown has seen through my attempts to remain unruffled by my hangover, all my strength has left. I slump in the chair, waiting for him to admonish me.

"I was wondering if you've taken a drawing class before?"

I blink as his words seep through me. I don't really know where this is going and I don't know if I like it. "No," I say, grimacing when my voice comes out as a croak. I clear my throat and quickly add, "I took some in high school, but this is my first time taking a college drawing course."

Mr. Brown nods and I watch as his smile somehow seems to grow. "Well, you're quite good."

"Really?" I ask. I take a moment to pinch myself, wondering if I somehow slept through my alarm clock. I grimace when I feel pain and my face flashes as I hear Mr. Brown chuckle.

"Yeah, you have a real talent."

"Are you sure?" I ask while leaning in, wondering if he's somehow made some sort of mistake. "It's only the second day. How can you tell already?"

Mr. Brown nods. "Oh, I can tell. I wanted to speak with you about an internship position."

I blink. Really, I must be dreaming. This keeps getting better and better.

"I know the semester has just begun, but I don't think it's too late to look into it." Mr. Brown slides a paper towards me, displaying the Eiffel Tower as well as the words 'Six Week Art Internship'. "It starts in July and goes until mid-August. As you can see it's in Paris."

"Are you sure?" I ask, my voice practically a whisper. "I mean, I'm just a Freshman. Wouldn't it be better to recommend one of your Juniors or Seniors for this position?"

Mr. Brown nods. "Oh, don't you worry. They'll be applying, too. But I believe in you." He winks while leaning back in his chair. "Apply for the program and build your portfolio. You'll need it when they ask you for an interview."

"Thank you," I whisper while standing, a smile tugging at my lips. "Thank you so much."

Mr. Brown raises his hands and shakes his head. "I haven't done anything. You're the one who needs to put in the work."

I nod vehemently. "Yes. And I will."

I turn on my heel, nearly skipping on my way towards the door.

"Oh, and Rachel."

I stop and turn around, a large smile on my face.

Mr. Brown winces as he says, "Maybe next time don't come to class smelling like a bar. I understand you're a Freshman and all and this is a bit of a party school, but even I have my limits."

I chuckle and nod. "Yes, of course, Mr. Brown. It won't happen again."

He twiddles his fingers in farewell as I open the door and step outside, feeling jubilant and filled with renewed energy. I turn as the door closes behind me, ready to take on my next class no matter how painful my body feels. I stop, my heart hammering in my chest as my eyes land on Josh leaning against the wall next to our drawing class with his arms crossed. He smiles at me, pushing away from the wall and stepping towards me.

"Hey," he says casually, as if somehow everything that happened last semester didn't.

Shit.

I turn on my heel and briskly walk down the hall.

"Hey, Rachel!" I hear him call, but I ignore him. There is no way he thinks after everything he has done that I would want to talk to him now. I can't. And I won't. I don't owe him anything. He's lucky I didn't tell the school board.

Hell, he's lucky I didn't go to the cops.

"Wait!"

I throw open the door and I don't stop.

"Rachel!"

I try to run, but there are too many students around and I don't want to make a scene. I should run though. I should run all the way to the sports store until I'm safely enclosed in Seth's arms. I look around, wondering if Lucas is around here somewhere. I know he has his writing class near here, but I can't remember if he has it today or not.

I feel hands on my shoulder, tugging me backwards followed by a, "Rachel, come on. Please talk to me."

I whirl around, fist raised and ready to break Josh's nose. His eyes widen in alarm and he immediately lets me go while raising his hands in defense.

Unclenching my fist I release the breath I have been holding and scowl back at him. "Leave me alone, Josh. I don't want to talk to you."

"Rachel," he says while stepping towards me.

I take a step back and I watch his shoulders slump, watch him sigh and look all pitiful. *It's all just a mask*, I tell myself. *He's nothing but a snake waiting in the shadows.*

"Rachel, I just want to say I'm sorry."

I shake my head. "No, you don't get to say that now," I nearly shout. I look around and find several pairs of eyes staring curiously at us.

"Rachel, please-"

I scoff. "You must be kidding me. After all this time you want to apologize to me. After everything you did to me. Pretending to be nice to me, just to get close." I laugh bitterly.

"That's not what I meant to happen."

"Oh, really," I say while circling around him. "So you didn't mean to grab me when I said no."

I watch him flinch as if I struck him.

"So you didn't mean to pin me down and attempt to force yourself on me when I was crying for you to stop."

Josh sighs. "Rachel, I'm apologizing. That's what I'm doing. Now, why can't you just let it go?"

"Because I fucking can't you asshole!" I stomp my foot, wishing his face was underneath it. "How can you possibly say that after everything you put me through?"

I turn on my heel, not able to look at him any longer. Just seeing his stupid face and his stupid glasses makes me remember how he grabbed my leg, making me trip and fall. I shudder as I remember him pulling my legs apart.

I don't want to hear his apology. I want him to stay as far away from me as possible.

***

A week has passed since Josh attempted to apologize to me after class. Unfortunately, I still haven't been able to get my mind off him and it doesn't help at all that we still share drawing class together. I don't even think he enjoys drawing. I seriously wish he would just drop it and leave me alone.

Thankfully, Lucas and I made plans to go out tonight to The Coffee Shop for Poetry Slam. Sitting in an old withered chair and desperately trying to find a comfortable spot on the torn cushion, I pause when I hear, "Lucas Brent."

I lift my head and turn towards Lucas, who has been staring nervously into his coffee cup since we first arrived. He hasn't seemed to notice that someone is calling his name up front and continues starting unblinkingly at his coffee, as if it somehow entranced him.

"Hey," I say while giving his shoulder a gentle nudge with my own. "That's you."

Lucas perks up and looks around as the person on the stage calls, "Lucas Brent? Are you here?"

Lucas jumps from his chair, making it slide across the wooden floor. I cringe at the screeching sound and the multiple stairs turning towards us. "Yes, coming," he says shakily while walking briskly to the front of the room.

I grimace as I watch him stumble in a few chairs on his way up. I have never seen him so stressed out before. Usually, Lucas is calm and collected. He always knows what to say, yet now he is acting like a high school student giving a huge speech in front of an auditorium filled with teachers.

Worry makes my skin tingle and my stomach twist while I watch him grab the microphone and sit on the edge of the stool. He smiles shakily, his gaze searching the cafe before he finds me. "He-hello," he stutters. He clears his throat, lowering his gaze down to the notebook he carries in his other hand. "I'm Lucas Brent." He chuckles awkwardly and the cafe resumes in its silence, while several customers gaze back at him, looking absolutely bored.

Oh, I hope this wasn't a bad idea.

I want him to be able to gain some confidence in his writing, yet now I'm wondering if I should have waited to bring him here. He's only read his work to me as far as I know. I don't even think the guys have heard his work.

Well, I guess it's too late to turn back now, I tell myself while propping my elbows on the table and placing my chin and my hands. "Come on, Lucas," I whisper while watching him open his notebook. "You can do this."

"Tonight, I'm going to read a short poem I wrote," says Lucas. He lifts his head and gazes back at me, offering this time a curt nod filled with strength. "It's about freedom."

I watch Lucas inhale and close his eyes for a brief moment before saying, "Like a bird, soaring and flying high in the sky…"

I allow his voice to wash over me, taking me away from my troubles with Josh and my worries for Hunter. I just listen to Lucas's words, feeling tears prickle my gaze as I stare at him. He truly is an artist, which is shocking since he hardly looks the part in his slim cut jeans and his black buttoned down shirt, which hardly contain the broad muscles of his chest and arms. I can't believe that after all this time, I am actually with this man, in a cafe, sharing art with each other.

It's like everything I have ever hoped and wished for.

Lucas's voice is calm, the words magical, pulling me into a different world where it's just me and him. And then, without even realizing it, he stops with a smile and a wink my way. I lone tear spill from my eye and I watch as he slowly stands and bows his head. "That's all," he says with a shrug. "Thank you for listening."

People around us snap their fingers while Lucas strides back to our table, dumping his body into his chair and tilting his head back. He draws in a deep breath and says, "That was unbearable."

I wipe my eyes and sniff. "No, that was beautiful."

He turns toward me and one side of his mouth lifts into a mischievous smirk. "You think so."

I chuckle. "I know so." I lean towards him and poke his nose teasingly. "I think you have nothing to worry about."

Lucas scoffs. "That was only one poem. And I'm supposed to create a whole book of them." He straightens himself and shakes his head. "That one alone took me weeks to write."

I slide my hand towards his, placing it on top, which catches his attention. "Then you better start writing. That award belongs to you."

Lucas nods towards the entrance. "Wanna get to-go cups and get out of here."

I smile and nod. "Sure."

I watch Lucas shrug on his black coat and take our coffee mugs to the front before grabbing my own. My gaze turns to the windows, finding the roads dimly lit by the lampposts and snow falling from the sky. I wrap my scarf around my neck and my shoulders tense in preparation for the cold about to slam into us.

"Ready?" I hear Lucas ask from behind and turn around, finding him handing my coffee over, now in a brown recyclable cup.

I beam up at him while wrapping my arm around his. "Ready when you are."

I hold tight to him as we exit, feeling the chill cut right through my layers and rattle my bones. "Oh, God," I murmur while trying to snuggle against Lucas's side. "Why did we go out again?"

Lucas chuckles while leading me down the snow-covered sidewalk. "Because you needed to take your mind off things, and I needed to get more confidence in my work."

I shake my head. "Definitely not good enough of a reason."

"Are you saying we should have stayed home and ordered a pizza instead?"

"Not necessarily," I say while giving Lucas a sly grin. "We could have done… other things."

Lucas turns to me and I watch his eyes dilate and his nostrils flare. "Oh, really?"

We turn a corner and I giggle as Lucas pushes me up against a brick building. His hip presses in-between my legs and his head lowers. My breath falters as my gaze catches on his lips, lingering just above my own.

"And what exactly, could we have gotten up to, Rachel?" Lucas whispers, his breath warming mine.

I angle my head up to him and I go up to my tiptoes, brushing my lips against his. "Oh, I don't know," I breathe. "Stuff."

Lucas chuckles and his free hand lowers to my hip, pulling me closer. My eyes flutter close and I yearn for his touch. Warmth pulls into my core as I wait.

Something vibrates and my eyes snap open. Lucas frowns and I see him questioning himself whether to answer his phone or not. He rolls his eyes and mutters, "Shit," while search his coat pockets, finding the phone and scowling down at the name on the Caller ID.

"Who is it?" I ask when his eyes widen.

"It's Hunter," he says before pressing the answer key and moving it to his ear. "Hey, bro, this really isn't a good-" Lucas's frown deepens. "Hunter?" He pulls his phone away from his ear for a moment, staring down at the Caller ID again before returning it to the side of his face. "Dude, I don't understand a word you're saying. Are you okay?" Lucas waits for an answer, his gaze meeting mine.

The worry I find there does nothing to halt the fear brimming within me.

"Where are you? Hunter?" Lucas sighs and kicks the building. "Un-fucking-believable," he mutters.

"Is he okay?" I ask while lightly touching Lucas's arm.

Lucas holds a finger up to me. "Millie's house? Why the hell are you- never mind. We're on our way."

"Is he alright?" I ask while Lucas hangs up and shoves his phone back into his pocket.

"Come on," he says while taking my hand and pulling me in the opposite direction of home. "It's about a ten-minute walk."

"Lucas, just tell me if he's alright," I say, my voice shrill, but I get no answer as Lucas drags me down the road towards Hunter with a dark scowl on his face.

13

LUCAS

"Dude, I don't- I don't, where am I?" I hear Hunter slur on the other line. *I don't know man,* I think in my head, knowing that isn't the greatest thing to respond with. I have never heard Hunter sound so trashed before. The dude liked to party, yet he kept himself together enough to find his way home. I barely recognize this person on the phone.

"Where are you, Hunter?" I ask instead, hoping to get his sluggish brain moving. Maybe it'll help him sober up a bit if he takes a look around and asks whomever is near him. Although, it's not even that late. Probably at most going on ten. How is he so fucked up this early?

Has he been partying all day?

Has he even gone to practice or class?

"I don't know man," I hear Hunter answer. There's some movement and then a groan. "Couch, lying on. I don't know- I don't know-"

"Un-fucking-believable," I mutter while shaking my head.

"There was a party yesterday. Millie's?"

My brow furrows. "Why the hell are you-" I groan and ruffle my hair, knowing whatever his answer it would just piss me off even more. It doesn't matter now. Get him home, yell at him later. "Never mind, we're on our way."

I hang up, not wanting to hear his stupid voice on the receiving end. I had barely seen him in the past week and sure, I had thought it strange at the time, but I also thought it might be best to give him his space.

I guess I thought wrong.

"Is he alright?" Rachel asks and I inwardly groan, wishing I had Seth with me to help the asshole home rather than her.

This is just going to make her even more upset. Hunter has been acting like a complete jerk to her since we got back from winter vacation and I know, if she isn't thinking about Josh, she is definitely thinking about ways to resolve her relationship with Hunter.

God this is all just a fucking mess.

"Come on," I say while taking her hand and dragging her behind me. "It's about a ten-minute walk."

"Lucas, just tell me if he's alright."

I shake my head, not wanting to talk at all right now. I can't lie to her. I know Hunter isn't fine. He hasn't been for a long time and I think now he has finally reached his breaking point. I know things at home with his mom aren't great, but I did think they were getting better. His dad was coming home more often, his mom was done with chemo.

I frown while sliding through the snow. The flakes are falling down even harder now and I scowl darkly at the houses surrounding us and the lampposts dimly lighting our path. I'm supposed to be on a date with Rachel and here I am, picking up my messed up best friend, who has been a jerk to not only her, but to me the past several days.

Something has to change.

I'm not going to be dealing with this shit forever. Either Hunter tells us what's up tonight or tomorrow, or... or...

I groan in frustration and run my hands in my hair. "Lucas," I hear Rachel murmur behind me.

"What?" I ask, louder than I need to while whirling around to glare darkly at her.

Rachel's eyes glimmer with unshed tears and I feel myself soften. I pull her close to me and hold her tight, pressing my head against hers while her hands wrap around my waist. "I'm sorry," I whisper into her ear. "I didn't mean to yell at you."

I feel her nod and she gently pushes me away. I watch her wipe her eyes, hear her sniff. I know she's worried and I am too. But, that's no reason to be so mean to her. We're in this together.

"I just need to know if he's okay," Rachel says shakily and I can tell she's close to breaking down.

"He's fine," I say while pushing her hair away from her face. "Just a bit drunk. We just gotta get him home. The sooner the better."

She nods. "Should I call Seth?"

I sigh and run my fingers through my hair. It might be a good idea, although I don't know if he can get here in time. "Not yet," I finally say. "I think walking will do Hunter some good." I take her hand and pull her towards me. "Come. We're almost there."

We walk the rest of the way to Millie's house, which is a two-story townhouse with a porch. I sigh while staring at the house, finding several girls sitting on the porch, covered in blankets, coats, and hats while sharing a bottle of wine. All the lights are on and the bass of some music playing in the background thumps loudly.

"Lucas!" I hear Millie, see her perk up from her place on the chair. She smiles brightly while waving her hand at us and lunges away from her friends and down the two steps towards us. "Fancy seeing you here," she says while sidling up close to me. Her gaze rakes over me, as if she's undressing me and I wonder for a moment, what I ever saw in this girl.

She is nothing compared to Rachel.

"Where's Hunter?" I ask while brushing past her and walking up the steps. My hand remains fastened to Rachel's and I watch her throw open the door.

"Ugh, that guy," I hear Millie say from behind us as we walk inside. "I have no clue."

"He has to be here, Millie," I say while looking around the place, finding a couple making out on a ripped up couch and several people drinking in the kitchen. "He called me like ten minutes ago."

I turn around and watch Millie shrug. "Haven't seen him in a while."

Rachel groans in annoyance and I watch her turn on her heel and storm up the stairs.

"Hey!" Millie shouts while following after her.

I follow them both and watch as Rachel looks through all the doors, suddenly reminded of another party not too long ago where we found Hunter completely messed up on a couch. "Stop!" Millie shouts while Rachel continues looking through the rooms.

Rachel frowns while crossing her arms.

"Find him?" I ask.

With one shake of her head, my shoulders slump and I stalk back down the stairs. Where the hell could he be? If he wasn't here, he could be anywhere. I take out my phone. Finding his number, I press the call pad and wait for his answer.

I frown when I hear ringing behind me. "Hunter?" I shout while looking around, finding nothing except the bathroom nearby.

"Wait a minute," I murmur while pressing on the bathroom door.

It opens slightly, but there is something pushing on the door.

"See, I told you he wasn't here," I hear Millie say behind me while I continue pressing on the door.

"Lucas," says Rachel and I see her hand appear and rest on top of mine. "I don't think he's here."

"Oh, he most certainly is," I say while pushing harder.

There's a groan on the other side and the door gives just slightly, showing blood stained tiles and dirty white tennis shoes. "Hunter!" I call.

"What?"

I tilt my head up, shaking my head and pinching the bridge of my nose. "Can you please stand up so I can open the fucking door?"

"He's here?" I hear Millie ask in surprise.

I sigh. Really, I have no time for these shenanigans. All I want is to be home, in bed with Rachel, maybe even playing some Mario Kart. But no, I have to deal with this bullshit instead.

"I can't," Hunter whines. "Everything hurts."

I slam my shoulder into the door and I hear a shout. "Fucking stand up now, you asshole and let's go!"

I hear some scrambling on the other side and the door suddenly opens. I feel my eyes widen and my heart completely stop as my gaze meets Hunter. His face is swollen in black and blue bruises and there's blood dripping from a cut in his lip. Blood drips from cuts on his knuckles and his white shirt is stained in blood, dirt, and what I could only assume is his own putrid vomit.

"Oh my God," I hear Millie murmur behind us.

"Hunter," says Rachel while lunging towards him and wrapping her arms around him.

Hunter doesn't say anything. His arms hang limply at his side while Rachel lifts her head up. "What happened to you?" She asks, her voice quivering. I frown at the tears streaming down her cheeks and a part of me wants to rip Hunter into two for making her worry so much about him. "Are you alright?"

Hunter stumbles in her arms and his gaze lifts to mine. His bloodshot eyes squint and confusion mars his face as he stares back at me. His lips twitch upwards into a strange grin and in a blink of an eye he bursts into laughter.

"I'm fine," he slurs while stumbling forwards. "Absolutely fine."

"Did Jerry do that to you?" I hear Millie ask, which makes me turn around sharply.

Her gaze turns to me, looking wide and horrified while I ask, "Who is Jerry?"

Millie quickly shakes her head. "You should get him home, Lucas."

I grab Millie before she can walk away. "Millie, who is Jerry?"

Millie shoves me away and runs into the crowd of party goers. I sigh and grab Hunter's arm, putting it over my shoulders and stepping towards the exit. "Alright, you asshole," I mutter while Hunter continue giggling crazily. "Let's get you home."

***

Walking home with Hunter is easier said than done. He continues stepping onto my feet, leaning into me. And the bastard is heavy. I keep looking over my shoulder, wondering if Rachel is fine. She follows us with her head down, making me frown. *Well, this turned into a pretty sucky night, now didn't it? I was supposed to take her mind off things and now she looks even more upset than before.*

I hate to say it, or even think it, but maybe it's time for her to call a quits on Hunter all together. He doesn't seem to be treating her right and I hate seeing her this way. I turn to Hunter and frown as I watch his head lull back and forth. Can't he see what he's doing to her?

I'm both happy and irritated when we finally arrive back to the apartment. Happy that I'm nearly free from lugging this guy all around town. Irritated that I have to lug him up the stairs.

"Pick up your feet, Hunter," I mutter while taking one step.

Hunter groans and his feet remain rooted to the ground.

"Hunter," I say, louder this time. "Pick up your fucking feet."

"You pick them up," Hunter groans.

"You've got to be fucking kidding me." My head lifts to the sound of a door opening and I sigh in relief as I see Seth coming down the stairs, dressed in bagging shorts and a sweater. He pads quickly down the stairs in his slippers and grabs Hunter's other arm. His worry and horror not lost on me as he stares at Hunter.

"I thought you were supposed to be home an hour ago," says Seth while helping Hunter up the stairs.

"I did, too, but I got a call from this guy." I nod towards Hunter who only bobs his head in agreement. His eyes are closed, but his eyebrows are pulled taught.

"What the hell happened to you, Bro?" Seth asks when we reach the landing. "Get into a little fight?"

Hunter's face contorts into a mixture of confusion and pain as he slurs out, "I don't remember."

"You don't remember or you don't want to tell us?" I ask in irritation while dragging his body into the open apartment door. Seth and I stride towards the couch and dump his body there while Rachel closes the door behind us.

"Can I do anything to help?" she asks while stepping towards Hunter.

"No, we got it," says Seth. "You should get to bed. You have your drawing class tomorrow right?"

Rachel doesn't say anything as she steps closer to Hunter. I move between them, taking her hands and pressing my lips against her knuckles. "Don't worry about him," I whisper. "Seth and I will take care of him."

She sniffs and nods and I watch her turn painstakingly towards her door. "Okay," she murmurs.

"Goodnight," Seth calls sadly while she trudges towards her door, her head still bent forward with shoulders slumped.

When I hear the click of her door shutting, I finally release and exasperated sigh, letting at all my frustration and worry in that breath.

"What the hell happened?" asks Seth.

I shake my head. "I have no clue." I throw an arm in Hunter's direction and scowl at his sleeping form. "He just called me up and told me to find him."

Seth kneels in front of Hunter, frowning down at his bruised face. "Should we call an ambulance? Maybe someone should take a look-"

"No."

Seth frowns while he rises. "But Lucas he looks-"

"I said no," I say forcefully and my skin begins to crawl as my eyes narrow on Hunter. "That could get him into more trouble."

14

RACHEL

The eggs are frying in the pan when I finally hear some groaning coming from the couch. I glance over my shoulder, my eyes finding Hunter rising from the couch while rubbing his head. His blond hair sticks to his face and there's scruff on his jaw. The swelling in his face has gone down, yet it's stilled marred by bruises and cuts.

I so desperately want to ask him what happened, but I know he will just push me away.

"Good morning," I call while trying to put on my best smile.

Hunter turns towards me, his eyes slightly swollen and squinting at me. "Huh?" He rubs his eyes and a painful hiss emits from his chapped lips.

"I've made you breakfast," I say while holding up the pan.

Hunter doesn't say anything as he stands. I watch him pass by me and walk down the hall towards the bathroom. The door closes and I return my attentions to the fried eggs I'm making with toast. It's a simple breakfast, but it should be a good hangover cure.

I hear the shower turn on as I turn off the stove and slide the eggs onto the plate. I smear avocado on my own and take a bite while taking out my cellphone and looking at my to-do list. Seth has gone on his run, although there is so much snow on the ground, I don't know how long he can actually go for.

I frown and make a face. *But, then again, he did go for a run every day we were in the mountains on that ski trip. So, obviously, snow doesn't bother him. Crazy bastard.* Lucas has already gone to class. I really want to talk to him about last night. Not about Hunter, but about our date. We barely had time to ourselves given that we had to go and rescue Hunter from whatever it was he got himself into.

 The door opens and I turn, watching a very wet, now toweled Hunter appear. "Hungry?" I ask while holding out his plate, but Hunter ignores me as he enters his room.

 I sigh and lower the plate. I don't know why I still try. He won't give no matter what I do. I take another bit of my avocado-egg toast and turn my attentions back to my hectic list of things to get done today. I need to speak with Mr. Brown about the internship program. After looking into it, I'm feeling a bit reluctant. There are so many talented artists in this school. I have no clue what to send in my portfolio, and what I currently have, won't get me anywhere close to my goals.

 The door opens again and I lift my head, finding Hunter looking fresh with his wet hair tied back in a man bun. He dumps his backpack near the front door and grabs one of Lucas's many coats.

 "Going to class?" I ask sweetly while approaching him.

 Hunter grunts while zipping the coat and grabbing his bag.

 I reach towards him, sliding my hand against his bruised flesh. His eyes turn to me, widening for a moment before he bats me away. "Stop, Rachel," he says harshly. "Just stop."

 I step backwards. I feel like I've been struck, yet he has barely touched me. Sniffing, I bite back me tears and give him a curt nod. "Sorry," I murmur while I watch him turn around and open the door.

 He doesn't say a word as he closes the door. My bottom lip trembles as I try to swallow my sobs, feeling stupid for ever thinking that he liked me.

 Steeling myself, I straighten and stalk back to my room, throwing on my coat and grabbing my bag. You know what, fuck him, I tell myself while sliding my keys off the counter and walking out the front door. If he doesn't want my help, that's on him. I'm over it. I deserve better than this. I have issues going on in my life, too. It's not just the 'Hunter Show' where everyone has to worry and care about him.

"So freaking selfish," I murmur to myself while locking the door. His eggs can rot on that counter for all I care. I'm done.

I don't know where my feet take me, but they don't take me to class, that's for sure. I look at the clock on my phone and see I have plenty of time before class starts. I guess I didn't really need to leave this early, but I don't want to be alone.

I sigh while walking through the small college town, my eyes catching on The Coffee Shop sign and I realize I am in desperate need of a latte. Sure, we have coffee at home, but I need a pick-me-up now more than ever. This morning, last night, this entire semester; all of it just freaking blows and I am so ready for it to be May and for the semester to end.

I open the door to The Coffee Shop and smile at the usual bell clanging above me, knowing it's a sign that soon I will have something yummy and warm taking all my stress and worries away. At least for the next thirty minutes. I look around while standing in line, smiling when I see Charlie and Lauren sitting in our usual corner next to the window.

Charlie catches my gaze, her eyes widening for a moment while I wave. "Hey!" I call.

She quickly looks away and leans towards Lauren. I watch her mouth move, watch Lauren turn around. Her eyes narrow on me and there's no smile on either of the girl's faces as they look at me.

I frown and slowly lower my hand. My stomach twists as I watch them quickly shove their notebooks and pencil cases into their bags. Something strange is going on, I think to myself while stepping forwards. My gaze remains glued to them as they shrug on their bags and walk towards the door, keeping their attentions off me.

"Hey!" I try again, this time leaving the line and following after them. "What's up?"

Neither of them answer as I follow them outside. "Hey!" I say while running around them, making them stop.

Lauren and Charlie look between them, a frown on their lips. Lauren lifts her gaze and I step backwards as she scowls at me. "What's going on?" I ask, my words coming out slowly. I don't know if I want to hear the answer.

Charlie shakes her head. "Rachel, maybe it's best if you just go back inside."

"No, what's going on?"

Charlie sighs and rubs her head while Lauren's scowl deepens.

"You know exactly what's going on," Lauren says darkly. "You've made Josh feel like a complete social pariah in our group."

"What?" I breathe. "What the hell are you talking about?"

"We know," says Charlie.

My eyes widen as I look between them. They know what happened between me and Josh? The asshole actually told them? "Are you siding with him?" I ask, horror filling me and making my voice sound shrill to my ears.

"Of course we're siding with him!" Lauren shouts. "Why wouldn't we?"

"He actually told you what he did to me and you're siding with him?" I ask, tears streaming down my cheeks. These girls are supposed to be my friends. They're supposed to have my back and instead they decide to team up with Josh, who almost raped me?

"What he did to you?" Lauren shouts. "You mean what you did to him! You should actually be ashamed of yourself."

"What did I ever do to him?"

"Alright, enough," says Charlie while placing herself in between me and Lauren. She presses a hand gently against my chest and makes space. "Let's talk about this later," she adds while looking around.

"Oh, I'm done here," says Lauren while whirling around and walking away.

"Lauren!" Charlie calls while sounding exasperated. She sighs and shakes her head before turning back to me. "Rachel, just give us some space, ok?" She says while staring back at me sadly. "It's a lot for us to take in."

"What do you need to take in?" I shout. "What did he even say? None of this makes sense."

Charlie sighs and lifts her gaze, staring upwards at the cloudy sky for a moment before returning her attentions back to me. "He told us the reason why he hasn't been hanging around, and the reason why you've been acting so weird when he does come around, is because you tried to kiss him."

"What?" I shout, my hands clenching as I feel rage boil over.

Charlie nods. "He also told us that you wouldn't take no for an answer." Charlie shrugs. "And then you trashed his place when you couldn't have things your way."

"Charlie-"

Charlie holds up a hand and whatever I want to say quickly dies in my throat. "Let's talk about this later I'm already late for class."

I watch her turn around and leave me in the cold, sniffing and trying to hold back my tears. The coffee forgotten, I slowly trudge towards my class, knowing there is absolutely nothing that could make this day get any better.

I grit my teeth as I think of Josh.

Well, there is one way I could feel a bit better, I think while tightening my grip on my bag.

***

I throw open the door and stride inside my drawing class, ignoring the loud thump the door makes against the wall as my scowl swivels onto Josh talking to one of the girls in the corner of the room. I ignore the stares as I stalk towards him, my hands fisting into tight little balls I imagine pummeling him with.

How could he say that?

How could he turn the tables around, making me out as the bad guy when it was him who had attacked me?

I stop next to him, my glare darkening as he turns towards me. A look of worry and confusion pulls his brows tight. I don't know what angers me more. What he said to Charlie or Lauren? Or the fact that he seems to think he's done no wrong?

"Rachel, what's-"

"What the actual fuck Josh?" I shout in his face.

I hear the girl Josh had been talking to step away from us while I watch Josh's eyes widen in recognition. He crosses his arms and leans away from me. "So, you spoke with Charlie and Lauren?" I ask while shoving a finger in his face. "How dare you! How dare you spin the tables on-"

"How dare you steal my friends away from me!" Josh shouts back.

"Steal your friends?" My mouth gapes open, trying to form words yet nothing is coming to me. There is so much I want to say to him. Asshole. Jerk. Rapist. But they all remain trapped within my throat.

"Yeah, Rachel," says Josh, stepping closer to me. An ugly smirk forms on his face and I take a step back, worried he will do something to me even though everyone is watching us. "They were my friends before you waltzed in. And they will stay my friends. Go back to your whorehouse Rachel. That's all you're really good for anyway."

I gasp and it takes everything within me to keep my hands from strangling him. Josh chuckles darkly and turns around.

"This isn't over," I whisper.

"Alright, class," I hear Mr. Brown say. I hear his footsteps and I know I should go to my seat, but my feet are just not moving. "Let's begin with-"

"You can't just go around campus spreading lies about me Josh!" I shout. I watch him ignore me as he reaches inside his bag for his pencil case. "You were the one who did wrong to me! You were the one-"

"Oh, shut up Rachel," says Josh while turning around and scowling up at me.

"Ok, what's going on?" I hear Mr. Brown ask, but I ignore him.

"I will not shut up! I will-"

"You'll what, Rachel?" Josh asks while sliding out of his chair, making it skid against the floor before falling over.

I hold his glare as he towers above me. I refuse to back down from this. I'm not going to allow him to bully me and spread lies about me.

"Alright, enough," I hear Mr. Brown, but I don't dare pull my gaze away from Josh. "Class dismissed." I hear everyone skidding their chairs back, picking up their backpacks, and footsteps towards the door. Josh turns away from me, grabbing his things, but I still don't move.

"Rachel, a word please."

I freeze as Mr. Brown's words halt my heart. Slowly, I turn around, finding my drawing teacher leaning against his desk with his arms crossed. He raises an eyebrow at me, making my stomach twist. I grimace when I hear Josh's chuckling behind me. A part of me wants to turn around and tell him to shut up, but I'm too afraid of what Mr. Brown is going to tell me.

I shouldn't have been so stupid. I should have left this mess for after class. God, what a crappy morning. Is this semester ever going to be normal?

Sniffing, I realize I am crying while I approach Mr. Brown and worry spreads through me as I wonder if he's going to kick me out of this class. I nibble on my bottom lip and cradle my bag closer to me.

"Yes, Mr. Brown?" I ask softly while lowering my gaze to the floor.

"What was that?"

I shake my head and close my eyes. "It was nothing. I'm so sorry I caused a scene."

I hear his sigh and my eyes snap open as he says, "Rachel-"

"It won't happen again. It was stupid."

Mr. Brown shakes his head. "I'm worried about you. What's going on between you and Josh? That obviously wasn't nothing."

My bottom lip trembles and I swallow a sob, knowing I need to leave now or I'm going to break down in front of Mr. Brown, whom I respect. I don't want him thinking I'm being some silly little freshman.

"It's nothing," I rush out while turning around.

I bump into a chair and nearly trip over it as I head for the door. Righting it quickly, I shrug on my bag and try very hard not to run towards my escape.

"Rachel, I'm only trying to help."

I pause, my hand hovering just above the door handle.

"If not me, you should at least try to talk to someone."

Tears stream down my cheeks while I slowly turn around. I don't know why, but there was something in his voice that made me want to open my stupid mouth. "Josh tried to," I sniff, not knowing if I can even say the words.

"Tried what, Rachel?" Mr. Brown asks calmly.

I feel my face scrunching up into an ugly mess as I croak out, "He tried to rape me." I swallow another sob while my head lowers. I'm trying desperately not to cry, but the tears keep coming. I inhale deeply, trying to control my breathing. A sob escapes and I curse myself for being so weak.

"Have you reported it?" I hear Mr. Brown asks.

I lift my gaze and see he's still leaning against his desk, but his gaze has softened. I shake my head and he sighs, uncrossing his arms while turning around and dumping himself into his chair.

"Rachel, you need to report it to the police. And the school authorities."

I shake my head. "It's too late. It happened last semester and-" I sniff while unzipping my bag. I know there's a tissue in here somewhere. "And in the end he didn't do anything."

"Rachel," Mr. Brown says sternly. "That still doesn't mean you shouldn't let it go. What if he does it again to some poor unknowing girl and actually succeeds?"

I shake my head, but I know deep down he's right. "No one will believe me anyway," I whisper.

"I believe you."

I watch Mr. Brown pinches his nose while leaning back in his chair and I feel guilty for making him feel so stressed. *I shouldn't have told him*, I tell myself. I should handle this on my own. I'm not a kid anymore.

"I'm sorry I involved you," I murmur.

"No, I need to know this," says Mr. Brown while turning back to me. "I did wonder why you acted so strange sometimes in class. Now it makes sense." Mr. Brown sighs. "Unfortunately, I can't kick Josh out of my class. I could, if you informed school authorities, but as of right now, I can't."

I nod. "You don't have to do anything, Mr. Brown."

"Do you have a class to rush off to after this one?"

I shake my head. "No," I say, a bit confused as to why he's asking. "I have a class, but there's a bit of a gap."

"Good. We can leave together. And I will arrive earlier. If he approaches you, I'll call you to my desk."

My eyes widen. *He's going to try to protect me? From Josh? He'd do that for me?*

"In the meantime, report it to the police and the school authorities," says Mr. Brown while pointing at me. "They might not do anything, but at least your conscious will be clear."

"Thank you, Mr. Brown."

He nods and with that I turn around and walk out into the quiet hall. Mr. Brown's words swim in my head as I walk out of the art department and into the bitter chilled air. What he said made sense, although I'm still worried about the repercussions. What if I reported it, but no one other than my boyfriends and Mr. Brown believed me? What if I became the university's number one 'girl-who-cried-wolf'?

I tilt my head back and look up at the cloudy sky. My eyes hurt. They feel swollen from all the crying. A thought tickles the back of my head that I never did get my coffee, and I decide I desperately need that pick me up while I decide what to do.

15

HUNTER

I sway on my feet in the locker room, wondering for a moment how in the world I am going to get through this game. I feel like shit. It's been about a week since Lucas and Rachel brought me home from that party at Millie's. I don't know what happened to my face. I remember drinking, meeting up with Drew and Jerry, taking some powdery substance. I recall dancing with some chick. I have no clue if it was Millie or someone else.

Everything is a blur.

I gaze back at myself in the mirror in my locker, stroking my jaw and turning my face from side to side. The swelling is gone. There's only a slight hint of bruising around my cheeks. My eyes are circled in dark shadows from lack of sleep. My cheekbones stick out. I grimace and look away, unable to see the disgusting piece of shit I've become.

I grind my teeth as I feel another pull in my shoulder. It seems to be getting worse these days and not only am I completely out of my painkillers, but the doctor won't prescribe me anymore. Apparently, I've had plenty and should be looking into other means to handle my pain. I roll my eyes and slam my door close. My vision blurs for a moment as I turn around. I lean against my locker, allowing the world to stop spinning around me while I slowly lower myself on the bench.

"Alright, gather around," I hear Coach say.

I don't move. My gut twists and I feel bile rise up my throat. Several glances are thrown my way, yet no one says a word as they circle around coach. I already know what he's going to say. There's no point in moving.

I'm being benched.

I close my eyes, allowing myself to rest for just a moment. I try to ignore Coach's voice and the names of teammates being called out, yet for some stupid reason I hold onto hope that he will call my name.

Stupid.

Idiot.

I haven't earned a place in today's game. I've missed so many practices and when I do show up I can barely do anything. *What happened to my dreams of playing in the NFL?* Is this really how I'm going to end my career? Being benched all because of my mommy complex and the pain in my shoulder. I'm better than this. I need to do better.

My eyes open when I hear footsteps leaving and the marching band playing in the distance. I rise and pick up my helmet, placing it under my arm while following after my teammates. No one says a word to me and I'm thankful for it. I don't need their pity or their apologies.

I know I messed up.

I hear something vibrate and turn around, finding that the sound is coming from my locker. Opening it, I rifle through my bag, finding my phone and the name 'MOM' on my caller ID.

"Are you coming Hunter?" Coach shouts.

"In a moment," I mumble while placing the phone against my ear.

I hear Coach's muttering, knowing he's irritated with me. I know I can easily be replaced, but after the weeks I've had, I don't think I can ignore her calls. At least, not any longer.

"Hey," I say sweetly, forcing a smile while I lean my forehead against my locker. "Long time no call. What's up?"

"Oh, I just wanted to send you good luck on the big day."

"Ask him why he's been ignoring your calls," I hear Dad shout.

I scowl at the sound of his voice, at the judgment I find there. Why is he acting so high and mighty? Just because he's there for her now doesn't mean he can act all self-important.

"Shush," I hear Mom say. "You can ask him when you call him. Sorry about that sweetie."

"It's fine Mom."

"We've just been worried and all. It's not like you to be so busy." I smile as I hear her chuckle. She sounds so warm and happy. It's just the thing I need on such a terrible day. "I was actually wondering if you'd met a girl."

I grimace and a sigh escapes my lips while an image of Rachel pops into my head.

"I reminded your father about when we met, how he would just turn off his phone and spend the whole day in bed with-"

I gag. "Ugh! Mom!"

She giggles on the other line and I smile. It's a good day, which doesn't happen often. Usually, she can barely stay on the phone for very long. It's great to hear her laugh and tease me again.

"Hunter, are you coming, or what?" I hear Coach shout down the hall.

"Coming!" I call back, tears prickling my eyes.

I don't want to go. Not when she sounds so good. I don't know when I will be able to get a chance like this again. "Mom," I say, my voice coming out as a croak. I close my eyes and force the tears down. "I have to go. Talk to you later?"

"Of course, sweetie. Have fun! I love you."

My bottom lip trembles and I clear my throat. "I love you, too."

I hang up and slide my phone back into my bag. Closing my locker door, a dark memory infiltrates itself

into my mind, whispering to me that I will probably never speak to her again. *That was your last time,* the voice whispers while I walk down the hall towards an angry looking coach.
You will never speak to her again.
As I enter the football field and find my place on the bench, my hands fist and I can't help myself from wondering if Jerry and Drew are having a party tonight.
***
Cheers surround me and my teammates high five each other, but all I can feel is dread and remorse as I type the words: *party tonight?*

My eyes remain glued to my phone, waiting for Drew's reply. He's seen the message, but I don't see the usual dots signaling his typing. I don't know how long I remain like that, staring down at my phone, waiting. The cheers lesson. The laughter subsides and soon it's just me standing in the locker room, probably looking absolutely stupid with my shirt off, staring at my phone.

No reply.

Dammit.

I throw my phone into my bag, hating myself for even bothering. Of course they wouldn't message me back after last time. I drag on my shirt, hissing as I feel another sharp stab in my shoulder. Grimacing, I throw off my pants and shin guards, shoving my garments with more force than need be into my bag. I can't message Millie. She's definitely had enough of me. My teammates would have asked me by now if I wanted to go party with them.

I should be partying with them.

We just won a big game. Why didn't they invite me out with them?

Probably because you've pushed everyone away.

I heave a sigh and stare at my phone lying at the top, willing it to vibrate. I know I should just go home. I should rest, maybe call my mom.

Maybe ask Lucas if I can borrow his car and go see her. It's not like I go to my classes anyway and I'm sure the bros and Rachel are sick of me. We could use the space. I could use the time with my mom.

My phone lights up and it vibrates. I lunge for it, sliding the screen up. My heart slams in my chest and a giddy rush makes my hands shake as I smile down at the message from Drew.

Bring money. Meet at Harper St. 22, it reads.

I type a quick response back while slamming my door shut. I nearly skip down the hallway. My body quivers and I grind my teeth as I anticipate the party, the drugs, the moment of escape I so need right now.

I throw the doors open and escape out into the chilled air. I look both ways, finding several people still in the lot, passing around a bottle of booze. Most of the lot is empty. Everyone must be in the bars or at a house party. I type in the address into my phone and make a note to stop off at an ATM along the way.

"Hey, Hunter!"

I frown and turn around. My frown deepens as I see Lucas, Seth, and Rachel striding towards me. Seth has gone all out and has his face painted in Aurora's school colors while Rachel is wearing Seth's university jacket. Lucas is wearing an Aurora university sweater underneath his long black coat.

All of them frown at me.

"Dude, we've been waiting forever," says Seth. "What took you so long?"

"I didn't know you were waiting."

"We always go party together after the big game," says Lucas.

Rachel smiles brightly up at me. "I was think we could go get some burgers."

"I have other plans," I say while slowly turning around.

"Alright, let's go," says Seth while charging forward.

I shake my head and roll my eyes. Typical Seth, always needing to lead the way when he has no clue where to go.

"No, that's okay. It's a small party," I say.

Seth slowly turns around and frowns at me. "Huh?"

I shrug. "You don't really know the people." I know I sound weird, but I really don't want them there with their judging, scrutinizing eyes. They wouldn't understand. "It probably won't be all that fun."

"No," says Lucas while grabbing my shoulder. "You're coming with us. I'm over this whole disappearing act."

I smack his hand away. "What is that supposed to mean?"

Lucas scoffs. "You really don't get it, do you?"

I cross my arms and look between the three. "I didn't ask for you to come."

"Hunter, we're your friends," says Seth while moving to stand next to Lucas. "Of course we're going to see your games."

"Even if you don't play," Lucas adds under his breath.

"Oh, fuck you!" I shout while whirling around.

"Fine!" I hear Lucas shout. "But don't call me next time when you find yourself in a bind. I'm tired of being your mother."

"Fine!" I shout, not bothering to look back. They all can go fuck themselves. I'm fine. I don't need them. I have Jerry and Drew. They have my back, more than those assholes anyway.

Who needs those assholes anyway?

16

RACHEL

I roll the pencil back and forth on the counter. It's a slow Friday evening and part of me is wishing I hadn't taken this shift, knowing I could be catching up on some TV or out with Lucas at a party.

However, ever since our spat with Hunter, I haven't quite wanted to be in the apartment. It isn't the same with Hunter always gone. I wrinkle my nose as I recall Hunter ignoring me when I made him breakfast. *And when he is there, he is quite the spoil sport.*

Lucas and Seth obviously feel the same. I lift my gaze and watch Seth sweep the floors, muttering something under his breath as he moves the dirt back and forth. He's been like that since Hunter left us outside the football stadium last weekend. It's been nearly a week since we've seen our Thor look-alike and I can tell Seth has been worrying about him. Although, he won't admit it to anyone.

I sigh and spin myself around in the chair. As I return to the computer screen, I notice its five minutes after seven. In less than one hour we can close the joint down and head home. Then what? Try to ignore Hunter?

"Hey," says Seth while perking his head up and leaning the broom against a shelf of running belts. "Let's go to The Coffee Shop after this. I don't feel like heading home."

I make a face and groan, remembering my last run in with Charlie and Lauren. Not only was my conversation with the girls completely messed up, but it also brought up memories of my big showdown with Josh in art class.

"Let's not."

Seth strides towards me, leaning against the counter while I focus my attentions on the computer screen. There's nothing really interesting to look at; just the running store's website and some photos I took of new gear coming out next month.

"Why not?" Seth asks.

I sigh and shake my head. "I don't want to talk about it."

"You'll feel better if you do."

I lift my gaze to his and roll my eyes as I see the smirk on his lips.

"Come on," he whines. "Let me take you out."

I chuckle and poke his nose. "You don't want to take me out on a date. You just don't want to go home."

"So?"

"I don't like to be used," I say while turning back to the website. I need to finish one more article on the bright pink compression socks we received last week.

"That's not what I heard," Seth whispers mischievously into my ear.

I lurch back in my chair, nearly falling out of it while Seth watches me, chuckling and helping me regain balance. "You are so bad."

"Have I changed your mind?"

I sigh and shake my head. "I don't know. I'm worried I'll run into Charlie and Lauren."

Seth frowns and wraps an arm around my shoulder. "Why are you worried about running into them? I thought you guys were close?"

I grimace, recalling Josh's stupid face and the words he told the girls. I still can't believe he did that. I don't understand why he would try to apologize to me one day and then ruin my life the next.

"Josh told the girls that I tried to take advantage of him."

"What?" Seth shouts.

"And when I confronted him in my drawing class, he accused me of stealing his friends."

I watch Seth roll up his sleeves. "That boy needs another punch in the face."

I chuckle and rest my hand on his. "That won't be necessary."

Seth shakes his head while tapping his chin. "Why don't you just tell the girls what happened? They will surely understand."

I sigh, feeling the need to cry again as I remember Lauren's scowl and Charlie's uncertainty. Maybe they'll believe me. Maybe they won't. I try to pull myself together and blink back the tears already beginning to form. I've already cried so much this semester. I feel raw, like someone has opened me up and I can never be whole again. "I told my teacher what happened. He told me to report it."

"That's what I've been telling you."

"I know." I purse my lips while I remember standing outside the police station yesterday morning. I almost went inside, but something held me back. I don't know why I can't just go inside and tell them what happened. Every time I think of that day, I remember how Josh grabbed me, forcing me down onto the floor, trying to take off his jeans.

A shiver ripples down my spine and I quickly stand and walk around the counter towards the stock room. My hands shake as the images continue to plague me and I lean against one of the high shelves, taking in deep, gulping breaths in order to calm myself.

"Rachel," I hear Seth, feel his hand on my shoulder.

I whirl around and smack his hand away.

Seth holds up his hands. "I'm sorry, Rachel." He takes a step back while keeping his hands up. "I won't touch you."

My shoulders slump and I feel terrible for pushing him away when he hasn't done anything wrong. "No, it's fine." I step towards him and wrap my hands around his waist, leaning my head against his shoulder. My eyes close, and I breathe him in. "I'm sorry for smacking you."

"It's fine, Rachel," he murmurs while nuzzling my nose. "I know you're going through a lot right now."

I nod and my hands tighten around him while his arms come over me, holding me close.

"I think your teacher is right though. You need to go. I can go with you if you need support."

My eyes open and I look up at him, catching his gaze filled with so much warmth. "Really?"

He smiles and strokes a stray lock away from my face. "Of course, Rachel. You know how much I care about you."

My hand comes around his neck and I pull him towards me, pressing my mouth against his. His tongue slides against my lips and I open myself to him, allowing him to deepen the kiss. My hands stroke his hair, tugging it slightly before caressing him once more. He moves us backwards until my back is resting against the shelving unit. I groan as I feel his hand come up to cup my breast and my legs part for him.

His hand slides away, and he grabs my leg, pulling it above his hip. I cling to him as my kisses become more desperate. I know we're at work. I know we shouldn't be doing this, but I want this. I want this more than anything right now; just a moment of bliss. A moment to forget all my problems and worries.

Seth grinds himself against me and I moan. I toss my head back, allowing him access to my neck. He kisses a path down to my collarbone, his teeth sinking into my flesh wonderfully before returning to sucking and licking. One hand cups my butt while the other slides up and palms my breast.

Something clangs in the distance, but I ignore it as I pull Seth's lips back to me. I bite his bottom lip and warmth pools in my stomach, tightening my insides as I hear a growl from him.

"Hello!" I hear someone call.

I stop, pulling away from Seth. Our eyes are glued to each other and I know I mirror the shock on his face as I hear the person ask, "Is anyone here?"

"Fuck," Seth murmurs while stepping away from me. "Just a moment!"

I giggle while we straighten ourselves. I don't know how I did it, but Seth's hair is standing up in tufts, as if glued their by hair gel. Seth turns to me and straightens my hair all while trying to tuck his shirt back into his pants with one hand.

"Go," I whisper while pushing him towards the stockroom door. "I can fix myself." My gaze falls to the tent in his pants and I giggle while covering my mouth with a hand. "Or maybe I should go?"

"No, I got this," says Seth while making a face and sliding his hands into his pants. I nearly burst out laughing as his face scrunches into a mixture of discomfort and irritation.

"I'm waiting!" The customer calls once more, a hint of irritation in their tone.

"Coming! Coming!"

I watch Seth leave while running my fingers through my tangled hair, feeling joy brim inside me. *At least I have Seth on my side,* I tell myself. I lean against the shelving unit once more and stroke my chin thoughtfully, wondering when I should go to the police station.

I should go as soon as possible, I decide while holding my head high and striding out of my hiding place in the stockroom.

***

The next day I lay in bed, trying to get some of my work done, but I can't focus. Seth and I decided to go to the police station on Monday. I stare down at the notes I've written over and over in my notebook detailing what happened between me and Josh that night. I scrunch up my nose as I try to block the memories from trickling back inside my protective walls. I need to get at least something done.

I roll over in my bed and stare up at the ceiling, deciding counting the cracks is a much better way to pass the time rather than drawing in my sketchbook. It's not like I have a giant project due and an internship to apply for. I groan, pressing my palms against my face and wanting to scream. This semester is turning out to be a real pain. I just wish I could talk to Lauren or Charlie about it.

I should have told them what happened with Josh. I probably wouldn't be in this mess if I had just been honest in the first place and done the right thing by going to the police.

Well, here I am.

I sigh and roll over onto my stomach, reaching for my cellphone lying on the pillow and swiping through my messages. I haven't talked to the girls since I saw them at the cafe, and neither of them have bothered reaching out to me.

Is this really the end?

They're just going to believe Josh's side and not listen to mine?

I scowl at my phone and bring up the chat group. *Over my dead body*, I think while typing a message to the girls: *Hey girls. Can we please talk? I want to explain to you what happened.*

I wait for a reply. I see Lauren has read the message, but isn't responding. Charlie still hasn't seen it. Maybe she's ignoring my messages? Maybe she's blocked me. My head falls onto the mattress and I groan against it while kicking my feet, wishing there is some way to fix this whole mess. I love hanging out with Seth and Lucas, but sometimes I need to be around other girls and talk about girly things. And art.

Sure, Seth likes photography, but it's not like I can debate with him technique or art theory. All that goes way over his head. And Lucas likes poetry and writing, which is an art form itself, but sometimes I just want to gossip and discuss fashion with Charlie and Lauren.

I pout at my phone, tempted to throw it at the pillow when I see Charlie has read my message, but isn't responding. Great. My only girlfriends and now they want nothing to do with me.

I straighten on the bed and rest my phone next to me, glancing at it for a moment before grabbing my sketchbook. *Well, at least I tried,* I think while sniffing and wiping at my eyes. Maybe next time I see them I should try warning them about Josh, just to be on the safe side. I would hate it if anything terrible happened to them.

I hear a ding and jump up, snatching my find and holding it close to my face. My eyes widen when I see that Charlie has responded: *We're busy finishing our art projects. We don't really have time to talk.*

My brow furrows and I purse my lips while typing back a quick message: *I understand, but it doesn't have to be long. It'll take five minutes. Max.*

I press send and wait for her to respond. Lauren is reading all the messages, yet not saying a word. I see the three dots pop up on the screen, displaying Charlie's writing, but it stops. I wait for it to pop up again, but everything remains silent on their end. Any hope I felt before goes crashing down as I continue waiting for them to respond.

They're probably discussing amongst themselves what they should say. Lauren is probably speaking through Charlie. I bite my lip, wondering if Josh is actually with them. All three of them are probably at the cafe working on their art projects.

My phone dings and I read the message: *We're at the art school. Room 302. Five minutes.*

I don't bother to reply. I jump up from my bed and shove on my boots. Grabbing my purse, I shove my cellphone inside before grabbing my keys and throwing open my door. I glance over my shoulder, wondering briefly if I have everything I need before I slam into something cold and hard.

I quickly turn, cringing when I feel my neck pop from the sudden motion. I still when I see Hunter standing in front of me, wearing sweats with his hair tied loosely into a ponytail. His face looks sickly; pale as if he has the flu. Dark shadows mar his eyes and his cheeks look gaunt. It appears like he has barely eaten anything in the last few days. I sniff and quickly cover my nose at the smell.

"Hey, Hunter," I say while stepping around him. "Do you need anything?"

His hand had been raised, looking like he was about to knock. I watch it slowly lower and his gaze dips to the floor while giving me a short shake of his head. My hands fist at my sides, knowing that something is up. He wouldn't be standing outside my door for nothing.

"Are you sure?" I ask. Inside I'm waiting for him to get testy or storm away and slam himself inside his room, but he remains glued to the ground.

"I'm sure," he murmurs, his voice sounding more like a croak.

My shoulders slump and I nearly slide my purse off and approach him. I hate seeing him like this. Usually, he's happy and the joy of the party, yet these days he seems more like the shadowed, hollowed version of himself.

I stop myself from taking off my boots and going to him. He can't do this to me. He can't be mean to me, yelling and shouting and refusing to tell me what's wrong and then expect me to drop everything to be there for him. I have my own shit, too. I shove my purse further up my shoulder, straightening myself as I turn on my heel and head towards my coat, lying in a heap on the couch.

"Alright, well let me know if you need anything. I'll be out for about thirty minutes."

"I won't be here," I hear him murmur.

I shake my head. My stomach churns and the hairs on the back of my neck stand up. Something doesn't feel right. I still reach for the door, still walk outside and close it behind me. With deft fingers, I button my coat and shiver as the wind whips pass.

I try to ignore my gut, pulling me back to Hunter; try to ignore that feeling telling me this is the last time I'm ever going to see him. *But what can I do?* I ask myself while stepping down the staircase, holding onto the banister so I don't slip and fall on my butt. I've been trying so hard to think of him, talk to him, but he keeps pushing me away.

I have to let go at some point. He's a grown man. He can make his own decisions.

I bite my bottom lip, still not enjoying the twisting of my stomach as I stride down the sidewalk towards campus. I don't know if it's Hunter, or the talk I'm about to have with the girls that's making me feel like I need to throw up.

Probably both.

Well, I can only solve one problem at a time. Since the girls are willing to hear me out, I will start with that and slowly make my way back to Hunter. I'll knock on his door tomorrow, see if he's home, maybe talk to him about what's been going on.

Maybe.

My heart is pounding in my chest when I finally see the art school coming into view. I try to think of the notes I wrote in my book, which was for the cops. I guess I can use the same notes to help me tell the girls what happened.

I reach into my purse and stop walking, finding only my wallet, keys, and phone inside.

I close my eyes and tilt my head up to the sky. *Great. Wonderful. I left my notebook at home on the bed, now didn't I?* I inhale a deep breath and count to ten before expelling it from my lungs. I don't feel any better so I do it again. I do it until my toes are numb and continue breathing in deeply as I enter the school.

I don't feel any better. My heart is still slamming in my chest. My whole body won't stop shaking and I don't think it's just from the winter air. I trudge up the stairs, which are currently covered in melting snow. I clamp my hand around the banister as I slip, nearly falling several times. I can't seem to focus on walking. I'm too nervous.

What if Josh is there?
What if they call me a liar?

I stop when I reach the third floor. I hear laughter coming from one of the rooms. It sounds like Charlie, but I'm not a hundred percent positive. It could be anyone.

What if they already left?

I lift my head and jut out my chin before taking in another breath. I force myself to step towards room 302. The door is already open and I poke my head inside, looking around and finding Charlie and Lauren sitting at one of the large tables. I'm so thankful Josh isn't anywhere in the vicinity, but I wonder if he's coming later or maybe he's already left.

Their bags and coats are strewn all over the other tables. Sketchbooks rest in front of them, but it seems they are looking at their cellphones while listening to some indie band playing in the background.

Some studying, I think while stepping inside.

Lauren lifts her head and her smile falls into a deep scowl. Charlie looks up, straightening in her chair as I approach them. She tucks her phone into her sweater pocket and rests her elbows on the table. She leans towards me while I slowly lower myself in a seat in front of them, feeling like I have just entered into a terrible job interview rather than a meeting with my friends.

"Hi," I say awkwardly while looking between the two.

Lauren scoffs and looks away while Charlie says, "You wanted to talk?"

"Yes," I say while my gaze slips to Lauren. She looks so angry with me. She's supposed to be my friend. "I want to tell you my side of the story."

Lauren rolls her eyes and I lean back in my seat, crossing my arms in front of my chest while I watch her. I don't understand why she's being like this. Sure. Josh told her some terrible things about me, but shouldn't she want to hear my side of the story? Whatever happened to innocent until proven guilty?

"Alright, well your five minutes have started," says Charlie while mirroring me.

I nod. "So, the both of you know that after I had a spat with Seth, Josh offered me a couch at his place."

Charlie nods while Lauren turns her narrowed gaze on me.

"Well, one night we decided to watch a movie together," I chuckle nervously while pushing my hair away from my face. "It was innocent, you know. And I thought, sure why not?" I grind my teeth as tears prickle my eyes. It's still so hard for me to talk about; thinking about how innocent I had been at the time. "Josh wanted me to drink. I can't remember what it was, but I told him no. He kept on insisting." I inhale deeply. My voice is getting shaky and slightly shrill. I take another breath, trying to calm my pounding heart.

Charlie looks worried. Her arms are no longer crossed. Her mouth is set in a firm line that makes her look older than her age. Lauren doesn't seem like she cares whatsoever. She's staring at me as if I'm a cockroach she needs to squash.

I swallow and urge myself to continue with my story. This is good practice for when I tell the cops on Monday. "So I kept saying no. As the movie went on, Josh started kissing me."

Charlie's eyes widen while Lauren scowls at me.

"I liked Josh at the beginning, but after my fight with Seth and getting kicked out of my apartment, I wasn't in the mood to start anything up. I told Josh no, but he kept pressing me." I grind my teeth as I remember standing up, remember him grabbing me and pushing me down on the floor. I whimper and shake my head. I need to get this out. I have to.

"So," I say with a shuddering breath, "I tried to leave, but Josh wouldn't let me. He grabbed me. I fell. He tried to climb on top of me. I remember- I remember him undoing his belt and-"

"Stop," says Charlie while placing a hand on mine. I look up and find her glimmer eyes watching mine. She sniffs and I see she's trying to keep herself from crying. "You don't need to continue. I believe you."

"What?" Lauren shouts while shoving back her chair and standing. She looks between us, scowling with her mouth ajar, as if she wants to shout or scream. "You must be kidding me. You believe her over Josh?" She shoves a finger into Charlie's face. "You know she's just trying to turn the tables."

Charlie makes a face, looking like she's torn between yelling herself and trying to remain calm. "Yes, I remember what Josh said, but honestly he didn't seem as choked up about it." Charlie nods to me. "She's trying desperately not to cry and here you are acting like a bitch. Do you really think she's a liar?"

Lauren nods. "Yes. She's a liar. Josh would never force himself on anyone. Josh is a good guy."

"Please," says Charlie while rolling her eyes. "Good guys can become bad guys. Trust me."

"You're really going to take her side?" Lauren shouts while turning her finger on me. "Even when she whores herself out to those assholes."

I gasp, my mouth hanging open. "I don't whore myself out. They're my boyfriends."

"And they don't force themselves on her," Charlie adds. "You know what, you're not thinking straight." Charlie shakes her head while running her fingers through her hair. "You're allowing your crush on Josh blind you to the truth. One of these days, you're going to get hurt."

Lauren scoffs and stalks towards the table with their things, grabbing her coat and bag. "I don't need this," she says while briskly walking towards the door. "I'm out of here." She slams the door shut.

Charlie sighs. "I'm so sorry," she says while grabbing my hand and giving it a gentle squeeze. She inhales deeply and I watch her eyelashes flutter while trying to keep herself from crying. "I knew something was up when Josh told me the story. Something about it didn't feel right."

"It's ok," I say while offering a gentle smile. "I know the two of you have been friends with Josh longer than me."

Charlie nods vigorously. "It still doesn't excuse me for the way I treated you." She inhales a shuddering breath. "Why didn't you tell us after it happened? We could have supported you. I could have been there for you."

I shake my head. "I don't know. I guess deep down I felt ashamed, and I felt like if I talked about it, it would become real."

"Have you told the police?"

I stay silent, but my face says everything.

"Oh, Rachel. You have to tell the police."

"I will," I say quickly. "On Monday, Seth and I are heading down to the police station."

She nods. "Do you need me to go with you?"

I pat her shoulder. "It's okay. Seth will be with me."

Charlie releases a shuddering sigh. "Alright. That's good. You know you can tell me anything right? I have your back."

My bottom lip trembles and I nod vigorously while wiping at my eyes. "I know," I say before breaking into a fit of laughter mixed with tears.

17

SETH

My hand tightens on Rachel's as we walk down the sidewalk. The police station comes into focus and I feel Rachel still at my side. Her steps halt and I wait for her to change her mind and turn around. She's been oddly quiet this whole morning, as if she's going through the motions. I turn to her, watching her stare at the station as if she's walking into a math test. Her brows are pinched together, and she keeps running her teeth over her bottom lip.

"Hey," I say while wrapping an arm around her shoulders and drawing her close to me. "It's going to be ok. I'll be there."

Rachel nods. "I know."

"You're doing the right thing," I say while taking a step forward, happy when she follows my lead.

Her arm slides against my back and she clutches at my waist as we close the distance between us and the station. "You won't leave?"

"If you want, I can come with you into the room," I say before pressing a kiss against her temple.

She nuzzles into me and I breathe in the fresh coconut smell of her hair. "I wrote down notes."

I chuckle. "So you told me."

"It's just so I don't forget anything."

There's a buzz and I watch Rachel slip her hand into her coat pocket, bringing out her phone. She smiles as a message from Charlie pops up.

"What's that?" I ask while nodding towards the phone.

"A cellphone, dumb-dumb."

I roll my eyes. "No. Your message. I thought you weren't speaking to the girls anymore."

Rachel sighs while sliding her phone back into her pocket. "I talked with them on Saturday."

I raise an eyebrow. "And now everything is fine?"

Rachel makes a face. "Not quite. Charlie believes me." She chuckles and pushes her hair out of her face. "She actually just messaged me: you can do it!" I watch her shake her head. There's a smile on her face, yet it doesn't reach her eyes. She looks like the saddest smiling girl I have ever seen. "Lauren on the other hand thinks I'm a liar. And a whore."

I stop in my tracks and turn Rachel around in my arms. "You are definitely not a whore."

Rachel looks away from me, her gaze focused on the ice covered sidewalk as if it's Picasso's finest work and not a freaking, boring slab of cement. "I don't know. What if they ask me why I was over in the first place? Then I have to tell them I got into a spat with you guys and then they might ask what my relationship is with you." She shrugs. "Maybe they will think I was asking for it."

"Rachel." I frown when she doesn't look at me and shake her shoulders slightly. Her tear stained gaze meets mine and I stroke the side of her face. "You are not a whore. Consent is consent and that bastard didn't have it. If they do ask, just say you got into an argument with me. You don't need to involve Lucas and Hunter. Hell, they wanted you to stay."

She nods, but I don't think she feels any better.

"Rachel, seriously, just because you are in a relationship with the three of us doesn't make you any lesser than a person. You told that asshole no, and he grabbed you and tried to take advantage of you. Everyone needs to know that."

Rachel nods again and straightens. "Yes, you're right," she says while lifting her head up. I watch her take a deep breath and stride towards the police station. "Let's just get this done and over with. The sooner I file the report the sooner I can put this whole mess behind me."

I follow after her. Lifting up my watch I notice the time. Track practice is soon, but I decide to shrug it off. Being there for Rachel is more important, and it's not like missing one practice is going to affect my game all that much. I'll just tell coach I got the stomach bug. I'm sure he'll understand.

We stride into the station. Looking around. I have no clue where to go or what to do. There seems to be a line of people waiting to be called to a front desk with others sitting in chairs lined against the frosted window. I follow Rachel towards the line, seeing that is probably the best place to be.

"It's getting late," says Rachel while looking at the time on her phone. "I thought this was going to be a quick in and out operation."

I smirk, thinking of something else that could be a quick in and out and receive a dark look from Rachel. She's getting better at reading minds… or me.

"You should probably get going."

"Don't worry about it."

Rachel fidgets as someone in the front is called to a desk. "I'm supposed to be at work in an hour and a half. I hope this won't take that long."

I grab Rachel's hands and give them a gentle squeeze. "You're worrying too much. It'll be fine and work will survive without you."

Rachel raises an eyebrow as if she doesn't believe me.

"Alright," I say while letting go of her hands. "If it takes longer I'll swing by and work until you're able to come."

Rachel smiles and shakes her head. "You're too good to me."

"I know," I murmur while counting the people standing ahead of us.

Five. Five people to wait through and then who knows about the others in the back and how long they'll take. An hour might not be enough. I fidget while looking around, trying to find something interesting about this place. I notice the no cellphone sign and scowl. How am I supposed to find something to do if I can't at least whip out my phone and play some games? Maybe I should have brought a book or something.

I chuckle to myself.

Like I ever read.

Another person is called to the front and I watch him walk impossibly slowly towards the desk. I don't know why, but it annoys the crap out of me. Another person is called and I tilt my head back, hoping the two people at the desks are quick.

My phone buzzes in my pocket and I quickly grab it, my brow furrowing when I see that it's Hunter's mom calling. That's strange. She might have called the wrong number. Someone clears their throat and I lift my head, finding a woman dressed in uniform scowling at me. She nods at my phone and then glances at the no cellphone sign.

I fight the need to roll my eyes and quickly shove it back into my pocket while forcing a smile.

Another person is called to the front. We're nearly there. I look at the time and see it's been thirty minutes. Well, I guess this isn't so bad, I think while glancing at Rachel, who keeps picking at her nails. I grab her hand and she looks up at me.

"It'll be fine," I reassure her.

My cell buzzes again and I groan, grabbing my phone, wondering if it is coach calling to complain that I'm late for practice. My eyes widen when I see it is Hunter's mom again.

"Excuse me, sir," says the uniformed lady. "There's no cellphones allowed."

"Yeah, I'm sorry." I hang up and shove it back in my pocket, but as soon as it's there it begins vibrating again.

Rachel watches me, her eyes perplexed and staring at my pocket. "Who is it?" She whispers.

"Hunter's mom," I say while turning away from the woman scowling at me. I'm not answering. Sure, I maybe should have turned it off, but she can't get me in trouble if it's not in my hand. Right?

"Hunter's mom?" Rachel repeats with widened eyes. "Maybe you should answer it. It could be important."

"But what about you? I'm supposed to be here to support you."

Rachel shakes her head. "It's fine. I'm nearly to the front."

My phone continues to vibrate as I stare down at Rachel, wondering if I should really leave her alone. It took me so long to convince her to finally file a police report. I don't want her to end up changing her mind and turning around.

"Don't worry," Rachel insists, once again reading my mind. "You have nothing to worry about. I'm going through with this."

I nod and slowly back away, nearly bumping into the uniformed woman, who seems to be watching me like a hawk.

"Excuse me," I say as sweetly as possible to her, earning an even darker glare before turning around and striding out of the station.

As soon as I'm outside I pick up the phone, once again seeing Hunter's Mom flashing on my phone's screen. "Hello?" I say as soon as I press the answer key. My stomach twists, knowing whatever she has to say, it can't be good.

Why isn't she calling Hunter? I wonder while pacing back and forth on the side walk.

"Hi," says a masculine voice. "Is this Hunter's friend, Seth?"

"Yeah," I say hesitantly. This isn't Hunter's mom. Unless his mom has come down with a very bad cold. "Who is this?"

"I'm his dad. Do you know where he is? I've been trying to call him since yesterday. He hasn't been picking up any of my calls. At first I thought he didn't want to speak with me, but he hasn't even been picking up on this number. Have you seen him around? I'm worried."

I shake my head. "No, I'm afraid I haven't." I make a face, wishing I could tell his dad how weird Hunter has been, but if he has gone missing I don't want to make his dad even more worried than he already is.

"Shit," I hear his dad mutter followed by sniffing. "I'm sorry," his dad says shakily. I hear a sob on the other line and I feel my heart pound in my throat as my stomach twists. "She died Saturday night and I need to tell Hunter," he sobs. "But I can't find him anywhere."

My stomach stops twisting and I feel a sense of numbness come over me. "Hunter's mom," I say slowly, "is dead?"

"She died in her sleep." I hear him sniff followed by the sound of blowing his nose. "I've been calling and calling, but he's not answering."

"Don't worry," I say while turning back to the police station. "We'll find him. We'll have him give you a call as soon as possible."

"You're so kind. Thank you."

I turn off my phone and throw open the door. Looking around, I don't find Rachel sitting at one of the chairs. They must have taken her to the back after she spoke with the front desk. Shit, I can't leave now. I'll have to wait until she comes out from one of those rooms.

I force myself into a chair, wishing I had ample space to pace, but the uniformed lady is staring at me, as if waiting to pounce the moment I take out my phone. Seriously, what is her deal? I shake my head, telling myself she's not worth the time to fret over. My leg bobs up and down and I can stop fidgeting with my fingers.

Hunter's mom died. I can't believe she's gone. I only met the lady a hand full of times, but she was sweet and nice and made really delicious cookies. This is going to kill Hunter, when and if we find him. I can't believe he's not picking up his phone, but the dude has been acting weird for the past month.

How am I going to tell him that his mom is gone?

"Seth?"

I look up, finding Rachel standing in front of me with a wide smile.

"Huh?" I blink. I am so out of it. I didn't even hear her approach.

"What do you mean 'huh'?" She says teasingly while grabbing my hand and pulling me up. "It's done. They took me to the back room immediately, and I filed the report."

I nod. "Great." I cringe, hearing the lack of joy in my voice. This is a big milestone for Rachel. I could at least act interested. I should be excited for her, yet I can't stop thinking about where Hunter is.

What if something terrible happened to him?

"What's going on?" Rachel asks while leading me out the door. Her frown deepens when we get outside and she turns towards me, crossing her arms as the wind whips her curly golden hair around us. "I thought you would be more excited for me."

I sigh and run my hands through my hair. I should just tell her I'm not feeling well and walk her to the store. She doesn't need to be involved in this. Hunter has been an ass to her since the ski trip. I don't need her worrying about him and she has work to get to.

But I don't want to hold information from her. Especially when she cares for the asshole.

"Hunter's mom passed away on Saturday."

Rachel gasps, her hand covering her mouth while her eyes glimmer with unshed tears. "Oh no," she breathes. "How's Hunter taking it?"

"That's just the thing," I say while rubbing the back of my head. "That was Hunter's dad. They can't find him. He hasn't been answering his phone."

Rachel's brows furrow. "What?" She asks. "But I saw him on Saturday before I met with Lauren and Charlie."

"Was that Saturday night?" I ask, feeling hopeful even though he could have ended up anywhere between Saturday and today.

She shakes her head and my hope deflates. "No, during the day."

I sigh and grab my phone, swiping through my contacts to call Lucas. I'm going to need some backup for this.

"Do you think something happened to him?" Rachel asks, her voice shaky.

I grimace while holding the phone to my ear, waiting for Lucas to answer. Hopefully he's not in class yet. "That's what I'm worried about."

Rachel stalks away from me, nearly running down the ice covered sidewalk.

"Where do you think you're going?" I shout while chasing after her.

"Hello," I hear Lucas say on the phone.

"I'm going to find that jerk face," says Rachel as she continues stalking away from me.

"No," I say while grabbing her hand and whirling her around. "You should get to work."

"What's going on?" Lucas asks.

I groan as Rachel's gaze on me darkens.

"I need to find him," she says. "Let me help you. I won't be able to focus at work anyway."

"Seth!" Lucas shouts. "Why are you calling me? Why is Rachel talking about finding someone?"

I pinch the bridge of my nose. "Hunter is missing. His dad just called. Is there any way you can help us look for him?"

"Yeah, of course," I hear Lucas say. "I'll call you if I find him."

"Perfect." I hang up and turn my attentions back to Rachel. "Alright, you can help. But don't expect anything good." I grimace while following Rachel, knowing that finding Hunter will be the easy part.

I have no clue what to do with what comes after.

18

HUNTER

My eyes open and I groan as light sprouts dots in my eyes. I roll over, wrinkling my nose when I find someone lying, clothed at my side. Lifting my body up, I swallow bile while looking around, finding several people sleeping around me. Mostly men, but there are a few women curling up with their pillows. I have no clue what time it is, but given the bright light it must be around noon or a little after.

I have no clue what happened.

I don't even know where I am.

Memories come back to me like a blur and I recall stumbling from place to place, some laughter, lots of drinking, taking drugs in a bathroom. I think I passed out somewhere along the way, only to reawaken drunkenly and continue on to the next party. Looking around at the people lying around me, I realize I have never met them before. They are probably some of Jerry and Drew's friends.

I cringe when the man next to me scratches at his arms. The black sleeve of his sweater rises and I see track marks all over his arms. I grab the arm of the sofa next to me and push myself up, wobbling on my feet for a moment while I try to control the dizziness in my air. I stare down at my barefoot feet, wondering where my shoes are. Feeling around in my jean pockets, I frown. My heart slams in my chest as panic begins to rise as I realize I don't have my wallet on me. Nor do I have my keys or cell phone. I shiver and rub my hands up and down my arms, nearly vomiting when I notice the green bile staining the front of my white t-shirt.

My stomach twists as I walk through the room, trying to ignore the soles of my feet sticking to the disgusting floor. I try not to look down. A faint memory on last semester and semesters before of living in a dump before Rachel came along comes drifting back, making me recall her sweet green eyes and the way she touched me gently.

I shake those thoughts away. I need to focus on finding my things. Or maybe, just figuring out where I am right now. I push the curtains to the side and groan as light suffocates me. I squint my eyes and try to look at the houses, not recognizing anything. There's not even a street sign, but I see some students walking on the sidewalk with their backpacks so I can't be that far away.

Turning away, I pad further through the house, walking down a hall into a kitchen where I find some people sitting in chairs with empty whiskey bottles surrounding them. I grab one, near gone but still several swigs left, and take a sip. It slides down my throat, burning through me, but settles the panic and settles my churning stomach.

All I want to do is find my shit and get out of this dump.

I just need to retrace my steps.

I take another swig of whiskey and try to think, which only makes my head pound harder. My hands tremble as I continue drinking. I remember holding my phone, frowning when I saw my dad's number lighting up on the screen. I cringe as I recall tossing it in the snow while walking alongside Jerry and Drew. We had been going to another party and Drew had laughed when I threw it away.

Fuck.

I don't think I can afford another phone.

But that doesn't explain what happened to my keys and wallet. I stride out of the kitchen, bottle still in hand.

Maybe I put them in my coat. If I find my coat, I'll probably find the rest of my things. There's no way I can walk out in the snow without any shoes on.

 I stop at the bathroom, taking a moment to relieve myself. I press my hand on the wall to steady myself. My head is still swimming and I don't know if it's from lack of sleep or from the whiskey. My whole body won't stop trembling. I feel so weak, as if at any moment I will pass out. I widen my eyes, trying to keep them open. I should at least make an attempt to go home today.

 I have no clue what day it is. The students walking outside the house is the only hint I have. So I assume it's either Monday or Tuesday. Hopefully not any later.

 God, coach is really going to kill me for missing so much practice.

 I chuckle and push my greasy hair away, knowing deep in my heart that at this rate I'm probably off the team. I'll lose my scholarship, and then what? Become a dead beat living off my parents? I don't know why, but I find the whole thing hilarious. Big star quarterback Hunter, falling from grace.

 I stop laughing when I turn and see my reflection on the mirror. I want to look away, but my eyes remain glued to the image staring me back. I don't recognize the man in front of me. The blonde locks framing my face hang limply and look brown at the roots from the grease coating my scalp. My right eye is blackened, and I have no clue what from. Maybe I got into a fight last night? My cheekbones stick out and my arms look scrawny at my side.

 I don't look like me anymore. I have no clue what happened to 'Hunter'. I feel like I'm an alien residing in someone else's body. Jerking away from the mirror I step out in the hall. My hands clench and unclench while I try to regain my composure, but my heart is pounding again and images from the following night keep flooding back in.

Jerry grabbing me by the scruff of my hair, jerking me towards him and shouting something I don't understand in my face.

Drew pacing around my body, holding out a hand. "Where's my money?" I remembered him asking.

I recalled giggling and Jerry kicked me in the gut.

A girl screaming at me in the bathroom. "What the fuck?" I remembered her smacking my shoulder and not caring. "You took it all and saved none for me!"

A shudder ripples down my spine and I don't care if I'm barely wearing anything, I walk as fast as possible towards the door, throwing it open and walking outside. I don't stop; even when the ice bites into the soles of my feet, I keep going, knowing that I can't step.

I need to go home.

I need to call my mom. Whatever it is that I'm doing, it has to stop. Now.

The wind gusts pass and I rub my hands up and down my arms, trying to ignore the burning in my feet as I continue walking down the sidewalk. There are hardly anyone on the streets, but the few I pass stare at me as if I have sprouted spikes and a tail. I ignore them while I stop at a stop sign and look both ways, wondering where the hell is home. I think I see the economic school in the distance so I should be about fifteen minutes away from home. Maybe. Although I have no clue if I can last fifteen minutes in the cold. My feet are already going numb.

"Where the fuck do you think you're going?"

I whirl around, my eyes widening as I see Jerry storm down the porch with a bat in hand. He twirls it around as he stalks towards me. I hold up my hands, not quite understand why he is scowling at me.

"What's going on Jerry?" I ask, cringing at the raspiness of my voice and how sore my throat feels.

"You know exactly what the fuck is going on!" Jerry shouts.

I shake my head. My feet give out and I feel myself falling. I groan as my knees crack against the ice on the pavement. "I'm sorry," I say, trying to ignore the desperation in my voice and the tears prickling my eyes. "I have no clue what's going on. Can you please just tell me where I am?"

"Where's our money, Hunter?" Jerry asks, stopping in front of me with the bat lying on his shoulders, ready to strike.

"I lost my wallet. I don't know where it is, but I can get you money. Anything you want."

Jerry smirks. "Lost your wallet, you say?" He spits on the ground in front of me. "That's what you said yesterday."

I nod vigorously before wiping the tears from my eyes. I can't believe I'm about to burst into tears in front of this guy. I don't cry. Hunter is strong. He's a man. He doesn't cry like a baby in front of others.

"You've been with us the whole time. You're fucking wallet is on the couch. You don't have shit, Hunter. You know you don't have shit."

"Please, let me call my dad."

"I'm tired of your excuses."

I have no clue what is going on. I can hardly remember what happened last week let alone this past weekend. Surely, I have something left in the bank to give him. I know I have something.

"Just give me until tomorrow," I say while slowly standing.

Jerry raises the bat and I look away, feeling pain explode through my bad shoulder. I bit back a scream and a low groan escapes my lips as I try to keep my mouth close. My hands grip at the ice. My flesh becomes numb and I lift my gaze, watching with wide eyes as Jerry slams the bat against my jaw. I fall onto the ground, spitting blood onto the snow. I try to stand.

"Stay down there you fucking piece of shit!" Jerry shouts while kicking me. "You owe us at least a grand if not more. You're paying up today. Whether you like it or not. You understand me?"

I keep my mouth close, knowing the moment I open it I would cry and beg. I nod instead while pushing myself up, ignoring the pain making my body shake.

"I didn't hear you, asshole."

I feel the bat smack against my back and my mouth opens, releasing a shout. I groan as my body hits the ground, and I lay my head in the snow, not bothering to get up as I hear Jerry step over me. He crouches in front of me, grabbing my hair and lifting me to meet his gaze. "Some football hero," he says while chuckling. He shoves me away and I remain on the ground, waiting and wondering what he will do next to me.

"You better-"

"He better what?" I hear a familiar voice.

I try to turn around and see who it is, but I'm in too much pain. I hear footsteps towards me while I watch Jerry smile easily at the person coming up behind me.

"This has nothing to do with you," Jerry says casually.

"This has everything to do with me. That's my roommate you're beating on."

Jerry sneers. "Well, your roommate owes us money."

"How much?"

My eyes close. Lucas. I inwardly groan. It's Lucas who has come to my rescue. A part of me feels relieved while the other part wants me to tell him to fuck off; I can handle my own problems.

I don't think you can, a dark voice whispers in the back of my head. One I haven't heard in a very long while.

"A grand," says Jerry while stepping over me.

I push myself up, using the stop sign to pull my body up. I lean against it while I watch Lucas pull out his check book and pen. Jerry's smile widens while he leers over Lucas's shoulder and a shiver ripples down my spine as Jerry's gaze lifts to mine.

"Make that two," Jerry says quickly before Lucas can put pen to paper.

Lucas scowls and Jerry shrugs, "for my troubles."

Lucas purses his lips, but he nods and writes on the check before tearing it out of the book and handing it to Jerry. "I don't want to see your face again," says Lucas.

Jerry chuckles. "Fair enough." He turns towards me and my grip on the stop sign pole tightens. "Until next time Hunter."

The hairs on the back of my neck rise and I watch Jerry turn on his heel back to the house, twirling his bat. Lucas grabs my arm and drags me towards his black SUV parked on the other side of the street.

"We have been looking everywhere for you," Lucas says between his teeth, his grip bruising on my arm. "Do you know how worried we've been? Not like you care."

I shove my arm out of his grasp and wobble on the ice beneath me, nearly sliding and falling on my ass. Lucas whirls around, his scowl set on me and I swear steam leaves his ears. I watch him, waiting for him to yell at me or punch me, but instead he turns around and stalks the rest of the way towards his car.

"Get in," he calls while slamming the door shut.

I trudge after him, knowing I can't walk home in the state I'm in. I slide into the front seat and lean back in the chair, closing my eyes and allowing the silence to settle over me.

"I do care," I whisper as the car starts.

"Well, you could act like it." Lucas groans and I crack open one eye, watching him wave a hand in front of his face while grimacing. "Dude, you need to take a shower." He glances over at me, his frown deepening. "Or maybe we should take you to a hospital. You really look like shit."

My stomach twists as I remember the last time I was in a hospital. An image of my mom surfaces and I realize it's been too long since I've heard her voice. I should call her as soon as I get home. Maybe I can borrow Lucas or Seth's phone.

"Hunter?" Lucas asks, his scowl turning into worry as he keeps glancing over at me as he drives us home. "Are you alright?"

"I'm fine," I murmur, turning my gaze out the window. "No hospital. I don't think anything's broken."

"What exactly did I just pay for back there? What mess have you gotten yourself in?"

My eyes slowly close. "Nothing. It's nothing."

I hear something slam, knowing its Lucas's hand smacking the steering wheel. My father often made the sound when he was pissed with me about my grades. "It's not fucking nothing, Hunter. God dammit. We've been so worried about you. At least promise me you're not going to pull this bullshit again."

I don't answer him, because I know I can't make that promise.

I hear his phone buzz and Lucas's exasperated sigh. "That must be Seth." I hear him fumble for the phone and my head lulls to the side, pressing up against the window and enjoying the coolness against my forehead.

"Hey," Lucas answers. "Yeah, I found him. Tony called me about thirty minutes ago. Told me he saw the asshole wondering outside barefoot. We're heading home now. Yep. See you soon."

I feel the car swerve to the left and begin to slow. Lucas puts it into park and I hear him open and close the door. My eyes open and I nearly jump out of the seat as

I'm met by Lucas's dark scowl. He throws open the door and offers a hand to me. I smack it away. I don't need his help. I don't need anyone's help. I'm fine.

Sure you are, comes that dark whisper again, taunting me. I grind my teeth, ignoring the piercing pain in my feet as they touch the snow. Shivering, I slowly wobble towards the staircase, feeling Lucas's glare boring a hole into my head. I grab the railing and pull myself up the stairs, taking them one at a time.

I reach for the door, but before I can grab the handle, it's thrown open and I see Seth glaring at me while Rachel hovers behind him.

"Where have you been?" Seth shouts, barely offering me space to get inside.

I shove pass him, nearly tripping over the shoes laying just within the doorway. Rachel steps back, her hands covering her mouth as I walk through the kitchen towards the bathroom.

I stop when I feel a hand on my arm. "Are you alright?" Rachel asks while I turn around. "You look-"

"Terrible?" I finish with a cruel smirk.

Rachel releases me and I continue on to the shower, cursing myself for being such an asshole to her. Not just to her. To everyone. They don't deserve this. I turn on the shower and strip myself of my clothes, making a note in the back of my head to throw away my t-shirt. I hear talking just outside the door, but I decide to ignore it as I step inside, groaning when the hot water meets my skin. It feels absolutely heavenly.

I lean my forehead against the wall and close my eyes while feeling the water pelt against my beaten body. My head feels like it's swimming. My feet are beginning to feel again. My shoulders shake. My bad side burns with each movement I make.

Maybe the hospital isn't such a bad idea.

I turn off the water and immediately hear shouting.

"We have to tell him," came Rachel's voice through the door.

"I don't know," came Lucas's voice. "He's pretty messed up. I think we drive him to the hospital first and then we tell him."

"I'm with Lucas on this one," Seth says while I grab a towel and rub it on my hair.

What are they talking about? What do they need to tell me? That I'm kicked off the team? I sigh and my shoulders slump while I lean against the sink, trying very hard not to look at my miserable body. I catch sight of a few bruises on my shoulder and hip.

"I don't think we should keep this bottled up," says Rachel, her voice sounding shrill and making my head hurt even more.

"He's going to be upset either way," I hear Seth say. "Might as well tell him after he's had some rest and detoxed a bit."

I roll my eyes and wrap the towel on my waist before grabbing the door and opening it. Everyone's mouths immediately shut and all eyes turn to me. "What is it?" I ask, dripping water everywhere while I walk toward them. "Just tell whatever it is you're hiding."

Seth sighs and rubs the back of his neck. "Why don't we get you into bed," he says while reaching for me.

I smack his hand away, not liking the way everyone is looking at me. As if they pitied me. "I'm fine," I say through clenched teeth. "Just tell me whatever it is you're arguing about. I'm a big boy."

Lucas shakes his head and turns around, grabbing his phone. "I'm going to call the hospital."

"I'm fine!" I shout, but Lucas already has the phone pressed to his ear.

"Hello? Yes I need to speak to a doctor."

I walk towards him, about to rip that phone from his ear and throw it out a window when Rachel steps into my path and grabs my arm. She easily guides me away from Lucas and towards my room. I don't have the energy to push her away anymore. My head feels like it's going to explode any moment and I'm too exhausted to fight.

Rachel pulls back my wrinkled blankets while I throw off my towel and crawl into bed. She settles in next to me, resting her back against the headboard and placing a pillow on her lap. I settle my head on top of it, sighing while she runs her fingers through my hair.

I really missed this.

I hear murmuring outside the room. Seth and Lucas are talking about something and I scowl, knowing Lucas is probably discussing the whole incident with Jerry. Like I really need them judging me right now. I lift my head, about to shout something at them when I feel Rachel's hand sliding against my cheek and pushing me back into the pillow.

"Don't worry about them," she says while continuing her tender touches. "Just relax for now. You're safe."

"I've always been safe," I say gruffly.

She doesn't say anything and I allow the silence wash over us. My eyes drift close and Rachel taps her hand against my cheek. "Don't go to sleep," she says softly. "You might have a concussion."

I groan and snuggle into the pillow while forcing my eyes open.

Seth stalks into the room and glances between us before saying, "Yeah, we're taking him to a hospital."

I shake my head. "No." I struggle as Lucas enters and approaches me.

"You have to go, Hunter," says Seth. "I have no clue how to help you."

"But- but-" My mouth gapes open. I can't tell them that there are drugs in my system, but I also can't go. If I do, I'll be in deep shit with the team… that is if I even have

a team to return to. They still haven't told me what secret they are keeping to themselves. "I can't go," I decide to stay, wrapping my arms around Rachel.
 Lucas tugs at my shoulder and I scream. My arms tighten around Rachel's waist as I hear her say, "Be careful with him. He's in pain."
 "He's being an asshole," says Lucas.
 "Come on Hunter," I hear Seth say while tugging on my hand. "Let's get you dressed and back in the car. We can't have you dying on our watch."
 "I'm not going to die," I groan. "Just let me be. I can't go. Lucas knows I can't go."
 I chance a glance and watch Lucas tilt his head back and rub his temples in frustration. "My dad knows a guy who can keep things… private. Alright? Does that work for you?"
 I slowly, carefully push myself up, hissing when I feel stabbing at my shoulder. "Yeah, that's perfect."
 Rachel helps me the rest of the way up while Seth digs through my pile of clothes, finding a reasonably clean black t-shirt and some black sweatpants. I inhale deeply while pulling the shirt over my head, trying not to cry out in pain.
 "Can I just borrow someone's phone real quick," I say while pulling on my pants.
 Everyone pauses, as if time suddenly stopped. Their gazes turn to me, looking worried and horrified. "What?" I murmur while looking round at everyone. "What is it?"
 Rachel looks at Seth and Lucas. I watch as the boys shake their head. Rachel's gaze dips to the floor while Seth turns to me. "Who do you want to call?" he asks slowly.
 My stomach twists and my heart slows. The hair on the back of my neck rises and I feel like I might faint or vomit. Something isn't right. The way they are staring at me isn't right. I don't even want to ask what it's about.

This can't be about coach or the team.

My mouth feels dry, and it's difficult to swallow; difficult to form words. I open my mouth, trying to say something, but it comes out as a raspy breath, "Mom."

Rachel doesn't look at me. Seth nods while Lucas sighs and turns around, unable to face me. I think I'm about to be sick. I force a smile, knowing whatever they are thinking, it can't be true. I hold out my hand, my lips trembling while tears come to my eyes. I quickly blink them away. I'm fine. Everything's fine.

"So," I say shakily, "can I use the phone? She'll probably want to..." Words drift away as I continue staring at them. Tears stream down my cheeks when no one reaches for their phone. Rachel lifts her gaze to mine and I see tears stream down her cheeks. Lucas leans against a wall, still facing away from me while Seth takes one step towards me.

"What's going on?" I ask while stepping away from him.

Seth holds up his hands. "Hunter, it's ok. Let me just-"

"Don't touch me!" I shout while stepping around him. "Just let me have your phone!"

Seth shakes his head. "I-" He sighs, his shoulders dropping. "I can't Hunter."

"Why not?" I cry. I wipe away the tears streaming down my cheeks. I'm trying so desperately to hang on, to be a man. I can't believe I'm crying like this, being so weak in front of my bros. I shouldn't be acting like this. I'm supposed to be strong and here I am crying like a child.

Lucas slowly turns around. The anger in his gaze is gone, and he looks at me with anguish. "Hunter-" he starts.

"No!" I shout while swiping an arm out, trying to keep them away from me. "I want to call my mom. Give me the phone. Now!"

Rachel lunges for me, wrapping her arms tightly around my waist and burying her face into my chest. "You can't call your mom," she sobs. "She's dead." She lifts her tearful eyes up to me. "She died Saturday night, Hunter."

My eyes widen and I feel my body going limp as I remember receiving my father's call. I threw my phone into the snow when he had been calling to tell me about Mom. While I was out getting fucked up, my mom died.

I hadn't been there for her.

I hadn't been there at all.

I fall to my knees and cover my face with my hands, sobbing into them everything I've felt up to this point; the anger, the hurt, the disappointment, the pain. Everything.

I feel Rachel's arms come around me. "I'm so sorry," she whispers into my ear.

I inhale deeply, trying to calm myself, but I can't seem to stop crying. I feel like a dam that's finally been released and there's nothing to do, but wait out the storm. More hands touch and surround me and I lift my head, finding Seth and Lucas also hugging me.

"It's going to be alright," says Seth. "You have us."

"You just need to talk to us," says Lucas. "We'll be there for you. We've always had your back."

I sniff and wipe my eyes while pulling away from them. "I haven't been doing well," I sob.

"We can tell," says Seth while patting my back.

"The cancer came back and my shoulder wasn't getting better," I take a deep breath as another sob threatens to escape from me. "I kinda lost it."

Rachel strokes my hair and my gaze locks with hers. I bit my bottom lip to keep it from trembling, but I still feel as if I'm breaking from inside out. "I'm so sorry," I whimper as I look at her. "I was so terrible to you and you were so good to me."

"Hunter, it's alright," says Rachel while pulling me to her. "I forgive you."

I nod against her and feel more arms pulling at me. Looking up, I see its Lucas. "We really need to get you to a hospital," he says while helping me up. "And afterwards, I'll introduce you to a therapist that can help."

I nod, allowing Seth, Lucas, and Rachel to help me out and into the car, feeling like the world is breaking and mending all at the same time.

19

RACHEL

I walk out of the apartment, smiling at the budding trees and the melting snow. I guess winter is ending. I sigh, closing my eyes and lifting my head, feeling the warmth of the bright sun stroking my face tenderly. With Hunter getting released from the hospital and my report against Josh being sent to the school authorities, I feel like I can walk easier; as if this semester is finally getting better.

I can't wait to see Hunter, I think while opening my eyes and continue my path down the sidewalk towards class. I've received a few text messages from him. Apparently his dad is getting on his case and is trying to get Hunter to drop the semester and pick it up next year when things have calmed down a bit. Hunter is pissed, but I think his dad is truly considering his needs. The guy has barely gone to class, let alone football practice. And I doubt he's going to be doing so well with his mom gone.

Maybe he needs some time at home to heal.

Of course, I can't just text that, knowing Hunter will probably blow up and shunt me out of his life. Seeing how he's just returned, I've kept my mouth firmly shut. For now. I cringe while shoving open the door to the art school, remembering vaguely how I sent in my application for the internship program in Paris last week. I nearly forgot with all the chaos going on. I'm supposed to hear from them soon.

"Hey!"

I turn around, recognizing the voice and wondering who is being this loud so early in the morning. My eyes widen on Lauren stalking toward me, looking like she's about to slam her fist into my face. I stop and move to the side of the hall so other students can get pass us, ignoring their curious glances.

 Lauren stops in front of me, scowling down at me as if I just dumped coffee all over her black sweater. "What is it?" I ask, my grip on the strap of my bag tightening. Of what I remember from our last encounter, we are still not talking. I have no clue what I've done to her now, since I've been pretty busy staying on the down low and concentrating on my school work. Briefly, I wonder if Charlie has spoken with her and she has come to offer her apologies for being such an asshole to me, but then again, why would she look so angry?

 I inhale deeply, trying to calm the anxiety making my stomach twist. Let's just get this done and over with I tell myself while watching Lauren scoff.

 She throws her head back as if her eye roll has suddenly took hold of her face. "Don't give me that innocent bullshit. You know exactly what's going on."

 I purse my lips and feel my brow furrowing into confusion. If I'm not careful, my face might stay this way. I feel like I've been pretty confused this whole semester. I can't think of anything I've done to Lauren in particular. Actually, I think the only thing I could be accused of these days is being rather boring. I haven't gone to many parties. I've been doing my work and focusing on applying to that internship program in Paris.

 I shake my head while I say, "I'm sorry. I really don't know."

 Lauren shifts back and forth while her gaze wonders to the group of students staring at us from across the hall. She leans in close to me, her scowl darkening. "I spoke with Josh," she whispers harshly. "He says you're ruining his life."

 My eyes widen and I feel rage brim inside me, making me want to grab Lauren and shake some sense into her. "Me?" I ask, trying to contain my anger. My fists clench at my side.

"He said you filed a report against him."

"I did."

"What the hell, Rachel?" Lauren shouts while leaning away from me, tossing her hands up in the air while she circles around. "How could you do that?"

My mouth hangs open. She has to be freaking kidding me? What does she mean 'how'? I clamp my mouth shut, trying to think of something to say, but I'm too angry. All I want to do is stamp my feet and scream at her for be a freaking idiot and a jerk.

"He might get expelled," Lauren continues. "Don't you understand what that means for him?"

I roll my eyes. "Good riddance," I spit.

I turn around, not wanting to listen to anymore of her bullshit. Why should I care what happens to him after all the crap he's put me through?

"Rachel!" I hear Lauren shout, feel her hand on my shoulder yanking me back.

I whirl around. "What Lauren? What more do we have to talk about?"

Lauren's mouth opens, but I don't wait for an answer as I say, "What he did to me was disgusting!"

"He didn't-"

"Yes, he did, Lauren," I say while shoving her hand off me. "And the sooner you realize that, the better." I cross my arms in front of me while I look her up and down. I shake my head. "I thought we were friends Lauren." I sniff, noticing tears are coming to my eyes as I watch Lauren's mouth open and close. I shrug. "I guess not."

I turn around and don't wait for an answer. I continue on to my class, opening the door and briskly walking to my usual seat. I dump my bag onto the floor and quickly wipe the tears from my eyes. *I don't need Lauren,* I tell myself while quickly grabbing my sketchbook and pencils. If she's acting like this now, then she never was a friend; just someone to hang out with.

Who needs her?

Looking around, I notice Josh isn't in his normal seat, sitting across from me. My attention turns to the door, waiting for him to stroll inside, maybe send me a dark scowl given the new situation. The door opens and my breath stalls, but instead of his dark head, a group of giggling girls enter followed by Mr. Brown.

"Alright, my fellow artists," calls Mr. Brown while striding towards his desk. He dumps his bag onto his table and I watch as several folders and papers slide from the opening and spill onto the desk. "Let's get started, shall we?"

I turn away from the door, realizing with a soft smile that Josh must not be coming today. Maybe it has something to do with the report I filed against him? Or maybe he doesn't want to see my face? Either way, I feel like things are getting even better for me.

Mr. Brown grabs a letter that slips out from his bag and his gaze locks with mine. Striding towards me, he sets the letter onto my desk, giving me a knowing look before turning back to the class.

"Can everyone please take out their projects for today?" Mr. Brown says while I grab the letter and rip it open.

My eyes widen as I quickly skim the contents.

I got the internship.
I'm going to Paris.

20

HUNTER

"I've made arrangements with your grandparents," I hear Dad say while I look out the window. "Your grandfather is being a big pain in the ass about all the funeral details."

I close my eyes, trying to stop the sob from welling in my throat. How can he talk about all this so easily? I inhale deeply to calm my pounding heart, wishing I could just drown out this unending pain with something. Anything.

"Hunter?"

I grind my teeth, my head lulling from side to side in the seat of the car while I try to ignore the breaking of my heart and the pain in my shoulder.

"Hunter?" Dad says louder this time, almost shouting.

An angry sigh escapes my lips and turn toward him. "What?" I say, my tone filled with bite.

Dad glances away from the road for a moment, his brow furrowed in worry. "I'd like it if you'd answer me when I say your name," he says.

I shake my head. He's nitpicking again. He's always nitpicking, talking, being absolutely annoying. "Whatever," I mumble while turning my gaze back to the window, watching houses pass us by. We're in town today. Dad insisted I remain home for a few days rather than return to my apartment with Seth and Lucas. Unfortunately, my friends didn't fight with my dad, thinking it best I get some family time in.

Like they know what's best for me.

"I really wish you would change your mind about school."

I ignore him. I don't want to stay home. I cross my arms to keep them from shaking. Home is so painful for me to be in right now. I keep seeing images of Mom in the kitchen, making breakfast. Or in the living room drinking a glass of wine while she watches that housewives TV she loved so much. Even being in my room, I can't help but picturing her striding inside with a basket full of laundry, dumping it all on my bed and demanding I clean up after myself.

I sniff and bite my bottom lip. Tears threaten to stream down my face at the memories. I sniff and wipe my eyes as Dad pulls into the parking lot. Quickly, I undo my seatbelt and throw the door open, stalking up the stairs and into the office.

"At least think about it!" Dad calls after me.

I look around in the office, not knowing exactly where to go or what to do. It's my first time in this place. I never needed a therapist before. I still don't think I need one now, but Dad insisted and Rachel messaged me that she thought it would be best if I at least tried one session.

The door jingles behind me and glancing over my shoulder, I see its Dad, following in after me. I purse my lips and I stare at him with a glare. "What are you doing?" I whisper, before looking around, catching the curious look of the receptionist sitting behind the desk.

"I thought I might as well have a look around," he says while striding pass me and towards the main desk.

"Why?" I murmur before dumping myself into a seat, crossing my arms and glaring at Dad's back.

"Hello," I hear him say, "we're here to see Dr. Forrester."

I roll my eyes. *We? When did this become a 'we' operation?* This is supposed to be for me and honestly if I had any say in it, I would have promptly told Dad to 'fuck off'. Unfortunately, I can't really say that to him, since he is my father and all. Well, on paper.

"Alright, here are some papers for you to fill out and she should be out in just a moment," the receptionist says with a smile.

My phone buzzes and I'm thankful for the distraction as Dad turns around and walks towards me. Dad bought me another phone after realizing that I had 'lost' mine. I didn't tell him the full truth, since I didn't want him to find out about what I had been doing at this point. The less he knows the better. It's a secondhand phone, but it works well enough and I can keep my old number. The only problem is getting everyone's contact details.

I frown when I look at the screen, expecting to see Rachel or one of the bros' names. Instead, I see a foreign number. Clicking on the text, the message opens and my frown deepens.

Hey sexy, wanna meet up later for some drinks?

It's obviously from Millie. Who else could it be? Rachel doesn't speak like that. My stomach twists while I stare down at the message, wanting to tell her 'yes' when I should be saying 'no' I shouldn't be drinking. And wherever Millie is, there is sure to be Drew and Jerry. What if Jerry told Millie to text me so he could get more money out of me?

What if he does more damage to my body than last time?

I had been lucky to come out of the whole mess with only a concussion and several, very painful, bruises. I groan at the memory, as if Jerry is still towering above me, slamming his bat into my flesh.

"Hunter, are you alright?"

I turn and see Dad staring at me with worry. He looks at me differently these days, like at any moment I'm going to break down. I worry that he suspects what's been going on, but I've decided I'm never going to tell him. He doesn't need to know. I nod and shove my cell in my pants pocket. "Fine," I say while leaning back in my chair, staring up at the bright ceiling light while waiting.

"You know, you can tell me anything."

I narrow my eyes. Doubtful, I want to say, but I say nothing.

"I know this is a very difficult time for you. It's a difficult time for me, too."

I nod, so he knows that I'm at least listening. My hands twitch and I feel this desperate need to either text Millie back or message anyone from my contacts list about any parties going on. All I want to do is drown out everything going wrong in my life.

The door opens and I tilt my head to the side, watching a woman in her forties walk into the reception. Her curly black hair is up in a bun and she smiles at me with dark eyes, gesturing towards a dimly lit room behind her. I see the hint of a white couch through the cracked door along with some white carpeting.

"Alright, Hunter," she says in a soft, soothing voice. "I'm ready for you."

My dad pops up from his seat and holds out a hand. "I'm Hunter's father, Tom. It's a pleasure to meet you." He holds up the papers awkwardly while I slowly rise from the chair. "I haven't finished filling everything out."

"Totally fine. You can hand them in when you're finished."

I roll my eyes while I shuffle into the room, hearing Dad call after me, "I'll be right outside. Maybe we can go for ice cream after."

My shoulders tense at the thought as a memory pops up of a time when I was about twelve years old; when we all went to get ice cream after my football practice. I sigh and wipe a hand over my face, trying to will the memories and the pain away as I dump my exhausted body into the couch across from Dr. Forrester's desk.

She pads in and closes the door quietly behind her. Her heels make zero noise on the carpet and she smiles at me while she strides towards her desk. I wait for her to take a seat, but she only grabs a stack of papers and a pen before walking back to the couch and taking a seat on the other side. I move immediately, trying to put at least two couch cushions between us. I feel awkward. This whole thing is frustrating. I don't need to talk to anyone. I've been having a tough semester. Everyone eventually gets a tough school year. How am I any different?

"So, Hunter," says Dr. Forrester. "What brings you in today?"

I shrug. "Nothing. My dad thought it would be a good idea."

Dr. Forrester nods. "So your father is worried about you." I watch her write something down, suspecting it's about my father. I fight the need to roll my eyes at how cliché all this seems. "Why is he worried Hunter?"

I scoff. "I don't know. It's not like he really cared all that much before."

She writes again. The sound irritates me so I quickly look away, finding several candles lit around the room. There's a lamp and a light above us, however they're not on. A book shelf sits to my right, behind the therapist. It's stocked full of books on relationships and parenthood, among other things. The scent of vanilla wafts towards me and I wrinkle my nose as I recall another memory of my mother lighting candles for Christmas.

"Well, he seems to care now," comes Dr. Forrester's soothing voice, drawing me back to her dark, soft gaze. "Why do you think he cares now? Did something happen?"

I open my mouth, but I don't know what to say. *Yes, something did happen. I fucked up and got so wasted my friends and family couldn't find me. A drug dealer beat the shit out of me for now being able to pay. I can't say that.*

I clamp my mouth close and go to rise. "I don't think this is going to work," I say while trying to turn away. I notice out of the corner of my eye that the therapist has stood. "I'm sorry for wasting your time."

"It's not a waste at all Hunter. I think it's actually quite brave that you were able to come in today."

I stop on my path towards the door. I turn around, completely confused. "How is this brave?" I ask, cringing at the bitterness in my voice. I'm angry and I don't know why. I shouldn't be taking it out on her. She's only doing her job. Of course she doesn't want me to leave. She won't get paid if she loses a client. I should just go.

"It's hard to talk about one's feelings," she says. "Especially men. Most men have been raised with the belief that feeling anything but rage and joy is a weakness and shouldn't be discussed. It's brave of you to come in today."

My hands shake. I want to shout, to hit something. I'm fine, I want to scream. Everything is fine. I still when I feel my cellphone vibrate and my thoughts immediately go to Drew, wondering if he's messaging me about another party. My teeth grind together and my fingers twitch as if there's a rope wound tightly around me and Drew is yanking on it furiously; dragging me back into his depths.

"Hunter, are you okay?"

I wobble on my feet.

"Why don't you sit down?" Dr. Forrester gestures back to the couch and I take the three steps towards it before dumping myself on the cushions.

My gaze focuses on the candles resting on the coffee table in front of me. I hear some clinking, but I don't turn towards the noise; needing to find some semblance of calm while I try to control my fingers.

It could be from Rachel, I tell myself. It could be absolutely nothing. Still, I don't reach for my phone, worried that I will lose all my strength and give in to that dark need.

"Here."

I look up and see a glass filled with water in front of me. Grabbing it, I guzzle down the liquid, enjoying the coolness against my throat. However, it's only a temporary fix and I find myself fidgeting again, trying to steer my thoughts away from Millie and Drew. My leg bumps up and down while my gaze returns to Dr. Forrester. I grimace when I find her leaning against her desk, watching me.

"I have a problem," I say quickly. "I don't really know how or why it happened. It just… started and then got worse as time went on."

Dr. Forrester nods. "Most bad habits start off that way."

"I don't want my dad to know," I say harshly.

"Whatever is said in my office doesn't leave my office," she says. "I'm legally bound to keep whatever you say private."

I nod vigorously while tapping my fingers against my knees. "Okay, well, I…" I don't even know where to begin. I'm searching for words but all and none come to mind at the same time.

"Why don't we start with the phone," says Dr. Forrester. "Who texted you? Or… who do you think texted you?"

"Millie," I say while leaning back in the couch. "She messaged me right before our session."

Dr. Forrester perks up, her eyes lifting in interest. "Is Millie your girlfriend?"

"No," I say while shaking my head. "Definitely not."

"And do you want her to be your girlfriend or…"

I make a face and Dr. Forrester stops speaking. She purses her lips and walks behind her desk, sitting in her chair. She leans forward while resting her chin in her hands, blinking back at me. "Did Millie do something to you?"

"No, not really," I say while lowering my gaze to my lap, feeling awkward and embarrassed. "I didn't want to be alone. And she made it so I didn't have to be."

"Did you have fun with this girl?"

"I don't remember," I say softly. I grimace as I realize it's the truth. This entire time I have been partying it up and I can't even recall what happened or if I even enjoyed it. The parties have always been the perfect distraction from my problems. "I just didn't want to think about it anymore. About my mother and her cancer."

"Did Millie help you forget?"

I shake my head. "No. I kept thinking of my mother which made me drink more." I release a shuddering breath while my hands grip my knees. "And eventually... I did more than just drinking." I lift my gaze and watch Dr. Forrester nod.

"Did it help?"

I purse my lips, remembering passing out in bathrooms and on floors, being unable to find my wallet and shoes, losing my coat, getting yelled at by Millie and hit by Jerry. "No," I say while shaking my head. "It didn't." I sniff, remembering getting a phone call from my dad and throwing my cell into the snow. "Actually," I say shakily, "it made things worse." Tears slip from my eyes and I quickly wipe them away. I try to regain control of my body, but I can't. My lips are trembling while I try to swallow my sobs. "I wasn't there for her," I rasp. "I wasn't there for my mom when she died." I bury my face into my hands. "I'm a terrible son."

"You're not a terrible son."

I lift my gaze and see Dr. Forrester holding out a tissue for me. I snatch it from her hands and quickly blow my nose, hating myself for letting myself go. Strangely, I feel better after crying and dab the tissue against my eyes. "I don't think I can ever forgive myself," I breathe.

"Cancer is hard. Losing a parent is hard, especially at your age. I can't snap my fingers and make everything difficult disappear from your life."

I nod while swallowing another sob.

"But I can give you the tools to help you take one day at a time." She nods towards the outline of my cellphone in my pants. "Starting with that. For our next session, I want you to write down a daily schedule you intend to adhere to and the names of the people you can trust to help you."

I chuckle bitterly. "You're giving me homework?"

Dr. Forrester nods. "If you want to feel better, you'll do your homework." I watch her grab a small note pad and write something down before tearing it out and handing the note to me. "I'll see you next week. Same time. Same day. Don't forget your homework."

I take the paper and nod before heading towards the door, already feeling a tiny bit lighter.

21

RACHEL

The bell on the door rings as I enter the sports store. It's an especially nice, sunny day and I'm hoping work moves along quickly so I can spend some of it getting some great photos of campus. My plan is to grab some merchandise after work ends and meet up with Seth so he can model them for our website. A part of me has worried what work would be like today, seeing how I missed my shift. Since I did call in and Sarah said it should be okay, I figure might as well get the awkwardness done and over with today.

Sarah perks up from the counter, her eyes widening on me while I stride towards the back. I wave at her while I smile and say, "Hey!"

"Hey!" She calls back while following me to the stock room. "What are you doing here?"

I throw off my jacket and punch in my card before unzipping my bag and pulling out my tennis shoes to change into. "I'm here for my shift, why?"

"So you didn't hear?"

I frown, pausing in unzipping my boots to meet Sarah's gaze. "Hear what?"

Sarah sighs and rubs the back of her head. "Alright, don't be mad at me, okay?"

"Be mad about what?" I ask while throwing my tennis shoes on the ground and crossing my arms in front of my chest.

Sarah grimaces. "You were... um... fired."

"Fired!" I shout, my voice shrill. "How did that happen? I called in. You said it would be fine. It was an emergency."

"I know," says Sarah while resting her hands on my shoulders. "I didn't do it, okay? I was totally fine with it. The store was completely dead anyway." She wrinkles her nose in distaste. "But Joe kinda had a cow about it."

I groan and roll my eyes. "I freaking called in. I would've gotten here as soon as possible but... but-"

"Shit happens, I know," says Sarah. "But Joe complained to the boss." Sarah sighs and shake her head.

"I'm sorry, Rachel. I really am."

I groan and grab my tennis shoes, throwing them into my bag before shoving on my coat.

"I thought you knew," Sarah calls after me. "Or else I would've called you!"

"It's fine!" I call over my shoulder.

It definitely isn't fine. How the hell am I going to pay for rent? Or all my lattes? And my candles? I need a job. I needed this job. I pause at the counter and turn around, memorizing the little running shop that had become part of my life. I'm not going to be able to work with Seth anymore. I'm not going to be able to joke around with him while mopping the floors and he won't tease me on my lack of knowledge on running.

Okay, I guess it isn't the end of the world. I can get a job anywhere else on campus.

It just really sucks to find out like this.

The door rings, reminding me that I should go. I turn around and my eyes land on Joe standing in the doorway. His tall, lanky form nearly takes up the whole doorway. My eyes narrow in a dark scowl as he has the audacity to lift a hand and smile awkwardly at me.

"Hey," he says as I stalk pass.

"Oh, fuck you, Joe," I mutter while throwing open the door and walking briskly down the sidewalk.

I stop, not quite knowing where I'm going. I need to make a game plan and fast. *Who could possibly be hiring in the middle of the semester? No one. That's who. Ugh, why did Joe have to open his stupid little mouth? And why did the owner have to be an asshole about it?*

It's not like I flaked out on work all the time, like Seth used to. I always came early, worked hard. I even came up with new campaigns for the website to get customers in. This whole thing is absolute bullshit.

"Rachel!"

I turn around, hoping to see the owner suddenly running down the street, begging me not to leave. I defat when I see Seth, walking briskly towards me with a coffee in his hand. He stops in front of me and holds it out for me to take.

"I wanted to surprise you at the store," he says while I take a very large gulp from the sweet latte. "Why are you out here?"

"They fired me," I say between gulps, wishing something a bit stronger was mixed with this. Like whiskey.

Seth's mouth hangs open, and he scowls. "What?"

I nod. "Yep. Apparently Joe complained."

Seth rolls up his sleeves and turns on his heel, stalking back towards the shop. "That bastard!" He shouts.

I run after him, grabbing his shoulder and turning him around. "Don't worry about it."

"But you're never late. You even come to work sick. It's absolute bullshit!"

I shrug. "I know." I hold the coffee up and take another swig. "But the coffee helps."

Seth purses his lips and I can see he's trying to decide whether to let the whole thing go, or stalk into the sports store and give Joe a whole new reason to complain. His shoulders slump and I see that he's decided on the former. "So what are you going to do?"

I turn around and continue down the sidewalk towards the small campus town. I feel Seth following at my side, feel his gaze watching me. "I don't know," I say while forcing a smile. "I have to find something though. Bills have to be paid."

"Well, I guess you no longer need to work on the website." My smile becomes real when I feel Seth's arm wrapping around my shoulder, drawing me close. "We could see if any cafes are hiring."

I wrinkle my nose. "I don't want to work in the food industry. That would just ruin food and coffee for me."

Seth chuckles while poking my nose. "Beggars can't be choosers."

I sigh, knowing he's right. I need at least something to last until May and then I can look into another retail store.

"There should be summer positions open, if you can last until then," says Seth while turning us further into the small town. My gaze lingers on an Urban Outfitters, staring at their window and wishing to see a 'hiring' sign, but there's nothing but cute clothes staring back at me.

"No, I need something now," I say, turning towards the Urban Outfitters anyway. Maybe they don't know yet that they need me.

The bell rings when I push it open and I feel the aura around Seth darken. Maybe he's realized that I may be in a mood for some retail therapy, I think with a smile. My gaze lifts to his and I chuckle softly at his scowl.

"What? So you can buy more of this crap?" He asks while gesturing towards a rack filled with oversized sweaters.

"Exactly," I say while picking up a giant white sweater and holding it close to my body. "Have you heard from Hunter?" I look around for a mirror and find one in the middle of the room. I want to change the subject away from summer. I haven't quite figured out how to tell them yet that I won't be around and I have the slightest hunch that Seth will take it the hardest.

I watch Seth nod his head in the mirror. "Yeah, he should be by today to pick up some things. I think he's taking the semester off."

"Really?" I ask while lowering the sweater from me. I can't believe Hunter is actually listening to his dad on something. It's good, though. I'll definitely miss him, but he needs the break. "Is he moving back in with his dad?" My heart squeezes with worry. I want him to stay with us. I hate this distance that's been growing, but I know he needs some attention. Attention that I'm not so sure I can give him right now.

"Just for a few weeks. He plans on coming back at the end of this month."

I nod. "Good."

Seth grabs several figurines sitting on a shelf and turns them around. "He'll actually need a job, too. Hey!" Seth perks up, his mouth twisting into a bright smile. "Maybe you guys can work together. The swimming pool opens in the summer. Maybe you both can work there and let me in for free!"

I chuckle and shake my head. "You're ridiculous."

Seth's hands slide against my hips and he nuzzles his nose against my neck. "No, I'm not. I'm amazing."

I turn around in his arms and wrap my own around his neck. "No to the swimming pool," I say before placing a chaste kiss on his lips.

Seth frowns and releases me. "Why not? It's perfect."

I sigh. "For you it is, but I don't think hanging out at the pool is my kind of thing."

Actually, it's totally my kind of thing. My fingers twiddle together, knowing I'm just going to have to come out and tell him. Now is better than never.

"Well, what would you like to do this summer? Lucas was talking about going to-"

"I'm going to Paris," I blurt out. I grimace while watching Seth's bright expression fall into a deep frown.

"Huh?" His mouth hangs open, and he stares at me as if I just told him that Brooks are the worse kind of running shoe in the entire world.

"I'm going to Paris," I say again, this time with my head held high and my back straight. "I got accepted into an internship program."

Seth's mouth opens and closes. He blinks and I can see he's still trying to wrap his little head around the whole idea of me not being around for summer. "Why didn't you tell me?"

I step toward him, but pause when he takes a step back. "I found out a few days ago. I didn't know how to tell you."

"Oh," Seth breathes. His mouth sets into a thin line as he stares down at me. "Okay."

"Are you alright?"

He nods his head a bit too roughly and his lips curl into a forced smile. "Fine," he says, his voice cracking. He clears his throat before saying, "Absolutely fine."

"So, you can see," I say with an awkward chuckle. "I kinda need a job now."

"Totally," Seth says. He looks weird, as if he's trying desperately not to cry while keeping a bright happy face.

"Seth-"

"I'm so happy for you," he says while pulling me into a tight hug. "You must be so proud."

I smile and hesitantly wrap my arms around him. My fingers slide against the hair at his nape and I close my eyes, enjoying the warmth and the tenderness in his hug. "I am," I whisper. "I just didn't want to upset you."

Seth pulls away from me and gathers my hands in his own. "I'm not upset," he says softly. "I'm a bit disappointed, since I wanted to spend this summer with you, but I can never be upset about this. You're following your dream. That's great. I don't want to take that away from you."

Tears prickle my eyes and I sniff while wiping them. "Thank you, Seth," I breathe while grabbing his hand. I lace my fingers with his and tug him towards the door. "I guess we should get a move on. I'd like to be hired somewhere by the end of today."

Seth nods while pushing the door open for me. "Don't worry, we'll figure it out together."

We walk down the steps and continue further into the campus town. My gaze keeps sliding to Seth as he asks shop after shop for me if they are hiring and I feel my heart swell, knowing I am really going to miss my bros while I'm away in Paris. But I can't focus on that now. We still have a few months left together before I leave.

22

LUCAS

I stare down at the thick manila envelope in my hands while pacing outside the mailbox, wondering if this is really a good idea. I have spent weeks working on my portfolio for the writing contest, trying to get the right rhythm for some of my works while also trying to convey emotion. If I fail, what then? I guess this is my first writing contest. It's not like I should expect first prize. I only started going to the poetry slams recently. I shouldn't expect to be the best writer in the world after a few classes.

Rachel believes in me. Rachel thinks I should do this. I stop pacing and face the mailbox. Taking a deep breath, I close the distance and open it, ramming the envelope inside and hearing it thumb against the metal container.

There, it's done. I turn on my heel and force myself back up the steps, ignoring the need to turn around and reclaim it. Just let it go, I tell myself while climbing up the steps to the apartment. Nothing good will come if I sit around and do nothing. I could get third prize, which would also be amazing.

I grimace, pausing before reaching for the door. I imagine getting third prize and my father suddenly getting wind of it. I imagine him calling me, telling me that I should spend my time focusing on better things, that I will always be considered lesser than when it came to my art.

I hear my phone vibrate and grab it, scowling down at the screen.

Well, speak of the devil.

I turn off my phone. I'm definitely not in the mood to speak to my father, especially now with everything going on. I open the door and force a smile at Hunter's dad swiveling around. He wrinkles his nose while his gaze slides to the sink full of dirty dishes. I fight the need to roll my eyes. Surely, this guy was once a college student himself. Not to mention, the place was worse off before Rachel came onto our lives.

"Hello," I say in a force cheerful voice. "You're still… here huh?"

Hunter's dad sighs and bobs his head up and down. "Yes, we're still here."

I close the door and stride further inside the apartment. I plop down on the couch and turn the TV on, hoping his dad gets the hint that I don't want to talk. Unfortunately, there doesn't seem to be anything on. I click through the channels, switching from infomercials to sitcom reruns I'm not interested in watching. I hear movement and flinch when Hunter's dad sits down next to me.

"Hunter is still looking for God knows what," his dad mutters while crossing his arms. "Oh! The game."

I set the remote down, settling on the WNBA. I'm not really a basketball fan, but I'll take it. My gaze slides to Hunter's dad, leaning against the armrest. The guy looks like an older, more conservative version of Hunter with blond greying hair clipped close and tired blue eyes. He's also big; tall and stocky with a bit of a beer gut around the waist. Glasses sit low on his nose and he sighs, pushing them upwards while watching the game.

"Are you about done in there?" he shouts all of a sudden, making me jump.

"I can't find it!" Hunter shouts back.

I grimace at the anxiety-filled tone Hunter's voice takes and I worry something might be gravely off. Dealing with Hunter beats dealing with his dad so I rise and stride towards his room. "I'll go check on him," I say with a forced smile.

Opening the door, I wrinkle my nose at the scattered dirty and wrinkled clothes around the room. Hunter sits next to the empty drawers, pressed against the wall. There's a bit more color in his face. His hair is washed and tied back in a man bun. His bruises are gone, yet he still looks haunted. Tears stream down his face and I feel like he isn't even looking at me, but looking at something else; something not visible to anyone but him.

"Hey, bro," I say, trying to be soothing even though I find this whole situation awkward as hell. I'm not really the hugging and coddling kind. That's more Rachel's thing, but seeing how she and Seth aren't home yet, I guess I have to man up and help Hunter with whatever it is he's going through. I lower myself, sitting next to him and grimacing when my head bumps the windowsill. "How's it going?"

Hunter blinks and groans while rubbing his eyes. "I can't find it," he rasps while tilting his head up to the ceiling.

"What is it? Maybe I can help," I say while looking at the clutter on his floor.

Hunter shakes his head. "It doesn't matter. I don't need it. It's just something-" He inhales deeply and releases a shuddering breath- "Mom gave me before I went off to college. I probably lost it at one of those house parties." He scowls. "I think I put it in my wallet." He sniffs and turns his bloodshot eyes towards me, offering a sad smile. I feel terrible for him, watching his bottom lip tremble while he tries to speak. "It was just a little good luck charm. A metal four-leaf clover." He shakes his head and covers his face with his hands. "I can't believe I lost it," he sobs.

I grind my teeth and force my awkwardness aside. This is my best friend. He's not being weak. He's mourning. "Come here," I say gruffly, pulling him to me and wrapping my arms around him. He cries against my chest, his shoulders shaking with each heave of breath he takes. I want to tell him that we will find it later; that it might be under his bed, but I can't make those promises. Not when his mom is gone, and he's dealing with that internal pain.

Eventually, we all have to learn how to let go.

I hear the front door opening and slamming shut and I roll my eyes, knowing Seth has finally returned home. I really wish he could be just a bit quieter.

"We're back!" I hear Rachel call.

Hunter's head pops up, and he quickly wipes his eyes. My arms fall away and I rise, holding out a hand for Hunter to take. "Not a word of this," I say sternly while holding a finger up to Hunter's face.

Hunter chuckles. "Of course not," he says before leading the way out of his room.

"I'm Rachel," I hear as we exit and I watch Rachel smile up at Hunter's dad, holding out her hand for him to take.

Hunter's dad frowns and shakes her hand. "You live here?" He asks. "With these guys? Do your parents know?"

Rachel chuckles while shaking his hand. "What they don't know doesn't hurt them."

Hunter's dad release her hand and shakes his head. "I can't believe you live here in this dump."

"Oh, you should have seen it before."

Hunter's dad turns towards us and he claps his hands together. "You ready?"

I turn towards Hunter, watching him grimace. "I guess."

"Actually," says Seth while stepping forward. "I was wondering if Hunter could hang out for tonight."

"Yeah, we were thinking about having pizza and maybe playing some Mario Kart," says Rachel cheerfully.

Hunter's dad makes a face. "I don't know. I think it would be best if-"

"Please, Dad," says Hunter. I turn to him, finding his gaze lingering on the floor. "Just for tonight?" He lifts his gaze, his eyes slightly swollen from crying. "It would be nice to hang with my friends for a bit before going back home."

I watch Hunter's dad, waiting for him to say no. His dad, to my surprise, bobs his head up and down and finally says, "Alright. Just for tonight. I'll pick you up tomorrow morning." He points at his son and says sternly, "Be ready by eleven. And you better not be hung over."

Hunter chuckles. "I won't be."

We all watch his father leave, the door clicking shut behind him before we all turn our attentions to Hunter.

"So," he starts, "pizza?"

"I'll order," says Rachel while grabbing her phone.

I smile and stride towards the TV. "I'll set up the games."

"Wait!" Shouts Seth while holding out his hands. "We need to have a meeting."

I frown and Hunter crosses his arms. "About what?" Hunter asks, sounding accusatory.

"Not about you," says Seth with an eye roll. "It's about Rachel." He gestures towards her, who is holding her phone up to her ear.

"Me?" She asks while pointing a finger at herself. "Why me?"

"It's about what you told me," Seth says through clenched teeth.

Rachel glares at him. "Oh, you must be kidding me."

"What's this about?" I asked while crossing my arms, not really liking where any of this is going. It's been awhile since we had a roommate meeting about Rachel, and the last one did not go well at all.

"Please don't tell me you want to kick her out again," Hunter groans. "I know I haven't been here all that much this semester, but I doubt she's done anything wrong."

Seth narrows his eyes at Hunter. "It's not that." I watch him slide his gaze towards Rachel, who is still scowling up at him. "Well," he says while gesturing to me and Hunter. "Tell them."

Rachel huffs. She opens her mouth to say something, but her face brightens. "Hello," she says into her phone, turning away from us. "Yes, I would like to order three large pizzas. Two pepperoni and one Hawaiian. Extra pineapples."

I gag and Hunter coughs. "Nevermind," I say while stalking towards the couch. "We're kicking her out. Anyone who eats pineapple on their pizza doesn't deserve to live here."

Rachel sticks her tongue out at me and I chuckle, jumping into the couch. Hunter joins me while Seth sits on the armrest. Together, we all wait for her to hang up and set aside her phone. When she turns around, her gaze widens as she finds all three of us staring at her.

"So," I start, "what's going on?"

Rachel groans and pinches her nose in annoyance. "Seth, seriously! Why did you have to say anything?"

"Because they should know, too."

Rachel shakes her head, resting her hands on her hips. "Yes, and I would've told them in private and in person."

"Can someone please tell me what's going on?" Hunter asks. "I thought we were going to have pizza and games."

Rachel sighs and I watch her purse her lips while she looks between Hunter and me. "Alright, well just so you know, I didn't want to tell you like this. And I *was* going to tell you!"

"Tell us what?" I ask, still completely confused.

Rachel twiddles her fingers together and I can't help but worry that something terrible has happened. "Okay, well, here it goes. I was accepted into an internship program."

My eyes widen and I feel my lips lifting into a smile. "That's amazing," says Hunter.

"That's so great!" I shout.

Rachel grimaces. "It's in Paris."

"Paris?" I repeat, my voice isn't more than a soft whisper.

She nods. "It's a summer program. I'll be gone about two months."

I can feel my smile falling. Two months? "When do you leave?"

"About a week after the semester ends."

"That soon?" Hunter asks. I feel him rise from the couch, watch him wrap his arms around Rachel. "I'll really miss you." I watch him press a kiss on the top of her head.

Rachel smiles and pats his back. "I'm not leaving, yet," she says. "We still have a few months. And it's only two months. It won't be that long."

I blink. I'm still in shock. I don't know why. I guess I thought we would all be spending summer together, hanging out by the pool and drinking cocktails. I should be happy for Rachel, but instead I fear what will happen to us. Things are already rocky between Rachel and Hunter. What if things become even rockier between all of us while she's gone?

"Lucas?" I hear Rachel say.

I quickly stand and force a smile. I come to her side and stroke the side of her face. "I'm so happy for you," I say, although deep down I'm already trying to think of a way to get to Paris. Maybe I could find a writing program. Maybe Dad has lawyer friends I could do an internship with. There has to be a way for us to be together this summer.

23

SETH

    I grab the last piece of pepperoni pizza and shove it into my mouth while listening to Hunter and Lucas race each other on Mario Kart.
    "God dammit!" Lucas shouts while Hunter laughs. "Will you stop throwing bombs at me?"
    I watch Hunter shake his head while he shouts, "Never!"
    "Bro, you are way too good at this."
    "Aww," Hunter taunts. "Don't be jealous."
    I chuckle and my attention slides to Rachel, whose head lulls from side to side. Her tongue slides against her bottom lip before darting back into her mouth, making me wish we were alone rather than hanging out with the two stooges. Her brows furrow together and her eyes flutter open briefly before closing again.
    It's about four in the morning and she keeps shifting from side to side to get comfortable while sleeping. I watch as her eyes completely open, looking around briefly before deciding to lay down completely. She slides her legs into Hunter's lap while resting her head on the armrest. Hunter doesn't seem to mind and I watch as his hand leaves the controller for a moment to rub her foot.
    I look away and continue munching on my pizza while sitting on the floor. Lucas scowls at the TV while pursing his lips. My brows furrow while I stare at him, knowing he's already thinking of a way to get himself to France. It's so easy for him. His dad is wealthy and can buy him a plane ticket. I'm sure Lucas knows people to stay with. If he doesn't, then his dad definitely knows someone.
    I wish it was that easy for me, but it's not. I come from a simple family; a family with hardly any money. The

only reason I can attend this school is because of my scholarship. I purse my lips, wondering how I'm going to be able to go with Rachel to Paris. It's not like my grades are outstanding. I barely get by. No one's going to offer me a scholarship to Paris.

I'll have to find my own way.

Hearing Rachel whimper, I finish chewing my pizza and swallow before standing and striding towards her. "Off to bed with you," I murmur while taking her shoulders and gently lifting her.

Rachel groans. Her curly blonde hair falls over her face while her legs wobble to stand. I grab her arm and rest it over my shoulders before leading her down the hall towards her room.

"Good night, Rachel," Hunter calls while glancing over his shoulder and watching us go.

"Nighty- fuck!" Lucas shouts.

I chuckle and shake my head while guiding Rachel down the hall. She can barely stand and keeps leaning against me as we walk to her room. I kick the door open and stumble inside, nearly toppling over before regaining my balance. I may be fast, but I'm not the strongest. Maybe it would have been better having Hunter or Lucas helping Rachel to bed, but I didn't want to interrupt their time together.

Usually, we have beers while playing Mario Kart and eating pizza. Considering Hunter's situation, we kept the party sober. It's definitely different, but I can complain. At least I won't have a raging headache tomorrow.

I dump Rachel's body into bed and watch her grab her pillow, nuzzling her head against it. I'm tempted to climb into bed with her and cuddle her, but my mind is going at high speed. I don't think I could get to sleep right now. I want to figure out a way to get my butt to Paris.

Turning on my heel, I stalk back down the hall and into my room, grabbing my laptop resting on the nightstand before jumping into bed. The mattress creaks with the movement and I kick off my shoes before shuffling my body backwards, leaning against the headboard.

    I might not be able to get a scholarship with my grades being how they are, but maybe I can find some kind of European marathon to join. And I can take more shifts at the running store. Rachel just got a job working at that cafe she's always going to. Maybe they will hire me as well. I just need to scrimp and save for the ticket. Coach will take care of the rest if there's a run I can join. He's always pressuring me to do things during my summer break.

    "Don't just drink your summer away," Coach always says. "Practice and make something of yourself."

    I roll my eyes at the sound of his voice. Even when I'm not at practice, Coach still has a way of infiltrating my mind. I type on the computer *Marathons in France* and wait for the search engine to load. My eyes widen on what I find and my lips curl into a smile.

    There's a marathon in July and it's held in Paris. The route is about twenty-five miles and the top ten contestants get awards. I can do that, I tell myself while snapping my laptop close. I'll just have to speak with a few people, but I can definitely do that.

***

    I wake up at nine, ignoring the exhaustion seeping through my bones while I force myself up and wipe the sleep from my eyes. I quickly dress in my track suit and tennis shoes before throwing open my door. Hunter and Lucas groan.

    "Ugh, what time is it?" Hunter asks while rubbing his head. His hair has fallen out of its man bun and hangs over his face.

    "Why did we sleep here?" Lucas asks while looking around.

    "You're the one who kept insisting on a rematch."

I chuckle while shaking my head. I guess it's a good thing I moved Rachel when I had the chance. I'm sure she would be feeling pretty terrible right about now.

"Where are you going, Seth?" I heard Lucas call.

"Yeah, it's like… too early," says Hunter.

I have no time to talk and barely utter, "Bye," before stalking outside the door and running down the steps. I need to remain focused. If I want to go to Paris, I need to talk to everyone today.

My first errand of the day is to speak with my coach. I run down the sidewalk, moving easily and not pushing myself too hard. It's just to warm up my muscles for practice. I keep practicing what to say, feeling nervousness take hold of me. I don't think I've ever been this nervous in my entire life.

My running shifts to a jog as I approach the field, watching coach pace back and forth while several of my peers stretch off to the side. I grimace. He definitely doesn't look like he's in a good mood. I sigh and jog towards him. Might as well get this done and over with.

"Coach!" I call while jogging toward him, stopping about a foot in front.

Coach slides his scowl towards me and shakes his head, already looking skyward as if my very presences pisses him off. "What is it Garcia?"

"I was hoping to have a word with you about something."

Coach snaps his fingers. "Make it quick, but not so loud. I have a hangover and the last thing I need is you making my headache worse."

"I found a marathon in France I'd like to take part in," I rush out. Coach's eyes widen on me, staring at me as if I my skin suddenly turned green. I don't wait for him to say anything. "It's about 25 miles and takes place in July. Top ten get medals."

Coach opens his mouth, but I don't let him get a word in.

"It'll look great for the school," I say with a forced smile. "I am your top runner and all. I could get that medal, do some interviews with the school paper, get the word out that Aurora's track and field has done it again. I can even pay for my own plane ticket. I'll just need your sponsorship and some money for my time there."

"Wait, stop," says Coach while holding up his hands. "You want to go where now?"

I make a face, already suspecting he's going to say no. "Paris," I say, my voice cracking, making me grimace more.

Coach throws up his hands. "Why Paris?"

I purse my lips. I probably shouldn't tell him the truth, but I can't think up a lie good enough, especially given the amount of sleep I got the night before. "Because my girlfriend is going to Paris," I say while sliding my foot back and forth on the dewy grass.

Coach groans. "You gotta be kidding me, Garcia."

I shake my head. "No, sir. I'm not."

"The money in the running program is for US based marathons. Not for Europe. Not for girlfriends."

"I know," I say quickly.

"And, I might add," says Coach while shoving a finger in my face. "You missed practice last week."

"I was-"

"Sick my ass!" Coach shouts. He shakes his head while scowling at me. I feel my heart cracking in my chest. This is stupid, I tell myself. I shouldn't be asking Coach to sponsor me on such an expensive trip. I should've known this would be fruitless.

"Now," begins Coach while crossing his arms. "The only way I can pay for this trip is if you buy your own plane ticket and find suitable accommodation on your own."

My brows pinch together in confusion. "What?"

"You heard me, Garcia," Coach says angrily. "Or have you suddenly become deaf? If you want to go, you need to handle those two things."

My head bobs up and down. "Of course," I rasp. I clear my throat and smile. "Thank you."

Coach groans. "Don't thank me, yet. Bring me back that medal. It'll look good for the team."

I smile and nod. "Of course, Coach. You can count on me."

I turn on my heel, running towards the track and feeling my body floating with joy with each step I take.

"Hey, Garcia!"

I turn around, running backwards while watching Coach's lips lift into a smile. "What?" I shout back.

"You should tell that girlfriend of yours congratulations. She's lucky to have a boyfriend like you."

I scoff, turning around and shaking my head. I don't know if that's a correct assumption. I've been an asshole to Rachel too many times to count on one hand, but slowly I'm making it up to her. I want to be a man she can rely on and look to if need be. I know she doesn't necessarily need me, but I hope, if any problems arise, she knows she can lean on me.

Well, part one of Plan Paris is done. Once practice ends, I'll need to go to the sports store and pick up some extra shifts. Maybe I can get Joe fired for being an asshole to Rachel? That will definitely open up some extra shifts for me to take.

I shake my head. That's probably not a good idea. Rachel will feel bad and Joe will probably find a way to get back to me. I smile, thinking of Rachel working at the coffee shop she always goes to. I can start there. If they offer me a job, Rachel and I can work together for the next few months.

And then once the semester ends, we can fly away to Paris. Together.

24

RACHEL

Charlie waves at me from inside The Coffee Shop, having snagged the cutest table resting right beside the window. I push open the heavy door, hearing the bell jangle as the door closes behind me.

"What took you so long?" Charlie asks while I dump my body down into the chair. I plop my purse down next to me on the windowsill and shrug off my coat. Thankfully, there's already a steaming mug waiting for me. I grab it hungrily, warming my chilled fingers against the ceramic cup before taking a tentative sip, enjoying the heat flowing through me.

I shrug while setting my mug on the wooden table. "I'm a busy girl," I say with a smirk.

Charlie chuckles while shaking her head, twirling a blond lock around her finger. "Have you spoken with Lauren?"

I make a face and lean back in my chair. "Unfortunately. She still hates my guts."

Charlie sighs and shakes her head. "That girl. I really don't understand what she's thinking."

I shrug, trying not to let it get to me even though I still feel the prickle of tears sting my eyes. "It doesn't matter," I say, knowing it's a lie. I really liked Lauren. I thought she liked me. Thinking about her makes it difficult to push away the tears. Sure, I hadn't known her for very long, but I could still remember us giggling while sitting in the back of class, drawing doodles on each other's notebooks, meeting for coffee at this exact same table, and discussing my complications with the bros.

I guess all of it was a lie.

I clench my teeth, knowing I'm about to cry. Pushing my dark thoughts away, I tell myself our friendship wasn't a lie. We did have fun together. Often times she did have my back, especially when it came to the bros. Our friendship just didn't have a solid foundation.

And not all friendships last forever.

I take another sip of my coffee, trying to console myself with the warm liquid as I hear Charlie continue, "She hasn't been replying to my texts and every time she sees me in the hall she turns around and walks the other way. She's eventually going to have to say something to me. She can't pretend like I've fallen off the face of the world forever. The art department is tiny. I'm sure we're all going to be in the same classes next year."

I grimace, recalling how Josh was dumped into the same drawing class as me. He hasn't been to class in a while though, which I am definitely thankful for. I have no clue if it has to do with me filing a report against him at the police department, or if he decided he doesn't care for drawing. I don't really care to find out either. Hopefully, he continues not attending and then I can continue thinking my life is normal.

"I hope she's not hanging out with Josh all by herself."

My heart falters at that thought and my head perks up. "Do you think she is?" I breathe. I clear my throat and try to ignore the twisting in my stomach. I don't think Josh would do anything to her. At least, I hope not. Every time I think about what happened I always think, maybe it was only a one-time thing. When I meet Charlie's gaze, I see the fear there which only makes the churning in my stomach worsen.

Charlie takes her phone out of her purse and begins texting. "Maybe I should shoot her a message, just to see if she's-" She doesn't finish her sentence and I notice the trembling in her fingers while she deftly stabs them against her phone's screen.

The bell on the cafe's door clangs and I glance over my shoulder, my eyes widening and my stomach feeling as if someone slammed their fist into me when I lay eyes upon the person standing about three feet behind me. I still, like a doe suddenly put in the spotlight, hoping he won't turn around or notice me. All hope deflates when I hear, "Josh! Over here!"

I inwardly groan and watch, as if I'm suddenly having an out-of-body moment, as he painstakingly turns around. His gaze lands on me and I cringe at the mixture of emotions taking hold of his face, recognizing shock and anger.

Quickly, I whirl around in my chair, locking eyes with Charlie, who seems just as alarmed as me if not more. I don't know why we're so surprised. This is a popular cafe; pretty much everyone goes here. It's not like Josh hates coffee or lives under a rock.

"Hey, Charlie," I hear him say, his voice making me want to both run and shout at the same time.

I take a deep breath and raise my gaze to him, my heart jumping into my throat when I realize he's watching me and not paying any mind to Charlie whatsoever. I watch him fiddle with his hands before shoving them into his skinny jean pockets.

"Hey," I hear Charlie say softly, hesitantly, as if she doesn't know what to do at this point.

"I didn't know you were going to be here today," Josh says, a hint of irritation in his tone.

I don't know if he's talking to me or Charlie, so I decide to shrug in response, hoping that's good enough for him. Why doesn't he just leave and go to his friends? I peak around him, noticing two men I've seen in the art department before; one with spiky blond hair and an earring and the other with brown hair and a black hoodie.

They're both watching us, waiting at the edge of their seats as if wondering what will happen. The fact that Josh has friends other than Charlie and Lauren is actually kind of shocking. I thought he only hung out with the girls for some reason.

"Well, you know, us girls just wanted to chat," Charlie says awkwardly.

I turn to her, watching her twirling her hair repeatedly around her finger. She looks nervous. Her gaze keeps switching from Josh to me and I feel bad that she's being put in the middle of this whole mess.

"You haven't been answering my texts."

Charlie's brows furrow, her nose wrinkles and her grip around her phone tightens. "I've been busy, Josh."

"Busy with her?" Josh's voice rises, his head nods towards me.

Charlie flinches. "Josh,"

"Yeah, we're having coffee," I interrupt while straightening my back.

Josh faces me, squaring his shoulders while he towers above. His gaze darkens, and he crosses his arms in front of his chest. "Why are ruining my life?"

"Josh," Charlie begins.

"I'm not ruining your life." I try to make myself taller, but it's hard when you're short and sitting in a chair.

Josh chuckles bitterly and gestures towards Charlie. "You took my friend away, I can't go to classes, because of what you said in your stupid report."

I blink. "What?" I don't really understand how any of this has to do with me. I filed a police report. I didn't go to the school board.

"Yeah, I can't go to classes now. A teacher went to the school board about me and they found the report you filed. So now I'm on probation."

If I could kiss Mr. Brown, I would. It had to be him. It just had to be. He was the only one I spoke to about my situation. I wonder when he went to the board.

"I hope you're happy now, Rachel," says Josh while throwing his hands into the air. "You got your revenge or whatever it is you wanted. I don't know why you think you need to make my life a living hell. It's not like I did anything to you."

My eyes widen and I slam my hands on the table, rattling the coffee mugs. "Now listen here, asshole," I say between clenched teeth while slowly rising from my chair, stabbing a manicured finger in his direction. "You don't think you made my life hell after what you did?"

Josh scowls down at me, jutting out his chin. "I did nothing."

I laugh bitterly, throwing back my head, earning some curious glances in our direction. "I haven't been the same since you attacked me, Josh," I say, my voice raising. I don't care who hears me, who's eavesdropping. Let them listen. Let them know that the sweet, kind Josh isn't who everyone thinks he is. "I can't go outside without feeling some sort of fear, I'm constantly looking over my shoulder, wondering if you or anyone else is going to grab me, take me, do something to me."

Josh looks around, his eyes wide with fear as several women frown in his direction. I see out of the corner of my eye, his friends quickly standing from their table and grabbing their coats and bags as if to make a quick getaway.

"You're the one who ruined my life!" I shout while shaking my finger at him, wishing I could stab it into his chest or smack him, knowing I can't. I don't want him to use anything against me, just in case he's called into court; just in case the board or the police actually decide to take me seriously. "I can't stop thinking about the way you grabbed me."

"Rachel, stop," says Josh while holding up his hands, still looking around at the cafe with worry. He takes a step back and I follow.

"No! I will not stop!" I shout.

Josh's blond friend grabs his shoulder and he nods towards the door. "Hey," he says casually, appearing calm given the situation. I notice he is trying desperately not to look at me. Really, I wonder how much these friends know. "Let's go."

"We can get a beer somewhere," says Josh's brunette friend.

I place my hands on my hips while Josh stills, his mouth gaping open as if he wants to offer some sort of excuse for his actions from that night. But there is no excuse; not for what he did.

"Fine," Josh says while shoving his shoulder out of his friend's hand. He smiles bitterly back at me. "It's your word against mine, Rachel."

I scoff and shake my head. "Go fuck yourself, Josh," I say while watching him and his friends head towards the door. I notice the brunette glancing uneasily back at me as I lower myself back into my seat.

"Well," I hear Charlie start.

I turn towards her, having completely forgotten that she is even here.

She smiles back at me. "That was interesting." Her hand slides towards mine and she grasps it, giving it a gentle squeeze. "You okay, girlie? That must have been hard."

I nod. "I'm fine. Absolutely fine."

Charlie makes a face. "Are you sure? I wish I could have done more for you. I was actually really shocked to see him. I should have-"

"You were fine." I shake my head and chuckle, filled with joy. I feel so light, as if a huge weight has been lifted from my shoulders and I lean back in my seat, smiling back at Charlie while crossing my arms. "I know it must have been hard. Has Lauren messaged you back?"

Charlie sighs and shakes her head. "No. I guess I'm officially on her shit list."

I give her hand a gentle squeeze before grabbing my coffee. "She'll come around, eventually."

Charlie nods. "Yeah." The word lingers in the air as sadness fills it. We both know she might not 'come around'. We both fear he will do the same to her, but at least something is being done. The school board is looking into it. Maybe I won't have to see him around the school next year.

"How is Hunter doing?" Charlie asks while tilting her head to the side.

I sigh and nod my head. "He is hanging in there. Trying to be tough."

"His mom's funeral is tomorrow, right?"

I grimace. "Yeah, it is." My gaze turns to the window, wondering how Hunter is really doing. He was still lying in bed when I left to meet with Charlie. I remember peeking into his room and he seemed to be staring off into space, his expression completely distant and unblinking. "I think he'll be ok," I say to Charlie's reflection in the window. "It'll just take some time."

25

HUNTER

  I clench my jaw while watching them lower her coffin into the ground. Dad stands at my side, dabbing at his eyes with an old handkerchief. I hear him sniffing beside me, but don't move to offer him any kind of solace. I'm barely hanging on myself. I can't remember the service. I only remember that I was there, listening to the pastor go on and on about a woman he hardly knew. Dad insisted on having a whole ceremony for her.
  I just wanted it done and over with.
  Now, watching her being lowered, I don't know what to think. I should have been there more for her. That's for sure. I should have taken this semester off as soon as I found out about her cancer's return. It was selfish of me to continue with classes and football; selfish of me to drown out my pain with drugs and alcohol.
  Tears stream down my cheeks and I wipe them away roughly, hoping no one notices. My eyes lift and I see Seth and Lucas watching me from the other side. I feel someone tugging on my hand and look down, finding Rachel standing at my side, holding my hand. She looks lovely in her black dress. Her curly blonde hair cascades down her shoulders. She smiles up at me and I force my lips up, hoping it resembles some sort of smile. Looking around, I notice everyone is heading back to the cars for the reception.
  So, I guess that's it. Mom is dead. She's been buried. What now? I wonder while allowing Rachel to tug me back to Lucas's SUV. We're all just supposed to eat and be merry? Talk about her life fondly? I don't know if I can do that. I feel so numb; as if time is slipping by and I'm only there physically, but not mentally.

The car door shuts and I lean my head against the window, watching the men in the distance shovel dirt into my mother's grave. I hear the car start, feel it move, but my gaze doesn't waver. I can't stop staring at the graves, wondering what I could have done differently in order to fix this. Could I have been a better son? Maybe I shouldn't have yelled at her when I was thirteen, and I was embarrassed about her bringing my forgotten lunch to school. She did yell at me pretty good then for being spoiled rotten and the next time I forgot my lunchbox she hadn't brought it. I smile, remembering how hungry I was.

Maybe I shouldn't have gone to college at all. I could have been home more often, taking care of her, making sure she was following all of the doctor's rules. At least, then she wouldn't have been so lonely while Dad spent all his days at work.

I grimace at the thought of my father. Maybe I shouldn't have fought with him so much. That probably stressed Mom out more than she needed to be. If I had been the perfect son for him, maybe Mom would've been around for a year or two more. Maybe we would've been a better family.

Maybe, I should have answered Dad's call rather than throwing my phone in the snow.

I whimper and turn away from the window, clamping my eyes close while trying to push those memories away. Every time I think about that night it only drives me to want to drink and drown out everything more. I should have answered. I should have been with her. I shouldn't have been out partying.

"Hunter?"

My eyes open and I see Rachel staring back at me with her worried green eyes. The car has stopped. Seth and Lucas are already out, heading towards the house.

"We're here?" I ask, my voice barely audible. I unbuckle myself and push the door open. My body moves sluggishly, as if I haven't slept in days, when in truth, I've probably slept most of my days away since Mom's death.

Rachel waits for me and we enter the house together, walking into the foyer I've known since I was a kid. The place is small, but it is home. Or at least it was. It doesn't quite feel like home without Mom here calling all the shots. A stack of shoes are piled up high to the side, and I slide mine off out of habit before traipsing through the brown, narrow hall, towards the kitchen. I hear several voices I recognize and find Grandma with several of my aunts, leaning against the counter filled with an assortment of food still wrapped in foil.

My mother's sisters dab at their eyes. My Aunt Loraine is shaking her head while my Aunt Margaret is sobbing while Grandma holds her.

"I can't believe she's gone," Aunt Margaret wails. "She was too young. Way too young."

Grandma's head lifts, her gaze locking with mine. Her hand reaches for me and I feel my body instinctively move away, as if she is raising her hand to strike me rather than console.

"Hunter, sweetie," she says in her old, gravelly voice. "Come here."

Aunt Margaret and Aunt Loraine immediately turn toward me and I feel their brown eyes dig into me, like they are a pack of wolves about to attack their weak prey. My hands clench, recognizing their eyes. They remind me of my mother's. Both aunts are older than Mom. It's like I'm looking at what her future would have been; greying hair, wrinkled hands and eyes.

I shake my head while turning on my heel, nearly ramming into Rachel. "Hunter?" I hear her call while I briskly stride pass her, shaking her hands from mine. I don't want to be touched right now. I only want to be alone.

"Hunter, sweetie, come back!" I hear Grandma call after me, but I can't.

I continue through the narrow hall and into the foyer before making a sharp turn up the staircase. I don't stop until I am in my old bedroom. I quickly close the door and lean against it, praying no one has followed me. My body slides down to the floor and my legs move in front of me while I tilt my head back, gazing up at the old posters littering my bedroom walls, reminding me of simpler days.

There's a red Ferrari poster hanging over my bed. Next to it is Brett Favre, holding a football. I always wanted to put up bikini women, but Mom never allowed me, hence all the football and car paraphernalia. There's a small window across from me. A wooden desk sits beneath it, littered with an old computer I doubt still works and several picture frames. I crawl towards my desk, slowly pulling myself up while I stare at the old pictures.

I grab one, holding it up close. It's a picture of me when I was ten with Mom wrapping her arms around me. I remember that day. It was winter, and we decided to go on a ski trip a few days before Christmas. It's weird seeing Mom with her long brown hair after years of her dealing with chemo. She looks so happy while holding me.

I grab several others, recalling Thanksgiving, when I was twelve and Dad allowed me to carve the turkey, and my seventh birthday when I had face slammed my birthday cake. These photos have sat on my desk for God knows how long. I never cared to look at them then. Now I can't stop myself. They're the only things I have left of her; the only proof that we were a happy family. Proof that Mom was happy before she passed.

I lower myself into the old chair, hearing it squeak with my weight. I rest the pictures back on the desk and lean forward, laying my head down on the table while staring back at the pictures. It's not fair. I don't understand why someone so good had to die. She didn't do anything wrong. She was always happy, always taking care of others.

She doesn't deserve a son like me.

I feel my phone vibrate and slowly close my eyes, knowing I shouldn't answer it. Everyone I need is here. Seth, Rachel, and Lucas are downstairs, probably wondering why I'm being such a drama king. Dad is probably already on the phone, speaking with my therapist about how we need to up my visits. I can picture Grandma talking to my aunts about my behavior; most likely more guests are arriving and wondering where the "football star" is.

I'm no football star. I'm nothing.

My phone vibrates again and I clench my fists, telling myself I don't need to answer it. I don't need to see who it is. I'm worried if I look, I'll answer, and if I answer, I'll find myself running out of this place and heading to the next big party, getting blackout drunk. I can't do that again. I need to be strong. I need to fight this urge, this need.

With one more buzz, my eyes open and my hand reaches inside my pocket, unable to fight myself any longer. I lean back in my seat. My fingers quiver as I type on the screen, seeing Millie's missed text messages. My finger hovers above her name. I don't have to look. I don't have to know. I can just ignore it and go back downstairs. I can be with my family, reminiscing about all the hilarious things we got up to. I can just put my cellphone back into my pocket and pretend like Millie never messaged me.

Despite knowing all that, my finger lowers, pressing against her name. There's a knock at my door and before I can read the messages, I hear my door squeaking open. Glancing over my shoulder, I see Rachel enter, followed by Seth and Lucas. They close the door behind them while Rachel strides towards me, taking my phone away and resting it on the desk.

"Are you alright?" She asks while sitting herself in my lap.

"Yeah, dude, we were worried about you," says Seth while sitting himself on my bed.

"You just took off without a word," adds Lucas. "Your Grandma makes a mean rhubarb pie by the way."

Rachel runs her hands through my hair and I lean into her touch, appreciating her warmth. "You should get something to eat."

I shake my head. "I'm not hungry," I murmur.

"Then you should come sit with us," says Lucas. "I don't think you should be alone right now."

I make a face. Actually, being alone is actually what I want. I open my mouth, but stop when I catch Seth's scowl. "We're not letting you be alone," he says. "Not this time anyway."

"Yeah, don't make us grab you," says Lucas while stepping closer. "I don't care if you kick and scream, we're not going to let you sit up here all by yourself." His gaze wonders to my phone. "And we're not going to let you leave without us."

I grimace, knowing they're right. I don't know why I keep pushing them away. They're my friends. No. They're more than that.

But I don't want them to think I'm weak. I've always been strong, brave; the perfect athlete. I don't know why, but allowing people to see the weakness in me is hard. It makes me feel less of a man, which is crazy.

"Stay with me," says Rachel while taking my hand. She places a kiss on my knuckles, before pressing her cheek into the palm of my hand. She blinks up at me with those beautiful green eyes of hers. "Be with me. With us. You can tell us anything, Hunter. We're here for you. Let us be with you."

"Yeah, bro," says Seth. "You're not any less of a man if you cry. Your mom just died. We won't think any less of you."

I turn to Lucas and watch him nod. "You don't need to pretend with us. We're family."

I nod, allowing those words to settle in me. I feel the resolves of my walls slowly crumbling down. My bottom lip quivers. I try to bite it, to hang onto something, but the tears are already slipping from my eyes. I sob, and press my hands against my face, trying to hide myself while I feel Rachel's arms wrapping around me.

She shushes me, her hands stroking my hair. Pulling me towards her, I nuzzle my face into her chest and continue sobbing. The bed squeaks and I feel Seth and Lucas around me, feel their arms wrapping around my body.

"It's going to be alright," says Rachel. "I know its hard now, but you have us."

I nod while wiping the snot and tears from my face, knowing I probably look like a mess. "I know," I whimper.

"What do you want?" Lucas asks while pulling away from me. "Pizza? Mario Kart?"

"Strippers?" Seth asks, earning a light smack from Rachel.

Seth shrugs. "What?"

Rachel rolls her eyes and Seth chuckles.

I pull Rachel closer to me, pressing my lips against her temple, her neck. I know now is not the time, especially since my whole family is right downstairs, but it's been too long and I really want to forget. Maybe I don't need booze and drugs for that.

"I want… you," I whisper into her ear. My gaze lifts to Seth and Lucas and for some reason, I feel incredibly awkward, like a virgin when I say, "I want… us."

Rachel smiles at me, leaning forward with hooded eyes. "Ok," she breathes before seizing my lips with hers.

My eyes flutter close and my arms wrap around her, holding her against me as her tongue strokes my bottom lip. It moves to my top, making my mouth drop open and allow her entrance. I groan, feeling her tongue slip against mine, igniting fires I haven't felt in all too long. She shifts herself in my lap, moving to straddle me on either side. Her hands cup my face. I hear ruffling around me. When I open my eyes, I see Seth and Lucas throwing off their suit jackets and unbuttoning their shirts.

Rachel releases my lips, leaning back while her thighs grip me. She pulls up her black dress, the garment going up and over her shoulders, displaying a black bra and matching thong. My cock twitches at the sight of her milky white skin and all I want to do is claim her lips again and drown my aching heart in her beautiful body.

She slips from my lap, smiling mischievously at me while moving to the bed. Lucas and Seth have already pulled off their pants and are standing in their boxers. I grab my suit jacket while rising, shrugging out of it. I still at the sound of footsteps padding up the staircase and my eyes whip to the door. Lunging for it, I quickly lock it, pressing my body against it while hearing the assailant rap their knuckles lightly against the door.

"Hunter?"

I grimace at Dad's voice, knowing this is definitely not the time and place to do this.

"Yes, Dad?" I clench my teeth, waiting for him to try opening the door. I have no clue what excuse I should give. We're having a séance? I need time alone with my friends? That actually might not be all that bad. I doubt Dad would think we were about to have sex in here.

"Are you ok?"

"Yeah, just with my friends." I glance over my shoulder, my eyes widening on Lucas removing Rachel's bra. His lips are on her shoulder, his eyes focused on me. Seth is slipping his fingers into her panties and I curse myself for not being with them as I watch her mouth open in a silent moan; wanting desperately to slide my naked body against hers.

"I'll be down soon, Dad," I say while trying to unbutton my shirt. My fingers are too awkward and I purse my lips, cursing them for not moving faster.

"Alright. Did Lucas get enough of your grandmother's pie?"

Fuck Grandma's pie, I think while ripping my shirt from my body and starting on my belt. Seth mouths Rachel's neck. His fingers are outlined by her black panties. I watch them moving back and forth, her body moving with him while her hand slides into his hair, gripping the locks while she gasps.

"Hunter?"

"Yeah, I'm sure he got enough Dad," I say while fumbling with my suit pants' buttons. "We'll be down soon." I grimace while stumbling towards them, hoping Dad has no more questions. I think I'm at my limit. There is no way I can deal with him any longer while Seth, Lucas, and Rachel are on my bed.

"Alright then," I hear Dad say and I don't wait.

I capture Rachel's lips, moaning against her while her body presses into me. My dick is hard and leaking. All I want to do is ram myself deep inside her and forget this pain. My hands cup her face. My fingers run through her hair, tangling themselves in her locks. I hardly notice Lucas and Seth on either side of her as I continue kissing her. My tongue twines around hers and I shudder, hearing her moan while her fingernails dig into my shoulders.

I pull away and looking down I see my cock is already poking out. While I pull my boxers down, Lucas claims her lips, his hands palming her breast at the same time Seth deftly undoes her bra. Her breasts heave with each breath she takes. The straps slip down her shoulders and she pushes her bra away, the material falling onto the bed, completely forgotten as I take her other, forgotten breast into my mouth.

Her hands grip my locks while my tongue twirls around her nipple, making it taut. My teeth nibble lightly and I hear her whimper. Looking up, a hand is clamped over her mouth and I smile to myself while warmth pits in my stomach. She sways while I continue my ministrations, loving each gasp she emits from those succulent lips of hers.

Seth's fingers slip away from her and I feel him moving on my right, taking my hand and pulling me to the head of the bed. An awkward laugh escapes me while he pushes my shoulders down until I'm lying flat on my back with my penis twitching for attention. Rachel crawls on top of me, her lips pressing against mine briefly.

"You look like you need some attention," she says between kisses, a playful smile on her lips.

"Desperately," I groan while grabbing my pillow behind me and nuzzling my head into it.

She smiles while slowly lowering her head to my cock, her tongue licking up the shaft and stroking against my sensitive tip. I bite my lower lip, trying to keep my groans soft so Dad doesn't come running up, wondering what's going on.

"You like that?" Rachel breathes.

My head bobs up and down. "Yeah," I say shakily, my eyes rolling to the back of my head while her mouth takes my head. My toes curl when I feel her sucking gently and a shuddering moan escapes my lips when her mouth slides, taking me fully in before releasing me.

Lucas hovers above her, stroking his own cock while watching. Seth positions himself behind her, massaging her ass. It's hard for me to pay attention to everything while Rachel continues sucking me; her mouth moving faster, her teeth lightly sliding against me in the most delectable way. I feel myself leaking, twitching; my body desperately trying to keep up with this mind-blowing pleasure. I feel myself moving with her, pumping my dick in and out of her mouth as if it was her vagina. It's so moist and wet and tight. Grinding my teeth, I hold onto the blankets beneath me, needing something to stabilize me as I feel my body riding wave after wave. I gasp, watching her head bob up and down.

"Stop," I breathe while grabbing her shoulders, not ready for this to end so soon. I know I told Dad I'd be right down, but I want more. I want to feel her tightening around me. I want to see her gasping and writhing above me.

Rachel's head lifts and I whimper, feeling my orgasm slowly deflate and my balls nearly shrivel up and die from the sudden halt, but I know deep down it's the right move. I want to be deep inside her.

I grab her shoulders and pull her towards me. My cock feels so wet. I worry the moment she sinks herself onto me, I'll come immediately. I need to calm down, but my heart is racing. I kiss her deep and hard, enjoying her lips on mine. Actually, enjoying them way too much. I push her back until she's staring at me, on her knees between Lucas and Seth, looking both confused and bewildered.

"I want to watch you," I say while leaning back against my pillow, touching my cock lightly while nodding to Seth and Lucas. "I want to watch you guys fuck."

Seth smiles, a slight gleam of mischief in his eyes. He doesn't wait. His hands grab Rachel's ass and he turns her towards him, claiming her lips while his hands massage her buttocks. Lucas busies himself with kissing her shoulder, his cock digging into her ass while his hands come around and grab her tits. His fingers pull them and I clench my teeth, hearing her gasp and whimper against Seth's lips.

Reaching over to my desk, I drag the drawer open, finding some condoms from a year ago when I moved home after the semester ended. They haven't expired yet. Thank God. I throw one at Seth, watching it bounce off his shoulder and land next to him on the bed. While Lucas continues to twist and pull her nipples, Seth's hands grab her panties, yanking them down before his fingers slide into her. I watch her body twitch and see her lean into Lucas's chest while Seth's thumb strokes over her clit hidden by the dust of curls.

Lucas's right hand slides away, stroking a path towards her ass and I watch him wet one finger first with his mouth before pushing in between her ass cheeks. Her body stills and my breath halts. My hand on my cock stops stroking, knowing I'm getting way too close when we only just started. She moans and I watch him continue to press it into her while Seth angles himself backwards.

Rachel slips to her knees and mouths Seth's cock, his hands pushing her hair away while she continues to suck him. His head goes back, his eyes flutter close and I watch her pump him in and out of her mouth while Lucas slips another finger into her ass. A moan escapes my lips as I watch them. My tip leaks precum and I use it to slick my cock, stroking a bit faster now.

Seth's head lulls from side to side while his hips thrust into her, moving faster now while Lucas aligns his cock with her hole. With one push, he stills, waiting for Rachel to adjust to his girth and length. She whimpers while her hands grip Seth's legs, nails digging into his flesh while she slowly moves backwards against Lucas's dick.

Lucas moans as her thrusts pick up. I watch his body move against her, gaining a kind of rhythm between them. I'm keen to join, but just as keen to watch, not knowing where to focus first; her mouth around Seth's cock or Lucas's dick thrusting into her ass. I can tell Seth is getting close. His whole body is shivering. His hands are fisting as if trying to remain in some sort of control. Lucas's body is moving at a feverish pace, slamming against Rachel while her body takes it.

"Oh, fuck," Seth mutters, fisting Rachel's hair in his grasp. Slurping and smacking sounds fill my ears. My balls tighten while I watch. "Rachel, your mouth is fucking fantastic."

"So tight," Lucas says between clenched teeth. His hands grip her hips and he slams her back into him, making Rachel cry out.

All of us still, our eyes flying to the door, waiting to hear footsteps or knocks at the door. The seconds seem to tick by like hours while we wait, wondering if Dad or even Grandma will come up, wondering what we are doing or what is taking us so long.

Rising to my knees, I wobble towards them, picking up the condom next to Seth and unwrapping it. We should probably speed things along, seeing how people are still downstairs, probably waiting for me to return. I pull the condom onto my dick while Rachel releases Seth's cock with a pop. I hear him whimper next to me, his brows pulled taut while his teeth grind. His hands slip to his aching tip and I can see he's having a hard time keeping himself together.

Lucas slips out of Rachel with a groan and I watch her climb towards me, pushing me down before placing her legs on either side. She angles my dick at her entrance and slowly lowers herself on me, taking my entire length deep inside her. A hiss escapes her. Her hooded eyes watch me while I lift my hips, moving at an entirely new pace for her while Lucas comes up from behind. Another hiss escapes her as he slips his dick into her. Seth kneels next to her, cock still in hand. Rachel leans over and takes him into her mouth.

I moan while I thrust into her, moving hard and fast. She feels so tight with Lucas moving from her other side. Her breasts dangle above me and I grab them, running my index and thumb over her tits and watching her spasm and shake as I pull them. Seth rams himself into her. His entire length going deep inside. I feel her tighten even more around me. My hand grabs her hip to keep her steady against me while the other reaches for her clit, circling around it while I thrust in and out of her.

Seth tosses back his head. "I'm coming," he whispers harshly. "Oh, fuck. I'm coming so hard. So fucking good." Cum slides out of Rachel's mouth while Seth thrusts into her two more times before slipping away. He gasps at my side while Rachel swallows. Her attention turns to me. Her hands stroking the hair away from my face before she presses her lips against mine.

I kiss her while sliding my hands up and down her body, touching her breasts before returning to her clit. I'm unable to decide where to administer my attentions, deciding I simply can't stop touching her. Her gasps and soft moans keep me going, making me believe I am the only man in her world.

I hear a moan and peak over Rachel's shoulder, finding Lucas clenching his jaw, his brows furrowed while his gaze focused. His hands stroke Rachel's back while he pulls out of her, having orgasmed.

Taking this moment, I roll her over and throw one of her legs over my shoulder, pumping as deep as I can into her. Her mouth gapes open as she watched me. My lips mouth her leg, sinking my teeth lightly into her flesh before sucking gently. Her walls are tightening. I know she's getting close. I know I'm getting close. My hips can't stop. My cock is twitching and I feel myself going over the edge.

"Fuck," I breathe as I feel myself come.

Rachel's mouth promptly closes and I feel her twitch, her whole body shaking while her hips meet mine before going lax.

"Did you come?" I whisper and she nods.

"I didn't want your family coming up here, thinking something weird," she says between gasps, pushing her hair out of her face.

I smile, kissing the tip of her nose first before moving to her lips. She smiles against me, kissing me back. I feel the ache from before seeping back into me while I push myself away from her, looking around for my clothes, instead finding Lucas and Seth leaning against the wall, staring dreamily in the distance.

"We should get downstairs before they suspect anything," I say, trying to sound teasing, instead sounding awkward.

I grimace while I stand, yanking off the condom and throwing it in the trash can under my desk. I should probably discard it somewhere else. Who knows if Dad goes snooping in here when I'm gone, but I'm too tired to deal with it.

"Hey," I hear Rachel, feel her hand on my shoulder.

Her fingers lace with mine when I turn around and once again, I try to force a smile with her. "Everything will be alright, ok? You have us."

I look between her, Seth, and Lucas. The bros are already grabbing the boxers, shoving their legs inside. She's right. I'm not alone when I am with them and having this moment, together, sober and happy; it's definitely better than any party I could ever go to.

I nod and feel a genuine smile take hold of my lips. "I know," I say while pulling her into a hug, my arms wrapping tightly around her body. "I know I'm not alone."

26

HUNTER

  Months have gone by since Mom's funeral. I'm once again living full time with the bros and Rachel, against Dad's advice. I know he's only worried about me, but I'm a grown man and I can take care of myself. I don't need him looking out for me all the time. My friends can do that easily and without making me feel like a two-year-old. He does insist on talking to me at least once a week to check in and see if I am attending my therapy appointments. Apparently, he has his own therapist now to help with Mom's death. I grimace thinking about it. It's still hard knowing she's gone, yet the pain isn't as bad as it once was.
  I'm walking down the sidewalk towards Dr. Forrester's office, enjoying the May weather and the greenery budding on the trees. The birds are chirping, kids are playing on the lawns, and several dogs are barking at one another. Next week is final's week and then the semester ends. It's strange how time flies so fast. I feel like it was only yesterday I was leaving Lucas's cottage after my fight with Rachel.
  Things, of course, aren't perfect. Every day is different. Yesterday, I spent most of the morning crying after finding Mom's recipe for green bean casserole in my backpack. I have no clue what it was doing there. She must have packed it amongst my things awhile back. I found it at the bottom of one of my side pockets when I was cleaning it out. Rachel had to calm me down.
  But that was yesterday.
  I don't know why, but today I feel renewed. It might be the sunlight or a goodnight's sleep. Or maybe it's because Coach hasn't given up on me and will let me play next year. That's probably it. I was expecting to be kicked

off the team, but apparently, given my previous record and my mom's funeral, he's decided to give me a second chance.

For now, that is.

"Hunter?"

I turn away from the blooming trees and find Millie standing several feet in front of me, dressed in a short denim skirt and a low-cut white crop top with some heels. She looks great as always, yet she seems thinner than normal, her skin more pallid. She smiles at me while closing the distance between us. Quite honestly I'm surprised she still wants to talk to me after all the hell we went through partying together. I've also ignored all her messages. However, I notice her smile doesn't meet her eyes as she stares up at me, looking expectant.

"Hey," I say awkwardly while rubbing the back of my head. "What's up? Haven't seen you in a while."

"Yeah, I know," Millie says in a high pitched voice while lightly smacking my arm. "You keep ignoring my texts. What's up with that?"

I shrug, not really wanting to explain myself. If I tell her my mom died, I would have to talk to her longer and I'm already running late to Dr. Forrester's office. "I've just been busy," I say, hoping to end our chat soon. I look at the time, noticing I have about ten minutes until my session starts. "Hey, Millie, I really gotta-"

"Drew was just asking about you yesterday."

My heart slams to a stop at the mention of his name.

Millie taps her chin thoughtfully. "And Jerry actually."

I clench my jaw, instantly remembering the last time I was around Jerry. My hands fist, recalling the baseball bat and him hitting me; me not knowing up from down.

Millie grabs my arm and pouts. "They miss you. You should-"

I push her away, knowing whatever she's about to say isn't good. "Sorry, Millie I have to go. It was nice seeing you," I call while running across the street, pushing myself to get as far away from her as possible.

Then there're days like today, which start off good, and then turn into me desperately trying not to drink. I shake the dark thoughts away, trying to ignore that need swelling within me, pushing me to chase Millie down and see what illegal things we could get up to.

I storm into Dr. Forrester's office, looking at the time and seeing that I have a minute to spare. The door opens and I see her smiling back at me, her lips lowering at the sight of me gasping and sweating.

"Good afternoon, Hunter," she says while stepping to the side and allowing me to pass. "Are you doing okay today?"

I shake my head while plopping down into her couch. "I was," I say while running my hands through my hair.

The door clicks close and she sits herself off to the side. Close, but not too close. "Do you want to tell me what happened?"

I grimace. "I ran into Millie on my way here."

Dr. Forrester looks through her papers. "Millie, who's the girl you used to go to these parties with."

I chuckle bitterly. "That's the one."

"Did she trigger anything?"

I groan and press my face into my hands. "She just reminded me of that time and that... need."

"The need to drown away your thoughts."

My hands slide away from my face and I lean back in the couch, my leg bouncing up and down maniacally. I'm itching to grab my cell, to call Millie, but I keep my hands in my lap. "Yeah, exactly," I say while gripping my hands. "Why am I not over this yet? It's not that hard. I should be better by now."

I watch Dr. Forrester shake her head. "It's always a long road, Hunter. You will always have these urges. The best thing to do is to figure out how to change gears, or keep yourself from giving in."

"Will it ever get any easier?"

Dr. Forrester sighs and shakes her head. "Afraid not. You're not the only one with triggers like this. Many people don't want to be alone. Many people have their own vices. Smoking, eating, or self harm. It doesn't have to be drugs and alcohol."

I nod, knowing she's right, but still wishing there is any easier way to fix me. I don't want to be feeling this way for the rest of my life. I don't want to be seeing Millie next year and feeling like I need to run in order to prevent myself from doing anything stupid.

"So, have you thought of a way to keep yourself busy after this session?"

I smile, happy to know I've done at least something right today. "Rachel is meeting me here and then we are getting some food at this burger joint we like. And then later we are meeting up with Seth and Lucas. Lucas won this big writing contest so we're celebrating."

"That sounds great."

I nod. "Yeah. Lucas, Seth, and Rachel; all of them are great. They've been really helpful during this whole thing."

"And football is going well?"

Thinking of football and Coach makes my shoulder twinge and I move it, happy to finally have the pain gone. "Yeah. I'm seeing a physical therapist so no more painkillers. I'm a bit nervous about next year though, seeing how it's my senior year. I need to make sure that I play enough to get spotted by the NFL scouts. I hardly played at all during January and February, so I will need to work harder next season."

I watch Dr. Forrester nod and write on her clipboard. "Just take one thing at a time," she says while she continues to write. "It's good to have goals, but you don't want to injury yourself again."

Talking with Dr. Forrester makes me feel like the world isn't going to burn down. I actually feel like I can be a person in this small room. Even though I still have issues with Millie and I still cry when I think about my mom, I also feel like I am slowly getting better. I am slowly becoming the man I want to be.

And I can't wait to be that man for Rachel.

"What are your plans for summer? Are you going to continue with training? Get a job? Do you have any goals in mind?"

I frown, thinking of what I am going to do while she is away in Paris. With everything going on, I haven't been able to save up any money. Lucas is going with the money he earned from his writing contest. Apparently, his dad has an apartment for Rachel to stay in. Seth can go with some money his coach last minute scrounged up.

But what about me?

27

RACHEL

Resting my hands on my hips, I frown at the suitcases in front of me, wondering if I packed everything I need. I had an earful earlier from my mom when I told her I wasn't going back to New York first before heading to Paris. I couldn't quite tell her that I wanted some ample alone time with Hunter without getting a hundred questions asked, so my excuse that I want to hang out with my friends was pretty frowned upon.

Oh, well. That's what happens when I pay for everything. I become my own woman.

Mom wasn't so pleased by that excuse either.

I heave a sigh and throw open my door, peaking down the hall to see if Seth or Lucas are ready, yet. The taxi should be here soon. I frown, wrinkling my nose when I hear Soul Caliber being played from the living room.

"Are you boys ready?" I call while stalking down the hall, my frown turning into a scowl when Seth and Lucas don't bother to answer.

"Seth? Lucas?" I cross my arms and tap my foot, wondering if they will answer if I go stand in front of the TV.

When they continue to ignore me, I stomp around the couch, positioning myself in front of them. They lean to the side, trying to fight each other while I scowl back at them.

"Boys!" I shout, reaching over and yanking the controllers out of their hands.

"Oh, come on!" Seth shouts. "We were almost done."

"Are you done packing, or not?" I ask while shaking the controller at him.

"All I need is passport, tooth brush, and tooth paste," says Seth with a shrug.

I gape at him. "That's all you packed?"

He smirks back at me. "Nah, I packed other stuff. I'm good to go."

I roll my eyes. "Please, tell me the other stuff you packed is actually clothes and not just condoms."

Seth's eyes widen and he turns to Lucas. "Did you pack the condoms?"

Lucas pats Seth shoulders. "Relax. Of course I packed the condoms."

My eyes narrow on both boys and I cross my arms, not particularly finding their antics funny whatsoever. "I hope you know I'm actually going to Paris to learn. Not just screw around." I turn away from them, walking towards Hunter's room. The door is still closed and I'm hoping he isn't too upset that we are leaving him all by himself. I don't want to leave him. It would be nice if all four of us could go to the most romantic city in the world together.

"Oh come on," I hear Seth say from behind while I knock lightly at Hunter's door. "Paris is the number one setting we *should* be screwing in."

I shake my head while I wait for Hunter to answer the door.

"Do you think you packed enough condoms?"

I glance over my shoulder, watching Lucas chuckle. "Paris sells condoms, you idiot."

I pinch my nose, already feeling a headache coming on. Paris with Seth is going to be really interesting. I have no clue what to make of it.

My phone vibrates and I smile when I see Charlie's message on the screen: *Have fun, girlie! Make sure to tell all the cute Frenchmen bonjour for me!*

Shaking my head, I respond with: *I don't think Lucas and Seth would like me speaking to strange Frenchmen.*

Charlie texts me back immediately: *They're not for you! They're for me! Just show them my picture and give them my number, just in case they ever find themselves in the area.*

I hear Hunter's door open and shove my phone away before turning around. Hunter smiles at me, his hands in his pockets.

"Is everything alright?" I cringe, knowing I should stop asking him that question. Ever since the funeral and the whole thing with Lucas finding him out in the snow, I feel like that's the only thing me and the bros ever ask him. "I wanted to say goodbye, but your door has been closed."

"Yeah," he says sheepishly. He nods inside his room. "I was hoping you could help me with something."

I nod and follow him inside. "Of course. What is it?"

I frown at the clutter in his room. There's clothes and tennis shoes everywhere with piles of trash littering the area around the trashcan, however, my gaze focuses on the bags and suitcases lying in the middle of the room.

"You're staying at your dad's?" I ask while motioning towards the bags.

Hunter shakes his head while grabbing several shirts from his bed.

"Are you going somewhere?"

Hunter chuckles. "Well, obviously. Which shirt do you think I should take?" He holds up a white button down and a gaudy yellow and orange shirt I have no clue where he bought from.

"The white one," I say while making a face.

He stuffs it into his suitcase without bothering to fold it, making me want to throw the lid open and rearrange everything neatly, knowing the inside was probably just as messy as his room if not more.

"Where are you going? Is there some sort of football camp you do?"

Hunter looks at me innocently while shaking his head. "No. I'm going to the airport."
I deadpan, placing my hands on my hips, wondering why he is being so cheeky with me. "Okay, wise guy."
Hunter chuckles and reaches for some papers on his bed. I notice his passport is also there, which is strange. He hands the papers to me and I stare down, my eyes widening upon the ticket I hold in his hand. My gaze lingers on the city, reading: *Paris*.
"You're coming to Paris?" I breathe, unable to control my voice any longer. I look up, watching him nod. My heart has completely stopped. "You're coming to Paris today?"
He chuckles and nods again. "Don't look so surprised. I can still leave the country, you know."
I lunge for him, wrapping my arms around his neck while planting my lips on his. He chuckles, his arms coming around me, holding me tight to him while he twirls us around. I end the kiss, meeting his blue gaze and feeling joy swell my heart. "I can't believe you're actually coming with us. How were you able to save up the money?"
Hunter shrugs while setting me down. "Dad bought the ticket. He's been feeling kind of bad these days about everything. When I was talking to him about it, he said he would help if I did some chores around the house for him."
I smile and nuzzle my nose against him. "I'm so happy."
"Why are we so happy?" I hear Seth call from behind.
Hunter and I turn, finding Seth and Lucas hovering at the doorway. "Hunter is coming with us!" I shout, feeling elated. This is the happiest news I could get today.
Seth's eyes widen and he turns to Lucas. "Are you sure you packed enough condoms?"

Lucas rolls his eyes. "We'll be fine." He leans against the doorframe, his lips twitching into a grin. "Happy to have you, Hunter."

"Will there be enough room?" Hunter asks, sounding slightly uneasy.

Seth scoffs. "It's Lucas. There's probably a thousand rooms in this so called apartment."

Lucas raises an eyebrow, but doesn't say anything, which makes me think that Seth isn't exaggerating.

"How did you convince your dad to let you go?" Lucas asks.

I'm wondering much the same. His dad didn't even want Hunter moving back into our apartment and now he's buying him a ticket to Paris. I know his dad feels bad, but I doubt he feels THAT bad.

Hunter chuckles and rubs the back of his head. "Well, we had a pretty big talk. Probably the longest one we've had in years." Hunter smiles softly. "It was a good talk. He's hoping I come back fluent in French." He turns his gaze to me and his smile broadens. "Or get a cute girlfriend."

I shake my head and go up onto my tiptoes to flick his nose.

"Ouch!" Hunter laughs before grabbing my hand and yanking me towards him, seizing my lips once more.

"Alright, taxi is here!" Seth shouts from the living room.

I quickly release Hunter and run to my room, throwing on my backpack and grabbing my purse and suitcase before scrambling through the hallway with all my gear. Seth stops, wearing only a backpack, and he shakes his head at me while scowling at all my bags.

"You must be kidding me," he mutters before wrenching my suitcase away from me and dragging it behind him.

I shrug. "I need to look cute."

Seth rolls his eyes.

"Everyone have passports?" Lucas asks while grabbing his keys and throwing open the apartment door.

"Check!" Seth, Hunter, and I call in unison.

"Alright!" Lucas shouts with a smile, watching as we trudge out the door with all our bags and suitcases. Hunter stops to lock the door while Seth curses my lack of packing skills underneath his breath, making me giggle.

"Paris, here we come!" I shout while punching my fists in the air.

Manufactured by Amazon.ca
Bolton, ON